THE DUKE'S PROTECTOR

The Duke's Guard Series, Book Two

C.H. Admirand

ARE YOU SIGNED UP FOR DRAGONBLADE'S BLOG?

You'll get the latest news and information on exclusive giveaways, exclusive excerpts, coming releases, sales, free books, cover reveals and more.

Check out our complete list of authors, too!

No spam, no junk. That's a promise!

Sign Up Here

www.dragonbladepublishing.com

Dearest Reader;

Thank you for your support of a small press. At Dragonblade Publishing, we strive to bring you the highest quality Historical Romance from some of the best authors in the business. Without your support, there is no 'us', so we sincerely hope you adore these stories and find some new favorite authors along the way.

Happy Reading!

CEO, Dragonblade Publishing

Additional Dragonblade books by Author C.H. Admirand

The Duke's Guard Series
The Duke's Sword
The Duke's Protector

The Lords of Vice Series
Mending the Duke's Pride
Avoiding the Earl's Lust
Tempering the Viscount's Envy
Redirecting the Baron's Greed
His Vow to Keep (Novella)

The Lyon's Den Series
Rescued by the Lyon

Dedication

For Scott Moreland, my fabulous editor, who encouraged me to write this series about *The Duke's Guard*. The men who swore a vow to protect the Duke and Duchess of Wyndmere and their family. *The O'Malleys, Flahertys, and Garahans would die to keep that vow.*

Author's Note

I love using family names in my books. In this book, there are two minor characters from my series, The Lords of Vice, *Madame Beaudoine,* modiste, and one of her seamstresses, Mignonette *de Chauret.*

De Chauret is an ancient spelling/variation of one of my family names: *Charette.* My great-great-grandfather, Oliver *Charette,* married Rosina *Beaudoine.* My great-grandfather, Joseph Augustin *Charette,* married Margaret Mary *Flaherty.* My great-great-grandfather, Patrick Henry *Flaherty,* married Anna *Garahan.*

Recognize the Flaherty and Garahan names? I thought you might. They are part of the Duke of Wyndmere's personal guard.

So, pour a cup of tea and settle into your comfy reading spot while I tell you a story…

PROLOGUE

THE EERIE SOUND of wood splintering and the crash that followed woke her. Disoriented, Mignonette de Chauret wondered if it had been a dream, while her mind replayed the terror she'd endured a fortnight ago. The shattered window and the intruders had nearly scared the life out of her.

Mon Dieu! Had they returned?

Hand to her racing heart, she listened, waiting to hear something—anything that would confirm, or deny, her fears. But it was impossible to hear over the pounding of her heart. She slowly rose from her pallet and crept to the door, opening it a crack.

The sound of heavy footfalls near the front of the shop had a ball of fear curdling in her belly.

Why were they here?

What were they looking for?

The sound of fabric rending brought tears to her eyes. Lady Aurelia's gowns were hanging in the wardrobe at the front of the shop, waiting to be delivered in just a few hours!

The soft glow from a lantern swinging shed light across the open space between the front of the shop and her room at the back. She slowly closed the door. Hands trembling, she slid the latch into place.

The pounding on her door nearly stopped her heart. *The must have seen her!*

She had to leave—escape! Frantically trying to think, Mignonette's gaze swept the tiny room, once…and then a second time. *The window!*

Sending up a prayer to her Maker, she climbed onto the table, grabbed hold of the windowsill, and slipped through into the darkness.

CHAPTER ONE

S EAN O'MALLEY READ the missive and handed it back to Earl Lippincott. "'Tisn't that I doubt King or his network of connections in London, but me gut tells me there's more to the vicious rumors circulating."

As head of the Duke of Wyndmere's personal guard at Lippincott Manor in Sussex, O'Malley doubted every claim. Required proof before he believed. As one of The Duke's Guard, he had stood firm between the vile and deadly threats against the duke, the earl, and their families, earning the moniker of *The Duke's Protector*.

Although he trusted the renowned Gavin King of the Bow Street Runners, O'Malley needed more information and had the connections on the streets to get it.

"My brother was quite adamant in his latest missive," the earl reminded him.

"The truth is a powerful weapon," O'Malley agreed.

For a moment, the anguish in the earl's gaze was laid bare before he blinked, and only the intensity remained. "The ability to reach all levels of society with the truth is essential to turning the tide."

"At last count," O'Malley stated, "ye have the staff from *six* households and the good people in their villages. Captain Coventry's military connections, and Gavin King and his Bow

Street Runners' wealth of contacts among the *ton*, as well as the working class, adds to our numbers."

"Your brothers and cousins have stood between our family and disaster too many times to count since my brother inherited his title," the earl remarked. "All that we hold dear is in the capable hands of the men of his personal guard. We are indebted to you, Sean."

The earl didn't say it often, but when he did, pride filled O'Malley at his words. "Ye know ye can count on the lot of us, yer lordship."

"I've put my faith and trust in you from the moment you had the audacity to argue with me about meeting the mysterious *Lady H.*"

O'Malley chuckled. "Ye were determined."

"I wasn't the only one. You and your men had my back then—even though it went against King's advice." The earl's admiration was evident as he added, "You and my brother's guard had our backs at Wyndmere Hall when that madman Hollingford and his miscreants attacked."

"Faith, ye weren't wrong to place yer trust in the likes of us."

"The recent kidnapping attempts shook the foundation of my brother's world to the point where he questioned Patrick's trust. Until this rumor began circulating about Aurelia again, I did not understand how that would be possible."

Their gazes met and held. O'Malley took the direct hit as it was intended—a cautionary warning of what may come.

"I cannot and will not stand by and let whoever is behind these ugly rumors go unchallenged!"

O'Malley knew then that the earl would be challenging whoever was behind the slanderous attack. "I'll stand as yer second, yer lordship. Me cousins, Dermott and Aiden, will guard yer back."

"Thank you, Sean. I know I can count on you."

Sensing the earl's anger had yet to abate, O'Malley changed the subject. "It may or may not have been mentioned in the past, but me and me kin are known to those of the working class…on both sides of the law."

The earl chuckled. "Just when I'm certain there is nothing you could say or do to surprise me, you do."

O'Malley was pleased the earl did not ask him *not* to use their less than savory contacts. He would use every means available to turn the tide of the vicious rumors surrounding the earl and his countess.

The earl warned O'Malley, "Nothing and no one will keep me from ferreting out who is behind these ugly rumors."

"'Tis only a matter of time before we do. Until then, we spread the truth—from the workers to the *quality*."

"What if it escalates and the truth is ignored?" the earl asked. "We both know it could happen."

"Leave it to me and the lads. We can be very persuasive." O'Malley grinned. "We've been known to hobble a man so he limps for the rest of his life. More than a time or two, we've had to resort to ensuring a man loses the use of his firing hand."

Surprisingly, the earl nodded. "I shall keep your offer in mind."

"I'm thinking 'twould be one less worry on yer mind if Lady Aurelia wasn't in yer enemy's crosshairs while we take care of this latest threat."

The intensity in the earl's gaze belied his easy tone as he replied, "I would feel better if I knew she was spirited away somewhere safe. That being said, I trust you to stand between my wife and unborn child and whoever is threatening them."

"I'm beginning to see why His Grace was conflicted about me cousin. 'Tis hard for a man to be in two places at one time."

The earl agreed. "Let us see what news King and Coventry bring. Then we'll meet with Finch and the rest of the household staff to finalize our plan of defense."

O'Malley slowly smiled. "Well now, ye might give a thought to laying out our plan of *attack*."

The earl inclined his head. "Until later."

O'Malley was in a fine mood as he let himself out the side door and began his sweep of Lippincott Manor's extensive grounds and the perimeter.

CHAPTER TWO

"WE HAVE HAD this discussion before," Earl Lippincott remarked. "What part of you need to rest with your feet elevated, do you *not* understand?"

O'Malley fought the urge to smile as the earl's petite countess put her hands on her hips and glared at him. His wife was giving her husband fits, reminding him of his ma. He smiled. Ma wasn't one to take orders from any man—especially his da!

The butler cleared his throat and announced, "Gavin King and Captain Coventry to see you, your lordship."

"Please show them in, Finch." Turning to his wife, he asked, "Would you excuse us, my love? We have a matter of some urgency to discuss."

Her eyes narrowed. "Obviously it involves me or else you wouldn't ask me to leave."

The earl frowned but was saved from responding as the butler stepped aside to allow King and Coventry to enter.

O'Malley stood at attention while the men greeted the countess and was taken aback when she asked, "Is there anything of import I should know?"

Coventry was quick to reply. "All is well, your ladyship."

Her smile faltered, but she maintained her composure as she bid those gathered goodbye.

When she closed the door behind her, Coventry asked, "Are

you certain keeping this latest crisis from your wife is wise, Lippincott?"

"Yes."

"Until we know more, it's best to protect her ladyship," King stated. "Once we have the culprit behind the heinous rumors, we can reevaluate the situation."

O'Malley was torn between telling Lady Aurelia the whole of it or keeping her in the dark. If it were his ma…well, it wasn't, and neither was the decision his to make.

"Out with it, O'Malley," the earl grumbled.

"Ye'd not be pleased to hear me opinion."

"When it involves my wife," the earl stated, "I rarely am."

O'Malley wasn't quite sure how to respond to that last comment. He had to remind himself he was there to contribute to their discussion regarding the protection of the earl's home and his countess—nothing more. His cousin, Patrick, advised early on that it was best to keep his opinions to himself unless called on to offer them. If asked a direct question, O'Malley would answer.

"Ye may want to confide in yer wife, yer lordship."

The earl was about to reply but a knock on the study door interrupted their discussion.

"Enter."

"Michael O'Malley to see you, your lordship," his butler announced.

As one, the men turned their attention to the man in charge of His Grace's London town house.

The earl met him halfway across the room. "What's happened, Michael?"

"I've been tasked with delivering an urgent message to ye, yer lordship."

"From?" King asked.

"A shop owner on Bond Street," Michael replied.

"Highly unusual," King stated.

"Who sent it?" Coventry was quick to inquire.

"Madame Beaudoine," Michael told them. "She asked me to

tell yer lordship in person that her shop was vandalized late last night."

"Was anyone injured?" O'Malley asked his brother.

"Not that I was told," his brother replied. "'Tis a bit of a mess inside and a handful of expensive gowns were shredded."

"But not every gown?" O'Malley inquired.

Michael glanced at his brother before he turned to the earl and stated, "Only the gowns ordered for Lady Aurelia were destroyed."

The earl hid his reaction to the news well, though O'Malley sensed the man had to be reeling from the shock. He watched the earl closely. The situation had just escalated from rumors involving Lady Aurelia, to the destruction of a shopkeeper's inventory—specifically, gowns designed for the earl's wife.

"Did someone interrupt the culprit?" King asked.

"Did he escape?" Coventry wanted to know.

O'Malley sensed there was more his brother had yet to confide. "Best tell his lordship the whole of it."

His brother nodded. "One of Madame Beaudoine's seamstresses was in the back room sleeping."

"I trust the Watch was summoned," King remarked.

"Aye," Michael replied. "But the intruders slipped away before the watchman arrived."

"I do not like the implication," the earl ground out. "Only my wife's gowns were damaged."

O'Malley agreed with the earl, "'Tis a blatant message to be sure."

"I believe I shall have a word with Madame Beaudoine," Coventry announced.

"I have some questions for the Watch," King told them.

"Did you follow my brother's protocol before you left to deliver Madame Beaudoine's message?" the earl asked.

"Aye, yer lordship," Michael replied. "I sent word to Bow Street on behalf of the duke as soon as I'd heard."

"Which one of my men relieved you?" King asked.

"Franklin."

The earl nodded. "A good man to have at your back. I know my brother would not expect anything less than having his standing orders obeyed, but I'll thank you on his behalf just the same."

"Me duty and me pleasure," Michael replied. "If ye have no further need of me—"

"Actually, I do," the earl interrupted as he yanked on the bell pull.

Finch appeared a few moments later. "Yes, your lordship?"

"See that Mrs. Wyatt prepares a meal for Michael and send one of the stable lads to take care of his horse."

"At once, your lordship."

Michael thanked him, saying, "I appreciate the offer of a meal, but I'd best be getting back to me post. No telling what else occurred while I've been gone."

"If Franklin needed help," King told the duke's man, "he would have sent word to Bow Street." King turned and stared at the earl for long moments before inquiring, "What are you thinking, Lippincott?"

The earl rolled his shoulders before responding. "I believe I shall accompany you and Coventry to London."

The knock on the open door interrupted the earl. "Is there a problem, Finch?"

"Her ladyship wishes to have a word."

"I do not have the time—"

Lady Aurelia swept into the room to confront her husband. "Make the time, because I'd dearly love to know what would possess you to hare off to London when I need you here!"

The room fell silent as the couple glared at one another. It was clear to O'Malley that Lady Aurelia had no intention of backing down. Needing to defuse the volatile situation, as it appeared no one else was about to, O'Malley spoke. "Seeing's how me brother is already here—I could return to London in his stead. I could see to matters for ye and be yer eyes and ears to handle the situation, yer lordship."

"Would you? Thank you, Sean." Lady Aurelia turned to his brother. "It's wonderful to see you again, Michael. Though from the dark expressions surrounding me, I gather you did not bring happy news."

O'Malley watched his brother's silent struggle to decide just what to tell the countess. Given her delicate condition, and to avoid prolonging her worry, he remarked, "Me brother had urgent news for King."

"Oh, does it involve me or my husband?"

Michael's face lost all expression as he responded, "Begging yer pardon, yer ladyship, but 'tisn't me place to say."

"You've just confirmed my suspicion," she said with a sad smile. "Thank you, Michael."

"Darling, why don't you accompany Michael to the kitchen. Mrs. Wyatt will no doubt have something sweet for you to eat while she feeds Michael."

The sadness in her gaze hit O'Malley in the gut. He could only imagine how it affected the earl.

An O'Malley to the core, his brother's expression softened as he offered his arm to Lady Aurelia. "Allow me to escort ye, yer ladyship."

Watching them leave, O'Malley felt unease creeping up from his toes. Turning to face those gathered, he warned, "Word will spread that there's a witness and the Watch had been summoned. We'd best not be underestimating whoever is behind this."

The men were quick to agree. "With your brother here," the earl began, "and Franklin in his place at Grosvenor Square, you can spend as much time as you need in London getting to the bottom of the incident at Madame Beaudoine's shop...and the rumors."

"Aye, yer lordship. I can leave immediately."

"Excellent." With a glance at the door, the earl murmured, "It appears I have a lot of placating to do."

"Although I have not been married as long as you," the captain remarked, "I have been a staunch friend to my wife and her son for over a decade. Talk to your wife. Trust her to be able to handle the situation."

The earl sighed. "I shall take it under advisement, Coventry."

The retired naval captain gave a swift nod before asking, "Would you risk having your wife ill-at-ease, worrying to the point where she and the babe become ill?"

O'Malley observed the abrupt change in his employer's demeanor.

The earl drew in a deep breath, squared his shoulders, and responded, "I shall speak to her directly." Turning to O'Malley, he remarked, "I'll expect daily reports from you."

"Aye, yer lordship."

"I'm interested in Madame Beaudoine's thoughts on what occurred," the earl told him. "And what the seamstress observed."

O'Malley made his way through the servants' door to the kitchen. He noted Lady Aurelia was not in the kitchen and hoped she was resting. His brother was busy plowing his way through a bowl of stew and a loaf of bread. "Hungry?"

Michael grinned as he took a bite of buttered bread. "Mrs. Wyatt's stew has taken the edge off me hunger. Do ye have a plan other than what his lordship asked of ye?"

"Aye. I cannot help but wonder when someone will venture back to the shop," O'Malley told his brother. "Would ye not want to silence the witness?"

Michael frowned. "Aye."

O'Malley nodded. "'Twill be a worry until I have a look around Madame Beaudoine's shop, the alley, and speak to her and her seamstress. How many does she have?"

Michael wiped his mouth with the linen napkin and placed it on the table next to his empty bowl. "Two, I'm thinking." He paused to drain his cup of tea, smiling when the cook refilled his cup. "Thank ye, Mrs. Wyatt. 'Twas a fine meal."

"You're very welcome, Mr. O'Malley."

"Ye'd best be calling me Michael or else everyone will be wondering which O'Malley ye're referring to—me or me cousin, Dermott."

The cook agreed, asking, "Did you save room for a bit of butter cake, Michael?"

His answering grin had O'Malley chuckling. "Best watch out for me brother, Mrs. Wyatt. Sure and Michael's the charmer in the family."

With a nod to his brother, he added, "Dermott and Aiden will fill ye in on the routine around here as there's more ground to cover and protect. They'll introduce ye to those on the staff ye haven't met."

"Watch yer back!" Michael called out as O'Malley stepped outside.

"Best be watching yer own, little brother."

O'MALLEY WAS GRATEFUL His Grace had horses stabled along the road north to London. He needed to make the trip as quickly as possible. The duke's horses did not disappoint as they covered the ground quickly between changes of his horse. Just shy of five hours later, he arrived at the duke's town house on Grosvenor Square.

He dismounted and rubbed a hand along the horse's neck. "'Twas a fine bit of a run we had those last few miles, wasn't it, Lad?"

The horse lifted his head and let out a loud neigh of agreement. The front door opened as he was leading the horse around back to the stables.

"O'Malley?"

He looked over his shoulder. "Aye, Jenkins?"

"I was expecting your brother," the duke's butler replied. "Has anything happened that I need to know?"

"I've news but need to see to me horse first. We traveled the last dozen miles between a cantor and a gallop, and I promised a bucket of oats for a job well done."

"If the news isn't urgent," Jenkins told him. "Stop in the kitchen. Mrs. O'Toole will have a meal for you."

"'Tisn't urgent. After I rub this fine fellow down, and give him the promised treat, I'll see ye in the kitchen."

A short while later, he'd demolished the shepherd's pie the cook placed before him. "That filled the hole in me aching gut, Mrs. O'Toole. Are ye sure ye won't run away with me? I could get used to having a warm meal like that every night."

"You and your brother are cheeky charmers, O'Malley." Her smile reminded him of his ma's. "Let me think it over."

He tilted his head back and laughed with delight. "Ma and ye would be great friends. If ye're ever in Wexford, she'd be happy to have ye for a long visit."

"I'll keep that in mind."

Jenkins entered the kitchen followed by King's man, Franklin, and O'Malley's cousin, Emmett. "If you've finished," Jenkins said, "we'd like to speak with you."

O'Malley rose from the table and pressed a kiss to the cook's cheek. "Thank ye again, Mrs. O'Toole."

Her cheeks flushed a bright pink as she waved the men out of the kitchen. "I've baking to do for this afternoon's tea," she told them. "Don't hurry back."

Stepping through to the main part of the house, Jenkins motioned to one of the footmen. "Stand guard at the front door until I return."

If the young man thought the request odd, he didn't let it show. "Aye, Jenkins."

Outside, O'Malley drew in a breath, surprised at the damp heaviness compared to the fresh air he'd become used to in Sussex. His cousin grinned. "'Tisn't like country air, is it?"

O'Malley shook his head. "I've grown used to lighter, sweeter air."

Emmett laughed in his face. "Sure and air ripe with the scent of horse and cow *shite* is the sweetest."

Giving his cousin a shove with his shoulder, he asked, "Any news to report?"

Emmett looked around them before replying, "Best to wait until we reach the stables."

CHAPTER THREE

"MIGNONETTE!"

"*Oui*, Madame?"

"Monsieur O'Malley is here to speak with you."

"I do not know a Monsieur O'Malley."

"He has come on behalf of Earl Lippincott."

Mignonette knew from the tone of her employer's voice that Madame was displeased with her reply. She did not look up from the froth of lace she was attaching to the neckline of a customer's gown. She asked, "A moment, *s'il vous plait?* I must tie off this stitch."

"*Oui, ma petite.* One cannot rush when dealing with delicate silk and lace."

Mignonette raised her head to see a broad chest clothed in black—the frockcoat and waistcoat were of the finest wool. Tilting her head further, her eyes beheld shoulders so broad she wondered if the well-made coat had a bit of buckram padding in it. Keeping that question to herself, she realized she'd have to stand if she wanted to see higher than the man's collarbone.

She rose to her full height just over five feet tall and was struck by the rugged beauty of the fair-haired giant with eyes a fascinating shade of cool moss green. His shoulders were impossibly wide...his smile charming. Shock held her rooted to the floor at the realization the man had simply stolen her breath.

"Monsieur O'Malley, may I introduce my right and my left hands, Mademoiselle Yvette Augustin, and Mademoiselle Mignonette de Chauret."

Addressing her seamstresses, she advised, "Monsieur O'Malley has questions for you, Mignonette, about the other night."

Her hands started to tremble as the unwanted memory returned. She clasped them at her waist and inclined her head, acquiescing. "Of course, Madame."

Her employer must have noted her unease. "You have nothing to fear. Yvette and I shall be right here." With a glance at the huge Irishman, Madame motioned for him to sit.

He smiled. "After yerselves, ladies."

Mignonette waited for him to begin his questions. She was no stranger to being interrogated and had suffered through more than one at the hands of those who had falsely accused her family of being involved with the notorious smuggler, Ruan. *They had not believed her.* Setting thoughts of her past aside, she clasped her hands in her lap, willing their trembling to stop.

"Ye have no need to fear me, Lass. I mean ye no harm."

She held his gaze as the truth of his words washed over her. "*Merci.*"

"I understand ye were here when intruders broke into the shop. Can ye tell me what happened?"

She cleared her throat to speak. "There was a loud sound in the shop. I thought I was dreaming at first, and then I heard what sounded like wood splintering."

"Then what?" he prompted.

She looked away as she confessed, "I was afraid. We'd had someone break into Madame's shop not that long ago."

He glanced at her employer. "Did ye report the other incident to the Watch?"

Madame shrugged. "I did not see the need. Mignonette was unharmed and a window was broken. Nothing more."

O'Malley mumbled beneath his breath, but Mignonette could

not hear what he'd said. *"Pardon?"*

"Thinking out loud."

"Ah."

"Were you injured, Lass?"

She hesitated before answering, "Not by the intruders."

He frowned at her and she shrugged. "I got up from my pallet and crept to the door. I wanted to see who was in Madame's shop. I heard more than one heavy footfall...and then I heard fabric tearing."

"Please tell me ye did not try to stop them."

Mignonette shrugged a second time.

"That's not a proper answer, Lass. Did ye leave yer room?"

"Oui."

O'Malley scrubbed a hand over his face, mumbling what sounded like a curse this time, but she did not recognize the word. "Why didn't ye wait?"

"For someone to walk past the shop late at night and hope that they weren't in league with the intruders?"

"An excellent question, Mignonette," Madame Beaudoine remarked. "Would you not agree, Monsieur?"

"Aye, but the Watch make their rounds at night—"

"I've never been out that late," the seamstress replied. "Madame warned me never to venture out alone at night, or else..."

"Or else," O'Malley prompted.

"Madame would not let either of us stay here," Yvette responded. "We had to promise."

"Yvette was the first to stay here until she could find lodging she could afford. Mignonette lives in the back room of my shop now. While it is not ideal for one to have to live where one works, the situation suits us. Does it not?"

"Oui, Madame," Mignonette replied. "I would never ignore your advice. I closed and locked my door but must have made a sound because one of the men pounded on it so hard it shook. I was forced to flee."

"Ye're going to make me ask ye again, aren't ye, Lass?"

The tone of his voice had her wondering if she had a reason to fear the man…his size was intimidating. "Monsieur?"

"Were ye injured?"

"Just bruised from climbing out the window."

His eyes widened at her confession, and she'd later swear their color changed to a yellowish-green. "And then what happened?"

"I hid in the doorway to the shop next door."

"When did ye return?"

She huffed out a breath. She disliked being questioned, but more hated not knowing if Monsieur O'Malley believed her. Finally, she answered, "When the Watch arrived."

Admiration filled him. "Ye're a brave lass. Though I cannot think it was the safest choice."

"Neither would it have been for her to remain in the shop," Madame reminded him. "Or for her to walk along Bond Street alone…at night…in her nightrail."

O'Malley's gaze locked with Mignonette's and an emotion she did not recognize flared to life in the depths of his changeable eyes.

An answering warmth swept from her toes.

He blinked and the heat in his soft green eyes cooled. "Ye have the right of it, Madame Beaudoine, 'Twouldn't be wise."

Mignonette snuck a glance at the handsome Irishman wondering what duties he performed for the earl. "I shall try to do as you say for the earl."

O'MALLEY DUG DEEP for the will to look away from the petite beauty who'd captured his interest the moment he stepped into the modiste's shop. Her eyes reminded him of one of Mrs. O'Toole's confections. He'd been on hand when the duke's cook had been stirring a pot of warmed chocolate—the exact shade of the young woman's eyes.

When Mignonette turned her head slightly to speak with Yvette, light from one of the sconces in the shop shone on her blue-black hair. "In all me life, I've only seen dark hair that shines blue in the light once before, when I was hired to work for the Duke of Wyndmere. Her Grace's hair is nearly the same shade as yers."

As soon as he murmured the words, he clamped his jaw shut. "I beg yer pardon, Mademoiselle. For a moment, I'd forgotten I wasn't home. 'Tisn't seemly to mention yer hair."

"And back home it would be acceptable?" Madame Beaudoine queried.

He sighed. "Among family, aye. Otherwise, nay."

"I am so happy to hear that you feel as if you are among family, Monsieur O'Malley," Madame quipped.

Embarrassment had him breaking out in a sweat. "Thank ye for yer time, Madame Beaudoine. Mademoiselle Augustin, Mademoiselle de Chauret, it was a pleasure meeting ye."

"You have nothing further to ask?" the modiste inquired.

"Not at the moment, but I may after I speak with the Watch. Would ye mind if I returned tomorrow?"

Madame inclined her head regally. "But of course, Monsieur." She held out her hand to him, and he bowed over it. "Thank ye." He spun on his heel, strode to the door, and stepped outside into the late afternoon sun.

"*Bollocks!*" he grumbled. "Ye've *shite* for brains."

The deep chuckle had him spinning around to find Coventry stepping down from a hack. "I was hoping to find you here," the duke's man remarked. "King wants to speak to us."

O'Malley was immediately on guard. "More bad news?"

"That remains to be seen," the captain answered cryptically.

"I'll follow ye on me horse."

"Excellent."

THEY ARRIVED ON Bow Street a short while later and were

ushered into King's office.

"Ah, O'Malley. What have you learned?"

"The lass lives in the back room of the modiste's shop."

King nodded. "Anything else?"

"This was not the first time the shop was broken into."

"Was it reported?"

"Nay."

Clearly unhappy, King frowned.

O'Malley continued with his report. "She was injured climbing out the window trying to escape from the intruders."

"Did she say how?"

"Nay," he grumbled. "The lass ignores questions she doesn't want to answer."

King frowned. "You'll have to encourage her to trust you with the truth."

"Is there anything else I need to know before I speak to her tomorrow?"

King frowned. "I questioned two of the watchmen responsible for the area in and around the modiste's shop. They were familiar with the proprietress and the two young women working for her."

O'Malley sensed he would not like what King would tell him.

"The watchmen were interviewed separately," King advised. "Both had the same information to impart. Though they had no proof that Madame's shop was connected to the free trade, one of the watchmen had overheard conversations and rumors that Mademoiselle de Chauret's family had ties with smugglers."

"Have ye uncovered any proof?"

King shook his head. "She has not been working for Madame Beaudoine long. I have one of my men working to discover if the rumors can be substantiated," King replied. "Until anything noteworthy in her past is discovered, we are in the dark."

O'Malley's gut clenched at the realization that King distrusted the seamstress when the man had not met or spoken to her. That the lass seemed uncomfortable when closely questioned, did not go unnoticed by him. But her reaction and other responses had seemed forthright to him. Based on her answers and his judgment of her character, he'd found nothing to suggest the young woman was involved in anything illegal…especially smuggling.

He hoped King did not uncover anything unsavory in her past, then wondered why in the bloody hell he cared. "I plan to return to the shop tonight and have a closer look at the perimeter, the alley, and the shops on either side of Madame Beaudoine's."

"Let me know what you discover."

He bid King and Coventry goodbye. His growing list of those to speak to included the watchman, and a number of his acquaintances in different parts of London. Two still worked as footmen for his former employer, Lord Chellenham. Others worked at various jobs throughout the city. One of them was bound to have heard news about the most sought after modiste in London having her shop broken into. He had no doubt the destruction of Lady Aurelia's gowns was tied to the ugly rumors that had started circulating again.

His gut was never wrong. After speaking to the watchman tonight, he'd have more questions to put to the petite beauty with hair the color of midnight.

CHAPTER FOUR

MIGNONETTE NOTICED A distinct difference in the atmosphere of Madame's shop the moment Monsieur O'Malley left. She'd felt safe when he was with them, and strangely unsettled the moment he'd stepped across the threshold onto the sidewalk.

She rushed to the window to watch his confident stride as he walked over to his horse, mounted, and rode away.

"Have you finished the gown for Lady Sterling?"

Mignonette ducked her head. Madame did not pay her seamstresses to laze about. She turned away from the window to reply, "*Oui*. I hung it beside the other gowns she ordered."

"We need to work quickly if we are to finish Lady Guddings' ballgown." She clapped her hands, signaling Mignonette and Yvette to gather the materials they needed to add the trim and the sparkles their most difficult customer insisted were an essential adornment to her gowns in order for her to dazzle her contemporaries. Thankfully, Madame was always able to discretely suggest small changes when the added sparkles bordered on poor taste. It would not do to have any of the *ton* discounting Madame's creations because of one lady's insistence on adding to them.

Hours later, they finished the orders and sent them off to be delivered. Madame bid goodbye to Yvette, and when it was just the two of them, she turned to Mignonette. "Are you afraid to be alone here tonight?"

Mignonette shrugged.

"You do not have to be brave on my account, *ma petite*. Know that you are always welcome to come home with me. You may sleep in the guest room," she suggested. "If you prefer, on one of the settees in the upstairs sitting room."

When her seamstress did not respond quickly enough, Madame shook her head. "*Mon Dieu,* you are stubborn! I should never have allowed you to stay in the shop!"

"But Madame," Mignonette rasped. "Where else would I go? I do not have enough coin to pay for a room of my own."

"I should have insisted you move in with me! That you were here when my shop was broken into has me lying awake at night instead of sleeping."

"I am grateful you've let me stay in the back room of your shop, Madame. I have been looking for somewhere to live, but cannot afford anything within walking distance."

"You know that you and Yvette are welcome to live in the shop until you have other lodgings."

"I am not afraid to stay here tonight," Mignonette insisted.

"*Alors!* It is against my better judgment, but I will allow you to stay."

"*Merci,* Madame!"

Madame put her hands on her hips and stared at her seamstress. "If anything happens, you will not open your door!"

"*Oui,* Madame."

"To anyone but me!"

Mignonette nodded.

Madame gathered her shawl and reticule and walked to where Mignonette stood at the front of the shop. Pausing in front of Mignonette, she cupped the young woman's cheek in her hand. "I was young and brave like you, once upon a time."

"Madame?"

Smoothing a lock of hair out of Mignonette's eyes, Madame

sighed, "*Mon Dieu*, I hope I am not making a mistake."

"I shall be fine," Mignonette assured her. "What reason would the intruders have for returning?"

Madame nearly told the young woman—*to silence a witness*, but she held her tongue. Biting back the need to share her worry, she smiled at Mignonette and bid her goodnight.

On the carriage ride back to her town house, Madame sorted through her worries. She would let Mignonette believe she would let her stay without protection. *Hah*! She would send word to Grosvenor Square alerting Monsieur O'Malley of her worry. Mignonette would not be left to her own devices and the possibility of having to face the intruders again.

By the time the carriage rolled to a stop in front of her home, she knew to whom she would send missives asking for assistance. Monsieur O'Malley was at the top of her list.

No one would harm *ses filles*—her girls!

CHAPTER FIVE

O'MALLEY HAD SPENT a few hours the night before keeping watch over the modiste's shop. Relieved that nothing untoward occurred, he was loath to admit the true reason for his relief—a petite woman with warm brown eyes and midnight hair.

This afternoon he had returned, determined to speak to Mademoiselle de Chauret at length to ask her about the infamous French smuggler—Ruan. The free trader had been spotted near the caves beneath the Penwith Tower, the duke's property in Cornwall. His cousin, Finn, who was stationed there had devised a plan to infiltrate the smuggler's gang. If O'Malley could supply his cousin with information ahead of time, all the better.

He opened the door to the shop and was greeted by Madame Beaudoine. "Monsieur O'Malley, to what do we owe the pleasure of your company?"

Madame's surprise was feigned, part of their ruse not to alert either of the young women to the fact that he was there at Madame's request and to protect them.

O'Malley smiled. "I've thought of a few other questions for Mademoiselle de Chauret. May I have a few moments of her time?"

"Mignonette! Monsieur O'Malley is here to speak with you again."

While they waited, Madame leaned close to confide, "I have

heard whisperings among the other shop owners. Your presence has not gone unnoticed. Will that put Mignonette in danger if the thugs come back?"

O'Malley kept a tight lid on his emotions, and a disinterested look on his face. "There is nothing to fear, Madame. I have not received information otherwise."

Madame Beaudoine frowned at him. 'Twas obvious the woman did not believe him. That was not his problem at the moment. The lovely lass walking toward him with a hesitant smile on her face was—to his heart…and his duties.

"Mademoiselle, I have a few questions for ye."

Her hands at her waist were clenched so tightly that her knuckles were white. "Of course.

"Is there somewhere we could speak uninterrupted, Madame?"

The modiste harrumphed but waved them toward the back of the shop where bolts of fabric were shelved. "I will not listen in on your conversation, Monsieur O'Malley." She narrowed her eyes, as she warned him, "However, I *will* be watching you."

He nodded, not willing to add to the woman's growing irritation at his request. When the modiste left them, he asked, "I understand ye haven't lived in London long, Mademoiselle. Do ye mind telling me where ye lived before and how ye came to work for Madame Beaudoine?"

The lass' eyes widened at his question, though she answered readily enough. "I used to live in Orleans."

"Before that?"

"A small town in the countryside when I was quite young."

"Was there a reason for yer leaving France?"

She looked away, and for a moment, he wondered if she would answer him. Finally, she glanced at him and replied, "My father was a tailor, my mother a seamstress. I worked in their shop. We were not rich, but we did not ever go hungry. The work was all to us."

He sensed she had a strong work ethic, her words confirmed

it. From the sorrow in her eyes, he knew her story was about to change. "Did ye fall on hard times?"

She shrugged. The elegant lift of her slender shoulder held his attention until she answered, "*Oui*, Monsieur."

O'Malley bit back on the need to rush her.

"*Mon Papa* was attacked one night."

On edge, he asked, "Why? Who attacked him?"

"Those who pretended to seek the truth, while lining their own pockets with the coin they demanded in return for their silence."

His mind raced, considering the possibilities. The one he feared was foremost in his mind. "Does the name Ruan mean anything to ye?"

Her face lost every ounce of color, leaving no doubt that it did. "Did yer father work for him? Did he store smuggled goods in his shop?"

Instead of answering, she whirled away from him, rushing to the front of the shop.

The modiste put her arms around the young woman, asking, "Mignonette, what is it?"

"I do not feel well."

O'Malley had no doubt the young woman spoke the truth. Lying always scraped at his guts until they pained him. "As soon as ye answer me question, I'll be leaving."

"Answer him, *ma petite*," Madame urged. "Then you may lie down."

Tears welled in the lass' eyes.

He wished to God he didn't have to insist she answer his questions. Bloody hell, it was his duty! The realization hit him between the eyes. This was the first time he thought of walking away from his duty.

If he did, more than the duke's family would suffer. The ladies of the shop felt safe...secure in the knowledge that word had spread along Bond Street that one of The Duke's Guard had taken a special interest in Madame Beaudoine's shop. They were openly pleased that the rumor would attract new customers as well as add to the layer of protection his presence supplied. He could not walk away from his duty, knowing Madame Beaudoine and her seamstresses were convinced they were safe because of him.

And what of his sworn vow? His brothers and his cousins were depending on him, as he did them. They had always been more than family, linked by blood. Working for the duke and the earl was proof of that as they fought to protect and uphold their vow to the duke.

O'Malley could not walk away without her answer. "Yes or no, Lass?" he queried. "Do ye know Ruan?"

The lass dissolved into tears. With a protective arm drawing her closer, Madame Beaudoine's eyes flashed a split-second warning before she pointed to the door. "You will leave at once, Monsieur!"

Knowing when to retreat to let them think they had won the day, he inclined his head, bid them goodbye and left the shop.

O'Malley brooded over the possibility that King's suppositions were not unfounded. Mayhap the lass' family *had* been involved with smugglers. Until she answered his question, he would keep his thoughts to himself. More than once, half an answer led to complications rather than resolutions.

He hoped the destruction of Lady Aurelia's gowns would be the end of Madame Beaudoine and her seamstresses' worries.

As he mounted his horse, he had a feeling it would not be.

CHAPTER SIX

MIGNONETTE WOKE WITH a start. Shaking the remnants of the nightmare from her sweat-slickened body, she bowed her head.

"Mon Dieu!"

The loud crack of wood giving way was followed by the sound of heavy footfalls echoing in the shop. Deep voices rumbled, punctuated by the sound of tables being overturned and fabric rending.

"Not again!" She slipped out of bed and reached for the pike she kept beside her pallet. No one would ravage Madame's shop again! Ignoring her employer's warning—breaking her promise, she crept to her door and peered into the darkened shop. In the faint light of a lantern, the sight before her hurt her heart. So many beautiful gowns tossed about like rags in the alleys back home in Orleans.

Anger bubbled close to the surface. So much time, attention and skill had gone into those gowns ground beneath the big feet of those heathens! Righteous indignation surged through her, setting her temper free as she opened her door. Her pike held high above her head, Mignonette let go a guttural cry of anger and vengeance.

The two huge brutes froze, giving her the advantage. With one thought in mind, she rushed toward them swinging her pike.

The larger of the two men blinked, then growled as he leapt toward her. The spell broken, she turned around and ran as he roared behind her. She had one chance to escape harm. Her mind raced, trying to decide if she should slip into the back room and bar the door or disappear into the wardrobe with the false bottom?

Tossing her pike behind her, she heard the brute trip over it and hit the floor. Pulling bolts of fabric from the shelf to slow the intruder down as she ran, she made it to the wardrobe and closed the massive double doors. Hands trembling, she lifted the trap door and slipped into the shallow space Madame had shown her and Yvette after the piece had been delivered a few months ago. Neither of them had understood the need to have a place to hide at the time. Now, she lay in the stifling darkness, breath held, heart pounding, praying she would not be discovered.

The doors were flung open, and clothing ripped from their hooks and piled on the floor of the wardrobe. The darkness that soothed her now felt like a grave as the trap door above her head bowed under the weight of the gowns tossed upon it.

The sound of heavy breathing had her holding her own. The intruder growled again, snapping her back to the present. She no longer felt safe. The brute punched the side of the wardrobe, cracking the wood. She felt the cabinet sway, and the wood give way. Shifting into a ball, she covered her head with her arms. Her last conscious thought was to pray she wouldn't be crushed to death.

SEAN O'MALLEY MOUNTED his horse and rode away from Bow Street. His meeting had gone as expected. He would have much to add to his report to Earl Lippincott when he reached Grosvenor Square. As he rode, he went over what he would say in the missive.

The duke's brother had not been surprised another ugly rumor about his family had begun to circulate through the *ton*. The earl and his brother had become accustomed to the constant attempts to discredit their family, though the target seemed to change from time to time. First it was the duke, then his duchess, then their sister. Recently it was their infant twins and now…the earl's countess. O'Malley knew another slur cast against Lady Aurelia's good name would have the earl rushing to join him in London to deal with the problem.

Taking his time, guiding his horse through the streets, O'Malley wondered if the latest *on dits* were an attempt at revenge. There were a few people that came to mind, but he required proof. His anger simmered. None of the attempts to discredit the duke and his family had been justified. Then again, neither had the vicious rumors spread about the duchess and the earl's countess.

Mindful not to confuse his mount by tightening his hands on the reins, he clenched his jaw to clamp down on his anger. There was no doubt in his mind the rumors that had begun to make the rounds among the *ton* were connected to the destruction in the modiste's shop. All he had to do was uncover who was behind the plot—and discover whether or not Mignonette had a connection to the smuggler.

Mulling over what he'd learned, and the plans King and Coventry were putting into place, he took a circuitous route back to the duke's town house. Though he'd been asked to leave the modiste's shop earlier that day, he would not shirk in his duty to protect the lass who made her home at the back of the shop.

The shops were closed, the street nearly deserted, magnifying an odd sound that had him glancing down an alleyway next to Madame Beaudoine's shop. The outline of two large men skulking there had him reining in his horse and tying him to a hitching post.

Light on his feet and quick with his hands, O'Malley pressed his back to the building and was edging his way closer when he heard a guttural cry. Years of fighting against those who would take what was dear to his family and friends had him reaching for the dagger in his boot. He hesitated as the first thug burst through the back door into the alley. O'Malley returned his dagger to its sheath and stood, facing the man. With a wicked right cross, he knocked the intruder off his feet. The man landed on his back, unconscious.

O'Malley spun around in time to fend off an attack from behind. Taking a punch to the gut doubled him over but allowed him to retrieve his dagger. "Do ye want to wager who's faster? Me and me dagger, or yer fists?"

The man grunted but stilled.

"Is it just ye two, then?" When the man refused to answer the question, O'Malley sighed. "Yers won't be the first throat I've slit." He slowly smiled, "Faith, it won't be the last."

"No…I mean aye, just the two of us."

O'Malley dragged the man to stand beside his fallen comrade.

"You didn't have to kill him," the man groaned. "We was just doing a job for a bit a blunt."

"Tell that to the Watch."

"You'd risk summoning the Watch after you killed Stanton?"

O'Malley nearly chuckled. "I've powerful friends in London. Ye're going to be meeting one of them shortly after ye've been transported to Bow Street."

"The Runners?"

"Aye. King's a friend of me employer. Mayhap ye've heard of the Duke of Wyndmere."

"Duke?"

O'Malley pulled a length of rope from the pocket of his frockcoat. "Turn around and put yer hands behind ye."

When the man didn't move fast enough, O'Malley yanked one of his arms into place and reached for the other. The man stopped fighting as soon as his hands were lashed together. "Stanton was a good man. We both lost our jobs on the docks. Shouldn't be a crime to lift a pint or two on the job."

"Even I wouldn't be drinking while doing me duty."

"With our midday meal—not off-loading crates."

"Well then, that's a different matter, isn't it?"

The man rasped, "We was only after another way to support our families when we were offered a chance to earn what we needed."

O'Malley hesitated. "There must have been another way. Ye chose the wrong one."

"No one would hire us on. The bloody tyrant we slaved for spread the word we wasn't to be trusted…drinking on the job, the liar!"

Stanton moaned as he started to regain consciousness.

"He's not dead?"

"Faith, I only tapped him lightly in the jaw."

The man came to, asking, "Brooks?"

"Don't get up," Brooks told him. "We're in it for sure this time, Stanton."

Stanton swore beneath his breath. "What'll our wives say?"

Brooks turned to face O'Malley. "How will we feed our families if they toss us in the gaol?"

O'Malley felt for their predicament. Sometimes life kept throwing roadblocks into your path. If his back was to the wall, and he had no other options, he'd do whatever it took to put food on *his* family's table. It wasn't right that it was the wives and children who suffered from the poor decisions and misdeeds of their fathers.

He'd been dubbed *the protector* years ago home in Ireland. He'd go to the wall for friend or foe, honest man or thief. If he decided to aid the men and their families, he'd have to place a word in the right ear. Otherwise, he'd be putting his position within the duke's guard on the line for known thieves.

The intruders' words hung in the air between them. O'Malley's family had gone hungry too many times to count. Da had been on the wrong side of the law simply because of their religion and ancestry. O'Malley's strong sense of family still rang true—he couldn't let another family starve because of a man's questionable decision in his time of need.

"I may be able to talk to someone, *if* ye cooperate while I summon the Watch." He helped the fallen man to his feet, and quickly tied the man's hands behind his back. "Was there anyone inside the shop?"

Stanton and Brooks exchanged a quick glance before Brooks nodded. "Aye. But I swear I didn't lay on hand on her."

Mignonette! O'Malley saw red. "Her?"

"One of the seamstresses surprised us, threatening us with a pike," Brooks replied.

"What else could we do, but scare her into hiding?" Stanton added. "We've never hurt a woman in our lives."

"Just men?" O'Malley suggested.

"Aye, but only if the purse for the job would put food on our tables."

"Wait here," he ordered. "If ye so much as move a muscle, I'll know. I won't regret taking a slice out of either one of ye!"

Trusting his words would be obeyed, O'Malley noted the door was hanging by one hinge as he stepped over it into the shambles of the dress shop. A soft whimper from across the shop had him moving toward what was left of a large wardrobe.

"Anyone here?"

The sound ceased.

"Lass. It's me…O'Malley!"

"Monsieur O'Malley, help me!"

"Hang on, Lass." O'Malley carefully pulled broken slats of wood away from the wardrobe door and peered inside—it was empty. "Where are ye?"

"In the false bottom," her soft voice rasped.

"God in Heaven," O'Malley swore. "Lie still. I'll have ye out in no time." Putting his back into the chore, he cleared away the piles of clothing and bits and pieces of wood. An ominous creek sounded above him. His hands shot out to the side to keep what was left of the wardrobe from caving in on them. Bent in half, he braced for impact as the roof of the wardrobe fell on him. He'd later swear he heard two of his ribs snap a heartbeat before pain speared through him, and his vision grayed. O'Malley locked his knees when they threatened to give way. *He had to protect Mignonette!*

"You there!" a deep voice rang out as a beam of light filled the shop.

The Watch had arrived. Relief filled O'Malley. He sucked in a breath through his clenched teeth to reply, "I was going to summon ye to take care of me prisoners outside."

"Don't move!"

"If ye're done spouting at me, I could use a hand."

The watchman moved to stand beside O'Malley, lifted his lantern high to shed light on what was left of the wooden cabinet.

"Who are you, and what are you doing in Madame Beaudoine's shop?"

"O'Malley. I work for the Duke of Wyndmere."

"You're one of The Duke's Guard?"

"Aye. Give a man a hand then, there's a wee lass trapped beneath me."

The watchman placed his lantern on the floor and set to work freeing him.

O'Malley's head felt light when the heaviest length of wood was lifted off his back. "Thank ye...what's yer name?"

"Nate," the watchman told him. "Can you stand?"

O'Malley straightened, ignoring the pain in his ribs. "Aye. Help me clear the rest of this."

The two men worked together silently, quickly. With the hinge cleared, O'Malley lifted the trap door. Light from Nate's lantern illuminated Mignonette's face. Covered with scratches— one of them deep, and white with fear, she was still the most beautiful woman O'Malley had ever seen.

He offered his hand to her. "Ye're safe now."

She hesitated before she put her hand in his. The calluses on her fingertips and strength in her hand belied how fragile she appeared. Her sharp intake of breath had him pausing. "What's wrong?"

A tear spilled across her cheek as she bit her lip. "Nothing, Monsieur O'Malley," she rasped. "Please, pull me free?"

O'Malley suspected a sliver of wood or nail may be the *nothing* she referred to. The sooner he got her out of her prison, the sooner a physician could take care of her. "Aye, Lass." Within moments, she was free and safe in his arms.

Though she trembled, she pushed against his hold as soon as they were outside. He set her on her feet, keeping his arm around her waist to support her. "Can ye walk?"

"*Oui.*" Strands of her black-as-midnight hair escaped from the braid that brushed against the small of her back. Her eyes were dark in the dim light from the lantern. Lips that had tempted him earlier in the day beckoned to him again. The urge to press his lips to hers nearly overwhelmed him.

This was not the time…not the place.

He dug deep to find his control. This woman was far too tempting. He had a job to do, and he'd promised the earl he'd not let a winsome woman tempt him. O'Malley had a feeling that promise would come back to haunt him.

He'd best keep his mind on the task at hand—getting a name from the intruders and uncovering who was behind the plot to discredit Lady Aurelia.

Confident no one knew how hard he fought to regain control, he stared at the alleyway as he ordered his thoughts. There were men to be handed over into the watchman's care—after he put one more question to them. Then, he'd have to return to Bow Street. 'Twould be best to have the conversation with King in person. He would have to explain so that King would understand why he wanted to help the two men who'd been paid to vandalize the modiste's shop.

On the one hand, it was because of similar circumstances that his family back in Ireland had faced, and a family that needed these men to provide for them in order to survive. On the other hand, if he were to pry the name of whoever paid the men to do the job—it would help them get to the bottom of this latest threat to the duke's family. O'Malley would be willing to wager that this event was connected to the ugly rumors circulating through the *ton* involving the earl's countess.

He guided Mignonette over to where the two men waited. Brooks and Stanton hung their heads. One sharp word from O'Malley had them paying attention to him. "Have ye something ye wish to say to the lass?"

Brooks was the first to clear his throat and speak. "We meant no harm. We was paid to shred the gowns and the modiste's stock." He shook his head. "I'm sorry you were injured."

Stanton added, "You scared the breath out of me when you screamed. I chased you to scare you, hoping you hadn't seen our faces." He paused to glance at his cohort. When Brooks nodded, Stanton rasped, "We've never hurt a woman in our lives."

O'Malley watched the expression on the young woman's face change from fear to understanding. Had she survived a similar situation? He'd dismissed King's suggestion of being involved in the free trade and had even gone so far as to ask if she knew Ruan, an infamous French smuggler, but her reaction wasn't what he expected. Nor was her lack of answer. Had she been a victim as these men were? He would spend the time to draw her out, all the while assuring the lass that he would continue to protect her from harm.

Why? The question popped into his head, and he nearly laughed aloud. Ma was always reminding him he was a glutton for punishment, never taking the easy road, always watching out for those in trouble or less fortunate.

"*Merci.* Thank you for apologizing. I am willing to extend your apologies to Madame, but need to ask why you were paid to destroy Lady Aurelia's gowns?" She hesitated before adding, "And why you returned tonight."

O'Malley felt as if he'd been punched in the gut a second time as the brave woman asked the questions he intended to. When they looked at one another and fell silent, he asked, "Were the two of ye trying to get out of paying for yer crimes by telling me tales of not being able to feed yer families?"

"No," Stanton replied.

Brooks shook his head.

The look of fear on the men's faces convinced O'Malley they had not lied to him. "Did ye intend to come back tonight to injure the lass?"

Again, they denied that they had.

"What did ye plan to accomplish?"

The men shared a glance before staring down at their toes.

"Well?" he demanded getting in their faces. "What were ye paid to do tonight besides finishing the job destroying the shop?"

Stanton lifted his head, and there was no mistaking the man's sorrow. "We was told to put the fear of God in her."

"Aye," Brooks agreed. "And to make sure she wouldn't talk."

"How?"

Stanton's nerves were visible as his Adam's apple bobbed up and down. "It was left up to us. The bloke who hired us said his client didn't care how we did it, but we was to see the seamstress lost her position. We had to agree, or we wouldn't get paid."

"How did you propose to collect your fee if you were caught and behind bars?" the watchman asked.

Stanton glanced at Brooks who replied, "We didn't think we'd get caught."

O'Malley's blood boiled as he faced the two men who'd asked for his help. "Am I understanding that the two of ye lost yer jobs and had to resort to destroying this shop and somehow planned to let it be known the lass was responsible so she'd lose her job?"

The two men shrugged. "Aye. She's not supporting a family. She's young and can find other work."

O'Malley turned to the petite woman by his side. "Do ye have family here in London?"

She shook her head before adding, "No. After the death of my parents, I was forced to leave Orleans to find work. I was fortunate Madame Beaudoine hired me and gave me a place to live."

The watchman spoke up. "Why don't we let the constable sort this out?"

O'Malley wanted to beat the bloody hell out of the two men staring at Mignonette. He reined in his anger. He needed a clear head in order to protect her and complete the job he'd been assigned.

"Are ye ready to tell me if ye've more than the scratches on her face and arms?"

She stared at her feet.

"If ye're certain ye don't need me to fetch a physician right away, I'll be escorting ye to the Duke of Wyndmere's town house after I've settled things with the constable and King."

"Do not bother about my injuries. They are minor. Please, take me to Madame! She must hear what happened from me." Mignonette swayed on her feet.

O'Malley frowned as he stared at her. Why wouldn't she trust him? "Are ye all right, Lass."

Nate held his lantern high to illuminate her face. "Where are you hurt, Miss?"

She shook her head ignoring their questions. "I must get to Madame—"

"We'll send word to her," O'Malley stated. "Trust me to help ye, Lass."

The young woman was silent for long enough to have O'Malley shifting from foot to foot. No one had taken this long to trust him in the past.

Why her?

Why now?

The feeling he was being watched had the hairs on the back of his neck standing on end. A glance around them didn't reveal anyone in hiding, though he could not see the other side of the street in the dark.

The watchman spoke. "I'll take these two with me and report

to the constable."

O'Malley hesitated. He had to be in two places at one time—he had to accompany the watchman in order to speak to the constable. He planned to encourage the constable to call on King on Bow Street. At the same time, he had to whisk Mignonette away to safety—the duke's town house. Mrs. O'Toole could take care of her injuries—and mayhap the lass would confide in the older woman, telling her what else ailed her. If need be, they'd send for the physician. His gut churned. He needed to speak to his cousin and send off two urgent missives: one to Earl Lippincott, and the other to Madame Beaudoine.

He informed the watchman, "My horse is out front. The lass and I will ride to Bow Street and speak to King. He could have his men deliver word to Madame Beaudoine and Captain Coventry."

The watchman agreed. "I'll flag down a hack if you wait here with the men."

"Aye."

With a nod, the man strode toward the street searching for a hackney coach to transport his prisoners.

O'Malley watched him walk away before glaring at the men. "I'll trust ye to keep yer word, if I'm to keep mine."

They agreed without hesitation. He turned to the woman and nearly swallowed his tongue as she shivered. Dressed in her nightrail and thin shawl, she had to be freezing in the damp night air. He tore off his coat and settled it around her shoulders. The surprise in her gaze changed to one of bliss as his coat did what he wished he could do—wrap himself around the barefoot lass with midnight hair and warm brown eyes.

Barefoot?

He cursed at his lack of thought to her comfort. Although he'd been doing his job, he should have at least insisted she put something on her feet before he led her into the alley. *Bloody eedjit!* The cobblestones were smooth, but cold to the touch. He'd ended up lying in an alleyway more than once since arriving in London all those years ago. The damp of night was the worst time to end up on your back on the cold stones—whether ye'd taken too much of the drink or been knocked off yer feet.

Mindful of her pride, he stated, "Ye'll catch yer death out here without a proper coat or shoes. Me coat will do for now, but yer feet, Lass…" he let his voice trail off while he waited for her to respond.

"They are cold. If you would wait for me, I'll go and get my shoes."

"There are bits of wood, splinters, and nails all over the floor. Ye'll tear yer feet to shreds. Let me carry ye inside and set ye down on one of Madame's chairs. Ye can tell me where I can find yer shoes."

Instead of acting like it would be a crime for him to enter her room at the back of the shop, she agreed. "*Merci,* Monsieur O'Malley."

Before she changed her mind, he lifted her into his arms and carried her into the shop. As carefully as he'd lifted her, he eased her into one arm, cleared off the seat of the deep blue velvet lady's chair and settled her onto it. "Just point the way."

"In the corner by the pallet."

Entering the room, he didn't comment on her spartan circumstances. His own were similar as he spent very little time in them. He wondered how many hours the lass worked at the shop. Surprised at the overwhelming need to take care of her, he retrieved her shoes. "Do ye need help putting them on?"

She shook her head. As soon as she slipped her feet into the shoes, she stood and met his gaze. "*Merci.*"

"Ye're welcome, Lass."

"Mignonette," she whispered.

Pleasure filled him at the offering of her given name. He nodded. "We'd best be going, Mignonette."

Nate was helping the men into the cab when they returned. The watchman glanced at her feet and nodded. "Would have been cold without shoes. Sorry not to have thought of it, Miss."

"I'm fine, Monsieur Nate."

The watchman was smiling as he stepped into the cab and closed the door. As the driver pulled away from the curb, O'Malley turned to Mignonette and could have kicked himself. Though he'd taken care to see that she had shoes on, she still wore her nightrail under his coat. How did it not occur to him the way she was dressed would tear her reputation to tatters before they arrived on Bow Street? "I'll stand guard outside the shop while ye go in and get dressed."

She stiffened as she laid her hand on his forearm. "*Merci*, Monsieur O'Malley. I was afraid to ask but was worried. I would not want to bring shame on Madame, or her shop, being seen in such a state."

He noted she did not mention *her* reputation—only Madame's. "Hurry now, Lass."

She returned to his side—dressed this time but weaving a bit. He was about to ask her what was wrong, when she held out his coat trying to return it to him. He glanced at the thin shawl around her shoulders and shook his head, motioning for her to put his coat back on. She did as he bid, then tugged on his arm. "We must get word to Madame!"

"Aye." He offered his hand, and she grasped it. He didn't let go until he'd mounted his horse and settled her on his lap. The rhythmic clopping of the horse's hooves on the street seemed to relax the woman in his arms. She must have fallen asleep. She was limp in his arms. By the time they reached Bow Street, her head was on his chest, and a feeling of peace filled him.

"O'Malley!" One of the guards outside hailed him. "Are you here to see King?"

"Aye."

Mignonette stirred in his arms but didn't wake. "We're here, Lass," he urged. Thinking she was afraid, he leaned close and whispered, "Ye've nothing to fear as long as ye're with me. Remember that."

Instead of the response he expected, she moaned and started to slide off his lap. Worry shot clear to the bone. "Lass?"

The guard rushed to O'Malley's side. "Who is she? How was she hurt?"

"Mademoiselle de Chauret." He handed her to the guard as he dismounted. The guard gently handed her back. O'Malley accepted the precious burden and added, "She was in Madame Beaudoine's shop tonight when the intruders returned."

"How was she injured?"

"I don't know what happened before I pulled her out of that bloody wardrobe! Take me to King."

Holding the lass to his pounding heart, O'Malley strode into the building and down the long hall to King's office.

The guard knocked and opened the door when King bid him enter. "O'Malley to see you, Sir."

King nodded to O'Malley, noting the limp woman in his arms. "Send for my physician."

Another man appeared in the doorway—one O'Malley recognized having worked with him before. "Jackson, bring water," King ordered.

"Aye, Sir."

With nowhere to lay the woman down, King motioned to one of the chairs. "Set her down there."

"I don't think the lass is able to sit up. I'll hold her until the doctor arrives."

King looked to the doorway when Jackson returned with the water and nodded. "What happened, O'Malley? Was this woman attacked?"

"I'm thinking she injured herself either when she hid inside the false bottom of one of Madame Beaudoine's wardrobes, or when I was pulling her free. It collapsed on top of us."

King studied O'Malley before suggesting, "See if you can rouse her." King poured water from the pitcher Jackson had just delivered and placed the glass on his desk.

O'Malley softly called her name, but she did not respond.

King removed his handkerchief from his waistcoat pocket and dipped it in the pitcher. Wringing it out, he handed it to

O'Malley.

As if she were one of Lady Aurelia's bone china teacups, he carefully smoothed the damp cloth on her cheeks and then her forehead. He called her name twice. She stirred but did not open her eyes.

"Have you checked the back of her head for injuries?" King asked.

O'Malley ignored the unease shifting through him and carefully slid one hand behind her head and found a lump. "Why wouldn't she tell me she was hurt?"

"If she was trying to hide from intruders, she may have been too frightened to notice," Jackson suggested.

"Ye could be right," O'Malley admitted. "She fell asleep before we'd reached the first cross street."

"She may have fainted," the older man remarked.

O'Malley lifted his head to look at King and swallowed against the lump of fear lodged in his throat. *How could he have not noticed she'd fainted on him?*

King rumbled to his man, "Fetch one of the cots and a warm blanket from the storage room."

When his man left to do his bidding, O'Malley inquired, "How long before the doctor arrives?"

"If he is at home, half an hour," King was quick to respond. "If not…I have no idea."

O'Malley's heart stuttered in his chest. "I'll be praying he's at home."

CHAPTER SEVEN

L ADY KITTRICK LIFTED the snifter of brandy, swirling the highly prized—*smuggled*—French contraband before bringing it to her lips. Savoring the flavor, she sighed as she set the crystal glass on the small table beside her. Any moment now, she'd receive word that the job had been completed.

She slowly smiled. The earl would have no idea who ordered such a strike against his countess. He would never uncover the truth. The man she'd hired to see to the task was known for his discretion and ability to keep his mouth shut. From their one and only meeting, she knew the man wouldn't get his hands dirty— he'd hire someone else to do the job. It didn't signify who destroyed the modiste's shop, as long as it was in shambles—and the witness taken care of.

She wondered how neither one of the men noticed they were being observed the night they destroyed the gowns belonging to Lady Aurelia. She'd been assured there would be no witnesses. But they were wrong. Did the seamstress live in the shop? Why else would she have been there after hours?

Unwilling to have her plans corrupted, she contemplated threatening her contact. She'd already told him to see to it the seamstress lost her ability to hold a sewing needle. What she could not fathom was why her request had been ignored. Reaching for her glass, she sipped, all the while wondering how difficult it would be to break one of the seamstress' hands—it was not as if she'd asked her contact to have both the seamstress' hands broken!

Sipping the potent brandy, she stared at the flames devouring the log in the fireplace as another idea occurred to her. Fires easily happened when one was careless. She could suggest the property be set ablaze after he'd taken care of the witness. If she happened to be in the shop at the time, then so be it!

Two hours later, a knock sounded on the door to her sitting room. "Enter!"

"Your ladyship," her butler stood in the doorway with a silver salver in his hand. "This missive just arrived via messenger."

"Give me that!"

When he complied, she snatched the sealed note from the tray.

The thugs sent back to the modiste's shop had been apprehended by the Watch! An unidentified man was involved in their capture. But more...the seamstress had been in the shop—again! This was the second time the man she'd hired had failed her.

This was not to be borne! He would pay for failing her—*after* he took care of the seamstress.

Melisande would have to go back on her word to never speak to a certain lord again. He may have bored her to tears in bed after a few weeks, but the man had a devious mind. She planned to see to it that those who failed her paid...and paid dearly.

"Is there a reply, your ladyship?"

"Fetch me something to write with!"

A quarter of an hour later, her missive was en route to Lord Brownwell. If she were to persuade him to help her, she'd best arm herself with her most alluring attire. Something soft, delicate, sheer enough to leave no doubt in the fool's mind that she was willing to share her bed again in order to procure his help.

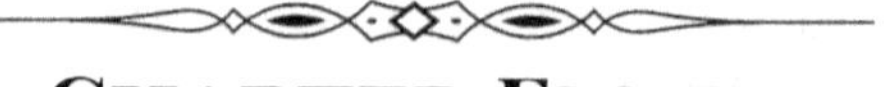

CHAPTER EIGHT

MIGNONETTE WOKE WITH a start. She tried to sit up, but a warm, strong hand urged her to lie still.

"Easy now, Lass."

The familiar voice soothed the worst of her fears. She felt safe with him but was unsure of her surroundings. Her gaze darted around the room, noting two men hovering nearby. "Monsieur O'Malley," she whispered, "where am I, and who are those men?"

Kneeling beside the cot, he replied, "My contact and friend, Gavin King of the Bow Street Runners and his physician."

She took in the information and tried to make sense of it, but her head ached. "And where are we?"

"King's office on Bow Street."

She'd heard Madame speak of the Runners and knew they were men who brought order to chaos on the streets of London from the slums to Mayfair and beyond. "Then, it is safe here?"

"Aye, Lass. 'Tis safe."

"Ah, so our patient is awake." The physician approached her. She took a moment to study the older man. His hair was iron gray, and his eyes a warm brown. He bowed and introduced himself, "Lieutenant Sampson at your service, Mademoiselle de Chauret."

"You are in the military?" She thought O'Malley told her he was a physician.

"Retired military, Mademoiselle." He slowly smiled. "I spent more than a decade serving in His Majesty's Dragoons, patching up his men."

When he paused, she nodded, and his smile deepened. "Now I patch up those who serve His Majesty in other worthwhile capacities."

"Ye've nothing to fear, Lass. Lieutenant Sampson examined the lump on the back of yer head. 'Twas the injury we feared the most. Now that ye're awake, he can tend to the cuts and scrapes on yer arms and side of yer face."

She lifted her hands, but before she could touch the angry scratches, O'Malley stayed her hands. "Let the physician tend to yer wounds first. Ye've far more than we'd first thought standing in the dark alley."

"Would you care to sit up?" the lieutenant asked. "Slowly," he added.

"If I may."

O'Malley eased a hand behind her back while the physician waited. "Now then," the older man said, "I'm going to start with the nasty abrasion on your cheek. Do you know how you injured it?"

Mignonette paused and tried to remember. "Everything happened so fast," she admitted. "I remember hearing the door to the shop crash open, and heavy footsteps."

O'Malley hovered nearby as the lieutenant deftly cleansed the wound on her cheek, ready to help or soothe, whatever she needed of him. "Then what happened, Lass?"

She would have ducked her head and ignored the question, but the physician had a hand beneath her chin as he smoothed something on her cheek. There was no way to avoid O'Malley's penetrating green gaze.

As if O'Malley knew what she was up to, he distracted her, saying, "'Tis a healing salve," he told her. "Then what happened?"

"I was angry."

"Were you?" King asked from where he stood behind

O'Malley.

"Madame has never harmed anyone. She is the most sought-after modiste in all of London and has spent years creating beautiful gowns. Why would anyone wish to damage her creations? We slave over every stitch."

"We?" King queried.

"*Oui*, Madame, Yvette, and me."

"Yvette?" King asked.

"Yvette Augustin, Madame Beaudoine's other seamstress," O'Malley remarked.

Mignonette could not keep the tears from welling in her eyes. She blinked but could not stop the first tears from falling. "To destroy her shop, rend the fabrics…it is unthinkable!"

"What may seem unlikely or unthinkable at first, eventually falls into place as we uncover the facts," King advised.

Ignoring the pounding at the base of her skull, she asked, "Has Madame been notified?"

O'Malley brushed the tears from her face. "Aye, Lass."

Surprised by his touch, she blinked, fighting to regain her equilibrium. "Please take me to her, Monsieur O'Malley. I must be there when she visits her shop!"

"I do not recommend any activity other than rest for a sennight, Mademoiselle de Chauret," Lieutenant Sampson declared. "Injuries to the head must always be handled with caution."

Her stomach roiled at his words. Her father had suffered a blow to the head when his shop in Orleans had been ransacked by the men searching for what was *not* there. He never recovered. "I must speak to Madame!" she insisted. Mignonette had to thank Madame again for giving her a job and a place to live before she, too, slipped into a deep sleep, never to waken.

She hadn't realized she was shaking until O'Malley grasped her hands in his. "Ye have to calm down, Lass. I promise ye'll have a chance to speak to her. Once the rest of yer injuries have been seen to, I'll be accompanying ye to the duke's town house."

"I cannot go," she protested. *What would Yvette and* Madame *think if she went anywhere with this man?* A shaft of unease slithered through her belly. She'd already been in his company unchaperoned for who knew how long. Worry filled her. What would Madame have to say about that? Would she chastise her, or worse...let her go? Mignonette's heart hurt, she would never willingly bring censure to Madame or her shop!

"You should have left me at Madame's shop," she rasped.

The physician smoothed more healing salve over the rest of her mild cuts and abrasions with a care she hadn't felt in a long time. When he was finished, she thanked him.

He nodded before stating, "O'Malley did the right thing. It is never wise to let a head injury go untended. You should be thanking him instead of adding to his duties."

Another tear escaped her guard. She glanced at the handsome man who'd rescued her. "Forgive me. I did not mean to ignore you. *Merci,* Monsieur O'Malley. I am sorry to be a burden to you."

He stared at her for longer than was seemly before he released her hands. "I'll be taking ye to His Grace's town house. I need to report in and send messages to His Grace and Earl Lippincott."

The softer side of O'Malley retreated as the protector accepted his duty.

"The hackney is here, Sir."

King acknowledged his man. "Thank you, Jackson."

"A carriage?" Mignonette turned to O'Malley, asking, "But what of your horse?"

"Ah, so ye remember part of the ride over here."

She frowned at him. "You cannot intend to leave him here, do you?"

"Nay, Lass. I'll be riding alongside the hack."

What he did not say had her wringing her hands. *He'd be protecting her. Did he anticipate more trouble?*

"I've given O'Malley further instructions, Mademoiselle. See to it you follow them."

"*Oui. Merci*, Lieutenant Sampson."

"You are very welcome." The physician helped her stand. When she wobbled on her feet, O'Malley scooped her into his arms.

Her breath snagged in her breast. Before she could demand he set her on her feet, she had the good sense to realize she'd only fall on her face. Reminding herself to breathe in and out slowly, she dared to glance about her. No one in the room seemed to be surprised by the fair-haired giant's swift movement or way he held her protectively against his broad chest.

"Don't forget to have someone sit with her," the physician reminded O'Malley. "Wake her every few hours."

"Aye, Lieutenant. I've been knocked on the head a time or two and understand the risks. I promise to follow yer instructions to the letter." He patted his coat pocket. "I've got them right here."

King walked alongside of O'Malley. "I'll be in touch. If something urgent arises, I shall send one of my men to you." To Mignonette, he assured her, "Do not worry, Mademoiselle de Chauret. O'Malley and His Grace's staff will take excellent care of you while we ferret out who is behind this atrocity."

Awed by the innate power of the man, she quickly agreed, thanking him. "*Merci*, Monsieur King."

He nodded as he stepped around them to speak to the man standing guard at the door.

Closing her eyes for a moment, she drew in a deep breath as she savored the strength in the arms holding her close against a heart that beat nearly as fast as her own. *Mayhap Monsieur O'Malley was affected by her nearness, too.*

King opened the door to the hack, and O'Malley settled her in the carriage. Watching him from the window, she was not surprised that he spoke to the driver before mounting his horse. O'Malley was thorough, leaving nothing to chance. A man who liked to give orders and see them followed. But he had not lorded his position with the duke over her or Madame for that matter.

He seemed sincere in his regard for her, Yvette, and their employer. Engendering trust by his deeds and the way he treated people…not demanding they trust him implicitly.

A warmth filled her when he glanced at her through the carriage window. With a nod, he mounted his horse. The clip clop of the carriage horses rhythmically hitting the cobblestones was oddly soothing. Glimpses of the man riding alongside the hack as he promised was a balm to her weary soul. In that moment, she gave what him what he'd silently asked for. *Her trust.*

It was time to tell him the truth. She had heard of Ruan. She feared the smuggler and his whispered promise to slit her throat before he gutted her. That was why she had fled France.

She trusted O'Malley to protect her and believed he had everything in hand for their journey to His Grace's town house—whether she wished to go or not was no longer a question. Mignonette would not gainsay him. Until she heard from Madame, she was in his care and that of Mr. King of the Bow Street Runners. She would do well to cooperate and not cause either of them any trouble. Looking forward to spending a few days in the servants' quarters of the duke's London household, she was prepared to offer her talent with a needle and thread to the duke's staff. It was the least she could do in exchange for staying there.

With a sigh, she leaned against the slightly worn leather seat and closed her eyes. Fear of slipping into the oblivion that had claimed her father, she pinched the inside of her wrist to stay awake. She did not intend to fall asleep until she had spoken with Madame.

Then if it be God's will, she would close her eyes and let the angels come for her.

CHAPTER NINE

T HE DUKE'S BUTLER greeted O'Malley as he dismounted. They stood side-by-side, watching the hack that slowed to a stop in front of them. Turning to O'Malley, the servant inquired, "Trouble?"

Reins in his hand, he warned, "Aye, there's been a bit of it, Jenkins. Can ye let Mrs. Wigglesworth and Mrs. O'Toole know I've a young woman in need of their care?"

Having worked closely with the O'Malleys and the men of the duke's guard, Jenkins quickly agreed. His questions would be answered in due time. One of the footmen stepped up to open the door to the hack, but O'Malley laid a hand on his shoulder. "I'll take it from here, if ye'd send for one of the stable lads to care for me horse."

"Aye, O'Malley."

Satisfied his requests were being taken care of, he ducked his head and stepped inside the carriage. Mignonette was awake, though her eyes were heavy with fatigue and pain. "Ye're in for a treat to be sure, Lass. Mrs. Wigglesworth will coddle ye, and Mrs. O'Toole will stuff ye with scones and the like until ye burst."

Some of the fatigue seemed to lessen at his words, but her pain and unease was still evident. "Ye have nothing to fear from anyone in His Grace's household. I know the staff personally and can vouch for everyone on it."

"Merci," she whispered. "But I do not intend to be a burden. I will earn my keep."

O'Malley frowned at the petite beauty. "Ye'll rest as Lieutenant Sampson ordered, Lass."

"I—"

"Ye'll rest or I'll have someone sit on ye to make sure ye do!"

Her eyes widened at the threat and, for a moment, he thought she'd refuse. Wisely, she did not contradict him, though a trace of fear lingered in the depths of her warm brown eyes.

He lifted her into his arms and carried her inside. The duke's housekeeper was ready and waiting for him. "Mignonette de Chauret is one of Madame Beaudoine's seamstresses," he told Mrs. Wigglesworth. "She is in need of your care—and me protection."

"Of course, Sean."

Taking Mignonette's hand, the kindly housekeeper gave it a quick squeeze then let go, proclaiming, "You've nothing to fear, my dear. We shall take excellent care of you." With a wave of her hand, she ordered, "Bring her into the downstairs sitting room, Sean. One of the upstairs maids is preparing a room for her."

Mignonette spoke up. "I do not wish to trouble you."

"It's no trouble at all," the housekeeper replied. "Mrs. O'Toole, His Grace's cook, will be in shortly with something to warm your belly."

O'Malley knew better than to argue with the housekeeper's orders and followed the duke's longtime servant down the long hallway.

"The settee will do for now. Don't you think, Sean?"

He glanced at the diminutive woman in his arms. "Aye. 'Twould be a perfect fit for someone so petite."

The housekeeper glanced at him and nodded without saying a word. She did not have to; he'd seen that knowing look all his life growing up with his ma and aunts. He'd have to exercise caution around the lovely Mignonette, or Mrs. Wigglesworth and Mrs. O'Toole would be after him to do more than protect the young woman. Hadn't they mentioned more than once it was past time he looked for a wife?

Setting that thought aside, he eased her onto the settee. Studying her face, he brushed a strand of hair clinging to her long eyelashes. What he saw in the depths of her eyes beckoned him closer. He shook the notion from his mind. For now, he did not have the time to do more than see to it she was taken care of. O'Malley had a job to do. He'd brought her to the safest place he knew of until he could speak to Madame in person. His gut told him the lass would be more comfortable with her employer and had planned to ask Madame if Mignonette could stay with her. Lieutenant Sampson had changed his mind. O'Malley would insist she stay at the duke's town house for the duration.

A soft moan called him back to the present. *Was she uncomfortable? Was she in pain?*

"What's wrong, Lass?"

She closed her eyes. A single tear slipped from the corner of her eye, sliding across the curve of her cheek. Before he could think to stay the action, he brushed it away. Leaning close, he asked, "Lass?"

"I should not be in here," she whispered.

Mrs. Wigglesworth fussed with the pillows until she was satisfied her charge was comfortable. "Of course you should be. How else can we properly care for you?"

"Don't you have a pallet in the servants' quarters or the pantry where I could stay...out of the way?"

O'Malley frowned. Was this what she expected? To be treated as if she were a servant in the duke's household. Putting the question to her, he did not like her reply.

"Don't you see? I am a seamstress in Madame Beaudoine's employ. I should not be in His Grace's sitting room being treated as if I am a member of society."

O'Malley ground his teeth together. This was going to be harder than he imagined. Why hadn't he thought of the ramifications of settling her into his employer's town house? Why hadn't he seen the stubborn streak beneath the woman's bravery?

"Until King and I deem it safe, ye'll remain under me protection. I cannot perform me tasks for the duke or the earl if ye don't cooperate, Lass. 'Tis the safest place in London. Ye'll remain here. King's physician has ordered ye to rest for a sennight, along with detailed instructions for yer care. Ye'll do as he says. Do ye understand?"

She stared at him for long moments without speaking. But he wasn't about to soften his words or change his mind. *She was his to protect.* Now, if only he could forget the curve of her cheek, the faint scent of roses that clung to her skin, and concentrate on his duties, they would get along famously while she healed. If not, he was afraid his head would be more than turned by the lovely lass.

He'd give her something to think about to encourage her to obey him. Locking gazes with her, he stated, "'Tis a scary thing to watch someone recovering from a head injury. They seem fine one day, and the next…" he let his words trail off.

Tears filled her eyes. He wondered if getting her to obey his dictates was as important as her healing. Although it was the truth, he hadn't intended to scare the lass to tears. He could kick himself…and would later if his cousin, Emmett, was willing to go a few rounds sparring with him.

It had been a few days since he'd had the opportunity to test his bare knuckle skills against his cousins at Lippincott Manor. His O'Malley, Garahan, and Flaherty cousins were all champions in their counties back home. There had been many times when situations called for quick thinking and a solid right cross or jab. Other times, a dagger, sword, pistol and rifle were the weapons they used. Training with all manner of weapons was essential in protecting the duke and his family. They'd be foolish not to sharpen their skills as often as possible.

He'd best speak to Jenkins and let him know the situation. The sooner he was able to speak to Madame and the constable, the sooner he could report back to the duke, the earl, and King with the latest information.

"There you are, Sean!" The duke's cook swept into the room with a tray. She placed it on the small table next to the settee and observed their guest.

"Mrs. O'Toole, meet Mignonette de Chauret."

"Yes, of course, one of Madame Beaudoine's seamstresses." She smiled at O'Malley. "Do not worry. We shall take good care of her while she recovers." Turning to Mignonette, she advised, "If there is something you need, do not hesitate to ask. The best thing for you is to rest and get well."

Mignonette seemed surprised but nodded in reply.

"I prepared a lovely bit of broth for you. If you finish every drop, along with the calf's foot jelly, we'll see about adding a bit of buttered bread. But," she cautioned, "that will have to wait for a few more hours." She handed her charge the first cup and waited to see if she would drink it.

When Mignonette finished the broth, Mrs. O'Toole slowly smiled. "Now then, the jelly."

The young woman delicately sipped at what O'Malley disliked...he thought it tasted noxious. She surprised him by finishing the cup and handing it back.

"If you do as you're told and rest, you'll be feeling more like yourself in no time."

Mignonette nodded, then winced.

"Ye'll have to remember not to move yer head for a bit, Lass."

"I never realized how often I move my head," she replied. "It will take some doing."

"If it hurts to move, ye'll remember. Rest now." He bowed, but before he took one step, he heard her soft gasp. He hunkered down next to where she sat. Panic swirled in the depths of her warm brown gaze.

"You're leaving?"

"I have duties to see to. Ye're in good hands."

She stared at her hands. "I am sorry to keep you from them."

Her unease was evident by the tension in her shoulders, the

white of her knuckles, and the way she ducked her head to avoid looking at him. He wanted nothing more than to stay with her until she felt comfortable here but couldn't spare the time. There was a culprit to apprehend, and once ferreted out, bring him to justice.

"Mignonette?" He waited for her to look at him. When she did, he reminded her, "Yer duty is to rest and recover. Madame would want ye to do as we ask."

"*Oui*, Monsieur O'Malley. She would insist upon it."

"Then Mrs. Wigglesworth and I will, too," Mrs. O'Toole announced from the other end of the settee.

"If ye need me, these lovely ladies know where to find me."

"Always the charmer," Mrs. O'Toole chuckled.

"You may trust Sean to keep his word," Mrs. Wigglesworth assured her.

"*Merci*. You are so kind. I shall try to do as you say and rest, but I cannot remember the last time I have had to be still for more than the time it takes to have a meal."

He knew the feeling well. Leaving the lass in the capable hands of the duke's cook and housekeeper, O'Malley took his leave when all he wanted to do was stay.

CHAPTER TEN

"WHAT AILS YE, Cousin?"

O'Malley snapped to attention at the sound of Emmett's voice. "What in the blazes do ye think? We've a devious person trying to cast aspersions on Lady Aurelia's character while at the same time trying to ruin the earl."

Emmett shook his head. "I know ye like a brother. We O'Malleys have hard heads, loyalty to our families, and the need to protect those weaker than us."

O'Malley grunted. Though his cousin was two years younger and an inch shorter, the family resemblance was striking. If you lined him and his brothers—the Wexford O'Malleys, up against his cousin, Patrick, and his brothers—the Cork O'Malleys, you'd have thought the eight of them *were* brothers.

Despite the close family connection growing up, he had no desire to tell his cousin what was in his heart just yet. Time enough *after* he figured out just what in the bloody hell his heart was trying to tell him!

"And," Emmett muttered, pitching his voice low so no one could overhear him, "to hear me ma tell it, when we meet the other half of our heart, we'll feel it in every part of our being."

O'Malley remembered his ma telling him and his brothers, *"Yer soul will cry out for hers when ye're apart."* Worried that he'd just heard his soul speaking to him for the first time in his life, he shook his head at his cousin. "That's a conversation best left for when we have time to raise a pint together."

Emmett shrugged. "How long will ye be here?"

"Until we uncover the bastard behind the rumors, the destruction of Madame Beaudoine's shop, and responsible for injuring the lass."

His cousin shook his head. "I knew it wasn't chance that ye'd brought a beautiful woman here to protect her." Not giving O'Malley the opportunity to reply, he continued, "Talk belowstairs is her hair is as black as midnight that shines of blue beneath the lamplight."

It was O'Malley's turn to shrug. He didn't have time for this. "I've places to be. Will ye be asking one of the footmen to stand guard with ye while I'm gone?"

Emmett bristled at the suggestion. "Do ye believe I need help?"

"Did I say that?"

"Ye may as well have."

O'Malley ran a hand through his close-cropped hair, making it stand on end. "There's a deep plot bubbling beneath the surface. Even King recognized the signs. It won't bode well for his lordship or his countess..." he let his voice trail off as thoughts of Mignonette filled his head and his heart once again.

"And the black-haired lass with the face of an angel."

O'Malley spun back to face his cousin. "When did ye see her?"

Emmett slowly smiled. "'Twere Mrs. O'Toole's words. I've yet to see her, but ye can be certain I'll be introducing meself while ye're gone. Wouldn't want her to feel as if ye'd abandoned her."

O'Malley's hands curled into fists at his sides. The need to haul off and clock his cousin in the jaw had him calling up his steely control. When he felt the invisible shields fall into place, he was able to reply. "Thank ye for watching out for her."

Emmett's eyebrows shot up. He'd not been expecting a reasonable response from O'Malley. *Good*, he thought. The Cork branch of the O'Malleys was a proud bunch. His cousin could stand to be taken down a peg or two.

"Ye can count on me," his cousin reminded him.

"And well I know it." Once an O'Malley swore his allegiance, he kept his word. The O'Malleys were just eight of the men that comprised the duke's guard. If the duke and his family had not been the constant target of more than one twisted member of the *ton* since the duke accepted the title, the eight of them would have been more than enough protection.

The attacks on the duke's family had only escalated after the duke wed Lady Persephone. O'Malley been grateful to have his Garahan and Flaherty cousins standing beside him in their bid to protect all the duke held dear. At times, the sixteen of them had not been able to cover the ground required to investigate rumors and follow leads whenever the family was threatened while an out and out attack had been launched.

Between Gavin King of the Bow Street Runners and Captain Gordon Coventry and his contacts, they'd been able to find the source of past rumors and fend off more than one attack—the latest of which had been three failed attempts to kidnap the duke's infant heir and daughter!

The earl's wife was expecting. No woman should have to bear the slings and arrows of jealous tongues, especially one carrying the earl's heir.

Feet planted, jaw taut, eyes blazing, he promised, "Whoever is behind these atrocities will not go free. We will find them and stop them."

"That we will, Sean," his cousin agreed. "Ye can count on it."

Relieved his cousin quickly agreed with him, he nodded. "I'll be away most of the day. If Madame Beaudoine should call, have Mrs. Wigglesworth insist Mademoiselle de Chauret is to remain here under doctor's orders."

"Aye." Emmett paused before asking, "What if the modiste is more like yer ma or me own and insists on taking Mademoiselle de Chauret with her?"

"See to it she does not."

His cousin's nod should have been agreement enough, and had been in the past, but this situation wasn't like any they'd encountered previously. "I'll have yer oath on it."

Emmett squared his shoulders and glared at him. "Ye bloody well have it."

With a grunt, O'Malley turned and strode down the long hallway in search of Jenkins. He'd apprise the butler of what might occur, while at the same time fill him in on the instructions he'd left with Emmett.

A quarter of an hour later, satisfied his orders would be followed, he mounted his horse. His first order of business was to meet with Coventry who would hopefully have more information about who had paid Stanton and Brooks to destroy Lady Aurelia's gowns in the modiste's shop.

The twinge in his gut reminded him of his pledge to the two men. He'd be paying a call on their wives, with a brief explanation of how they came to be locked in a cell, and O'Malley's promise to take care of them until they were released. Only God knew how long that would be.

Calculating how much of his pay would be required to provide for both families before meeting Mrs. Stanton and Mrs. Brooks was pointless. He'd need to see for himself what their circumstances were and how many children he'd be feeding.

He pulled up outside of the building Coventry and his new wife and stepson lived in. It looked different in the daylight, brighter and more welcoming. Tethering his horse, he strode to the front door. Stepping inside, he bypassed the door to the larger downstairs apartment where Coventry and his family lived to head up the stairs to the captain's office.

His knock was answered immediately. A dark look and brief nod greeted him instead of the surprise he expected. "I've been waiting for you. King sent word a short while ago that he has a lead for you to follow."

"I wasn't expecting any news until later in the day. What have ye got for me?"

The captain didn't bother with niceties, and O'Malley hadn't expected any. Time was of the essence. Reputations were at stake, and possibly the life of the earl's unborn child. "Rumor has it we may be under the wrong assumption that it is a man behind the latest heinous rumors."

"What has King uncovered?"

"Do you recall a member of the *ton* by the name of Lady Kittrick?"

O'Malley's gut roiled at the name. "Aye."

"King thought you would. I gather her connection to the earl was one-sided?"

"Aye. Though he didn't mention meeting her before the night of the Blakley's ball, he had a bit to say about her after calling on her the following day."

"And?"

"Garahan and I accompanied him there. My cousin was the one to rescue one of the lady's servants. Poor lass had been tossed out their kitchen door to the curb, landed hard on her hands and knees."

"Ah, the scullery maid who His Grace hired and sent to Wyndmere Hall."

"Aye, where she remained until she accompanied Lady Calliope to Chattsworth Manor as her lady's maid."

"She wasn't the only servant to leave Lady Kittrick's employ after the earl's visit," Coventry remarked.

"Aye, Garahan mentioned the butler having been sorely abused as well."

"Offering to aid the aging butler was second nature to the duke and the earl," Coventry stated. "Apparently, Lady Kittrick never gave a thought to the backlash she'd face for having let two of her servants go without a farthing or recommendation."

"The duke always considers every aspect of a decision before acting."

"Aye," the captain agreed. "Both His Grace and his lordship were accustomed to the way their father treated his staff. Instead of retiring the elderly staff on half-pay when His Grace assumed the title, he kept them on. Treating them more like the family they had become."

"'Tis just one of the many reasons why me brothers, cousins, and I hold His Grace and his lordship in high regard."

Coventry's green eye gleamed as he smiled. "I have had the pleasure of knowing His Grace since I was injured at Trafalgar."

O'Malley glanced at the captain's black eyepatch and sling, nodding. He'd heard bits and pieces of the man's bravery in battle and subsequent injuries.

"He is the best of men, as was his father, the Fourth Duke of Wyndmere." Coventry paused. "We seem to have drifted a bit from the matter at hand."

O'Malley waited for the captain to continue.

"Apparently, the woman had more than a brief meeting in mind concerning the earl."

"Did she now?"

"At the time, it was rumored she was tiring of her current protector and on the prowl for a replacement."

O'Malley sighed. "She'd decided on his lordship."

Coventry frowned. "When the earl did not shower her with attention, as she was accustomed to in those she chose as her latest conquest, she became fixated on him. When the earl married, there was more than one *on dit* circulating that the lady had made him an offer that he apparently refused."

"But would his turning her down be reason enough to lash out at the earl and his countess?" O'Malley would never understand the so-called ladies of society who were married to one lord but spent a good deal of their time in the bed of another.

"Unfortunately, as society dictates, once a woman reaches a certain age, she is considered on the shelf," Coventry remarked. "Once a married woman becomes a widow, she is considered fair game to any in search of a dalliance—or acquiring another lover."

"I've heard as much when employed by Chellenham. It wasn't a rumor that he had three paramours at one time. Each one kept for a specific reason that I was sworn never to discuss with anyone."

Coventry shook his head. "Chellenham's predilection for the, shall we say, women of uncommon talent, is well known. As is his insistence that he end his association with a woman once she's reached the age of nine and twenty."

"I'd thought that to be a falsehood. I'd been on hand more than once to help…retrieve… Chellenham. Four flights of stairs in one night, added to the man's weight, put a strain on me back."

Coventry's lips twitched as he tried not to smile. "He is a bit on the corpulent side."

"Fat is what me ma would call him."

Coventry's snort of laughter eased the tension in the room. He cleared his throat. "Although the *ton* rarely speaks of a man's paramour in polite company, the age of one's paramour is also dictated by society."

"Ye'd think they'd have more important things to worry over," O'Malley mumbled. "Like helping those scraping to get by to feed their families."

Their gazes met and held. "I did a little digging regarding Stanton and Brooks."

O'Malley's ears perked up. "Did ye now?"

Coventry inclined his head. "Stanton has a wife and two small children. Brooks' wife is expecting their fourth child."

O'Malley frowned. Blast, he hadn't expected that many mouths to feed. But a promise was a promise. "I'd best be going, I've a number of stops to make before I call on Madame Beaudoine."

Coventry handed him a slip of paper. "The men live in the same building. It's in a rough section of town."

O'Malley shrugged. "Won't be deterring me from paying a call."

"I didn't expect it would, though you might want to have

someone accompany you."

"I'd best be paying this call alone. I wouldn't want to bring trouble to either family."

"Just send word if you change your mind."

"I will. Thank ye, Coventry."

"My pleasure, O'Malley."

The men shook hands and O'Malley retraced his steps. He untied his horse, mounted, and headed to the underbelly of London.

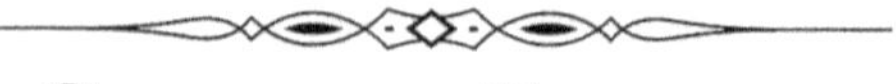

CHAPTER ELEVEN

"WHERE IS SHE?" Madame Beaudoine swept past the startled butler, heading toward the duke's sitting room.

He motioned for one of the footmen to take his place in the entryway and chased after the modiste. "Madame, if you will wait, I'll announce you."

She paused to gape at him. "She is my seamstress, not the duchess."

Jenkins caught up to her as the modiste stepped through the open doorway to the sitting room. "Madame Beaudoine to see you, Mademoiselle de Chauret."

"*Alors,* Mignonette! What happened to you?"

"Madame!" Relief swept up from her toes as tears welled in her eyes and spilled over. "I am so sorry. I did not mean to leave your shop unattended…but you see—"

Her employer waved a hand in front of her as if to dismiss Mignonette's words. "Let us not speak of it now. My carriage is waiting to whisk you off to my home where you should have been taken."

Mignonette wiped at her tears with the backs of her hands. "I was not given a choice."

Madame was reaching for the quilt covering Mignonette's legs when she stopped and frowned. "Who is this person who did not give you a choice?"

"Monsieur King, or was it Monsieur O'Malley?" She met her employer's gaze and then stared at her clenched hands resting in her lap. "I am afraid my mind was a bit fuzzy, you see—"

"Mademoiselle de Chauret suffered a blow to the head," Jenkins informed her from where he stood in the doorway. "She is under strict orders not to be moved while she recovers."

"Whose orders?" the modiste demanded. "I should have been consulted. Mignonette is more than just a seamstress who creates lovely gowns. She and Yvette are my family!"

"I beg your pardon, Madame Beaudoine," he apologized as Mrs. Wigglesworth entered the room followed by a servant bearing a tea tray.

"Ah, Madame Beaudoine," the housekeeper remarked, "you have arrived in time to keep Mignonette company while she has her meal."

The modiste eyed the tray containing a small plate with a few slices of bread on it alongside of a mug. "She will never recover if you serve her bread and water. She needs to keep up her strength…not diminish it."

The housekeeper glanced at Jenkins. "Would you have Mrs. O'Toole prepare a tea tray for our guest? I am certain Madame Beaudoine could do with a nice cup of tea."

"Brandy would be more like it," Madame muttered just loud enough for Mignonette to hear.

She glanced at the housekeeper but could not tell by the woman's expression if she had heard Madame or not.

Normally, she would agree with her employer. While Madame owned and ran her own shop and designed exquisite gowns that were all the rage, she was not a physician. Mignonette would do her part to regain her health by doing as Lieutenant Sampson dictated beginning with resting and eating the invalid's diet.

Relief swirled through her as Madame settled herself on the settee across from her.

"Now, tell me everything."

Never one to ignore when Madame gave an order, she told her in as much detail as possible what had occurred.

"Providential that Monsieur O'Malley was nearby. He is more than capable of coming to one's rescue, is he not?" Before Mignonette could respond, Madame continued, "I met Monsieur King recently when I delivered the wedding gown to the new Viscountess Moreland." She paused to tap the tip of her gloved finger to her chin. "I shall never forget the countess' bravery that day—or that madman holding a pistol to her head!" She collected herself to continue. "But I do not wish to upset you with such things. I am here to take you home with me."

Mignonette was momentarily at a complete loss for words. *Viscountess Moreland being held against her will by a madman? A pistol to her head?* She remembered helping to create her gown. A sick feeling threatened to sweep up from the bottom of her stomach at the image her employer planted in her brain.

Mentally shaking her head—it would have pained her if she actually had—she reminded herself, unlike the countess, Mignonette had only suffered fear and uncertainty. The intruders were huge, but not armed with the intention of harming her. Drawing in a deep breath, she lifted her chin. She'd had the wherewithal to hide from the culprits who had dared to return to ransack Madame's shop!

Mrs. O'Toole entered the room, followed by a servant bearing a large tea tray with all the accoutrements, including a plate piled high with sweet confections. She could not remember when she'd eaten last—aside from the broth and jelly. Her mouth began to water.

"Madame Beaudoine," the housekeeper remarked, "you are just the person Mignonette needs to see right now."

"Am I?" the modiste asked, "then why would Jenkins try to stop me from taking her home with me?"

The housekeeper poured tea and served a berry tart topped with a dollop of rich clotted cream to Madame, while the cook handed the mug of savory beef broth to Mignonette.

"Lieutenant Sampson's orders, Madame," Mignonette was quick to respond.

"A lieutenant?" Madame paused with the teacup halfway to her lips. "Why would a military man have the authority to give you orders regarding your health?"

Mignonette's hands tightened around the warm mug before answering, "He is Monsieur King's private physician, retired from serving His Majesty for many years." When the modiste did not give any indication that she had been swayed by Mignonette's explanation, she added, "He attended to me last night as if I were his patient."

Her employer's eyes narrowed as she studied Mignonette over the rim of her teacup. "Have you been injured other than the nasty scrapes and bruises on your pretty face?"

Mignonette shook her head and winced.

"Shaking your head at me is not a proper response." Madame set her teacup on its saucer. "From the look on your face, I understand the need for caution now, *ma petite*. A head injury is not to be taken lightly."

Mrs. O'Toole hoovered nearby with her hands at her waist. *Was she afraid to leave her alone with Madame?* Surely the duke's housekeeper would know that Madame would never want any harm to come to her or Yvette.

Before Mignonette could speak on her employer's behalf, Madame rose to her feet and waved her hand to encompass everyone in the room. "I shall allow you to remain here until Monsieur Sampson has declared you well enough to travel."

"*Lieutenant* Sampson," Mignonette corrected.

Madame inclined her head. "*Lieutenant* Sampson."

Slipping the quilt off her legs to stand, Mignonette rasped, "I would rather go with you."

"Mademoiselle de Chauret," a deep voice grumbled from the doorway. "Where do ye think ye're going?"

Mignonette's gaze met that of the man standing on the threshold of the room. His coloring and features were familiar.

His height and the breadth and depth of his chest had her wondering how he was related to her rescuer. "Are you Monsieur O'Malley's brother?"

"His cousin," the man replied. "Emmett O'Malley at yer service."

Even though she'd just said she would stay and follow the physician's orders, the overwhelming need to be in surroundings she was accustomed to—among those of her station in life, she could not help but ask, "Then you will assist me to Madame's carriage?"

His eyes were a much deeper, brighter green than her rescuer's moss green eyes. The longer she waited for him to reply, the more they hardened. Was he angry because of her question, or was it something else entirely? Uncomfortable enough ensconced in the duke's sitting room as if she were his equal in society, Mignonette ducked her head and stared at her hands.

"Not today, *ma petite*," Madame reminded her. "You gave your word, as did I. You shall remain here until the physician releases you from his care."

The hard expression on Emmett's face softened enough that Mignonette sensed he must have been concerned for her.

Turning to the housekeeper and cook, Madame inclined her head. "I cannot thank you enough for taking care of Mignonette. If there is anything you need from me, please send word immediately."

"You are quite welcome, Madame Beaudoine," Mrs. Wigglesworth replied.

"Do please extend my thanks to His Grace and his lordship as I understand from Monsieur O'Malley—" she paused to glance at Emmett to add, "the *other* Monsieur O'Malley. We have them both to thank for their hospitality."

Relief evident in the depths of his eyes, he replied, "I'll pass yer thanks along to me cousin." He bowed to the women and strode from the room.

"I would be happy to tell His Grace and his lordship for you," the housekeeper agreed.

Madame surprised Mignonette by bending and placing a kiss to her forehead. "Rest and get well, *ma petite*."

Mignonette smiled as Madame swept from the room as if she were royalty. She missed her already.

"If you'll excuse me, Mademoiselle," Mrs. Wigglesworth said, hurrying after the modiste. "I'll show Madame Beaudoine to the door."

"Of course." She stifled the urge to giggle at the incongruous sight of the older housekeeper rushing to catch up to the much younger Madame. When her employer wished, she was swift of foot. There were times when she and Yvette had to run to catch up to Madame.

Alone, Mignonette leaned against the pillows, hoping no one else would come calling and discover her where she had no right to be. The strain of her situation increased the throbbing at the base of her skull. Another worry coursed through her as she remembered how her father had suffered before he slipped away from them before reason returned. Her stomach was not queasy, and her eyesight remained clear. Reminding herself those symptoms combined were the reason her father had succumbed to the blow to his head, drifting to sleep and never awakening.

Closing her eyes, she remembered the little things Monsieur O'Malley did the night before. He'd wrapped her in his greatcoat, swept her into his arms, carrying her over the debris inside the shop so she would not injure her bare feet until he'd retrieved her shoes.

A small smile eased the tight line of her jaw as she recalled the look on his face when he realized she'd been wearing her nightrail and wrap beneath his coat. Once she was dressed, he lifted her onto his horse. She did not remember much after leaning against his broad chest, encircled in his arms. His warmth penetrated his coat and her clothing, lulling her to sleep.

MIGNONETTE WOKE TO the sound of raised voices. Slowly opening her eyes, she glanced about the room, but she was alone. Scooting up so she was once again sitting, she brushed the strands of hair out of her eyes. For the life of her, she could not remember if she'd taken the time to comb the tangles from her hair the night before. Should she ask the kindly housekeeper for a looking glass to repair her appearance? *Alors!* She must look disheveled after all she'd been through. Why hadn't anyone mentioned it to her?

"I'll not have the lass disturbed," a very familiar voice rumbled from the other side of the closed door. *Was O'Malley standing guard outside of it? Was she in danger? Had someone tried to enter without permission?*

"I promise not to waken her—if she is asleep. I have brought some things she will need if she is to remain here for more than a day."

Mignonette recognized Yvette's no-nonsense voice and wondered if O'Malley would let her in.

"If ye leave them with me, I'll see to it she gets them."

"I will do no such thing!" Yvette sounded affronted. "Mignonette would not want anyone pawing through her things."

Before her fellow seamstress could get into any trouble on her behalf, she called out, "Monsieur O'Malley, I am awake!"

The door swung open to reveal the too-handsome man who'd never been far from her thoughts. "We did not mean to wake ye," he apologized. With a hard glare at the young woman standing beside him, he added, "Mademoiselle Augustin wishes to see ye."

Remembering not to move her head too quickly, she replied, "Thank you, Monsieur O'Malley. I would like that."

Yvette shifted the basket on her arm, and swept her skirts closer to her side, so they did not brush against the man blocking her path.

Mignonette swallowed the urge to laugh at her friend's obvious disdain for the man—or was it simply because he'd tried to tell her what to do? Neither of them did well with dictates, but for

Madame's sake, they endured whenever she handed out orders as it was expected and part of their job. But from anyone else, they would stand their ground.

With the toss of her head, Yvette ordered, "Leave us."

Not wanting to insult the man who'd rescued her, saw to it her injuries were tended to, and delivered her to a safe place to recover, she smiled at him. "If you wouldn't mind, Monsieur O'Malley, I feel well enough and would like to spend a little time with Yvette."

A mix of emotions simmering in the depths of his light green eyes darkened them the longer he stared at her. Unsure if it was anger or something else entirely, she dared not blink—nor look away.

Finally, he gave a brief nod. With his hand on the knob, he started to close the door, then paused. "If ye have need of me, Lass, I'll be right outside."

Her heart lighter than it had been moments before, she slowly smiled. Her rescuer was back. "Thank you, Monsieur O'Malley."

Yvette rounded on her the moment the door closed behind O'Malley. "Tell me everything!" her friend demanded. "What really happened last night? Madame won't tell me a thing!"

Mignonette sighed. "Someone broke into the shop."

"Again?"

Mignonette nodded. "I was afraid, but at the same time angry."

"You did not do anything foolish, did you?" her friend asked.

She sighed louder this time. "Are you going to batter me with questions, or are you going to listen?"

Her friend frowned at her before telling her, "Do not leave anything out."

She told of being woken from a deep sleep, the fear that coursed through her knowing someone had broken into Madame's shop again. Her worry that this time they would destroy it.

Yvette listened intently while Mignonette relayed how she'd ended up being tended to by the personal physician of one of O'Malley's friends on Bow Street of all places. She expected questions, but her friend surprised her by not asking any.

Instead, she handed Mignonette the basket she'd brought with her. "Madame and I picked out a few of your better gowns—not what we would normally wear while working, your nightrail and a few other things." She paused and reached for Mignonette's hand. "We are both so worried about you but know you are receiving excellent care here at the duke's town house." With a glance about her, Yvette added, "And in such sumptuous surroundings. Have the servants been treating you kindly?"

She gripped her friend's hand like a lifeline. "How the daughter of a tailor and a seamstress landed in the Duke of Wyndmere's sitting room will be a tale to tell for years," she told Yvette. "I do not remember much of the journey from Bow Street to here, but I do remember insisting that I be taken to the servants' quarters."

"Apparently they ignored your request."

"Monsieur O'Malley can be quite stubborn. If only he could understand how uncomfortable it is to be in here...I do not belong here." Glancing about her, she noted the highly polished mahogany tables, exquisite fabrics covering the matching settees and occasional chairs, the draperies. Wealth and title were evident throughout the room. Every piece of furniture, the rugs, the drapes—even the vase holding blush-colored roses. Mignonette was not used to such opulence. What she would not give to be in the little back room of Madame's shop on her sleeping pallet!

"Would you like me to ask Monsieur O'Malley to have you moved to where you'd feel more comfortable and able to fully relax?"

She shook her head. "I doubt he would listen. He was quite adamant." Distracting herself from what she could not change, Mignonette looked through the contents of the basket and gasped, *"Papa's* book of poems!" Holding it to her heart, tears glistened in her eyes as she reached for her friend's hand and squeezed it. "Thank you for remembering. I shall be able to sleep tonight now that I have it with me."

Yvette's eyes welled with unshed tears. "You mentioned this treasure so many times, we knew you wouldn't rest without it."

A knock sounded on the door before it opened and O'Malley stepped into the room. "I have to leave, but me cousin, Emmett, will be—" his eyes narrowed on her face. "What's wrong, Lass?" O'Malley strode over to where they sat. "Does yer head pain ye? Shall I have Jenkins send for the physician?"

Wiping her tears with the backs of her hands, she assured him, "Nothing is wrong."

He looked from one woman to the other. "Then why is Mademoiselle Augustin crying, too?"

"Happy tears, Monsieur O'Malley." Mignonette held up the small, worn book for him to see. "Yvette and Madame packed my father's book for me."

The look in his eyes softened, taking in the worn spine of the book. "Well then, if ye're certain ye aren't in pain, I'll be taking me leave."

Before she could stop herself, Mignonette asked, "When will you be back?"

With a smile that had her heart stuttering in her breast, he told her, "Well after the evening meal. If ye need anything, Emmett will see to it until I return."

She hesitated before agreeing.

"Ye can trust him."

"I will. Thank you for worrying about me."

His gaze held hers for long moments before he took his leave, striding to the door without a backward glance.

"You have feelings for him," Yvette stated.

She lifted a shoulder in reply, not sure if she could trust her voice not to crack as the tears she held at bay threatened to fall.

"No matter," Yvette huffed. "I am sure you will forget all about the handsome guard as soon as you are back where you belong."

Mignonette held her silence.

Yvette stood, smoothed her skirts, and warned, "Do not lose your heart or your head to that one."

Too late, Mignonette thought. *I already have.*

CHAPTER TWELVE

O'MALLEY WAS TORN as he and his cousin discussed Mignonette's protection in detail. He wanted to be the one protecting her from harm.

His cousin sensed there was more to it than that. "Never thought to meet another woman with hair as black as midnight," Emmett remarked. "'Tis just like Her Grace's hair," he added, "shining a deep blue beneath candleflame."

O'Malley shoved his cousin to get his attention. "She's not to be trifled with," he ground out. "Or ye'll answer to me. She's a beautiful woman—don't be playing on her situation or her emotions!"

Emmett studied him before giving a brief nod of agreement. His cousin's next words surprised O'Malley. "Anyone with eyes in their head can see she's taken with ye, Sean."

He thought she felt gratitude toward him, nothing more. *Was his cousin right?*

Emmett's hand clamped down hard on O'Malley's shoulder, breaking through his reverie. "She'll be leaving in a few days to return to her life as a seamstress. Try to remember that."

The swift jab to his heart was unexpected. Mayhap his feelings ran deeper than he'd already acknowledged. "Aye, ye're right. Between the two of us, we'll see to her protection."

Emmett nodded.

"I'm off to meet with Coventry. I've sensitive information to relay."

"About the wives and families of the bloody bastards the constable hauled off last night?"

"They'd lost their jobs," O'Malley reminded him. "The talk went against them from the start. It spread through the docks until no one would hire them. What else could they do? They had to feed their families." He drew in a deep breath and let it go. "What else could me da or yours have done?"

Emmett locked gazes with him and O'Malley saw what he'd been waiting for…understanding. "Watch yer back, Sean."

He sighed deeply. At times, his cousin knew him better than he knew himself. "Aye. 'Tis a circumstance so close to what's been happening back home I cannot ignore it and walk away."

His cousin understood without being told that O'Malley already added the two families to those under his protection. "Ye cannot save the world, Sean."

He squared his shoulders and straightened to his full height. Emmett did the same, and O'Malley grumbled, "Stick yer chin out at me again, and I'll be planting me fist on it."

His cousin cracked his knuckles and slowly smiled. "I've missed the last few days sparring with ye." With a deep sigh of resignation, Emmett told him, "It'll have to wait for a bit, but depend on it—I'll be the one knocking ye on yer *arse*."

O'Malley laughed in his face. "It won't be happening any time soon."

Emmett shook his head at him. "Later. Speak to Coventry, he's got a level head and sees things from our point of view more often than not."

O'Malley agreed and turned to go.

"See that ye remember what nearly happened to yer da," Emmett reminded him. "And what happened to mine."

His cousin's comment had him looking over his shoulder to give his word. "I will."

Head whirling with possibilities of how to take care of two

women who didn't trust him to keep his word—and feed the five children between them, O'Malley made his way to the stables. He saddled his horse and rode out to meet with Coventry. They would need to discuss possible plans in detail before either of them met with King. As a man of the law, he'd be hard to sway to their way of thinking.

With a quick prayer to his Maker, hope filled O'Malley the closer he got to the corner of Hart and Lumley.

COVENTRY MOTIONED FOR O'Malley to take a seat. When he did, the captain asked, "What did you have in mind?"

For some reason, the calm tone got under O'Malley's skin. "I've been working out a plan and discussed it with Emmett."

"And?" Coventry prompted. "Does it include asking His Grace to get involved and have the two men responsible for shredding his sister-in-law's gowns and destroying Madame Beaudoine's shop be set free without paying for their crimes?"

O'Malley clenched his teeth to keep from shouting at the man. It would not do any good. He'd worked closely with the captain, and knew he was always level-headed under pressure. It was why he'd come to him first, hoping his point of view, added to O'Malley's ideas, would sway King from throwing the two men behind bars and tossing away the key.

He decided to fill the captain in on what he'd observed during his visit earlier with Mrs. Brooks and Mrs. Stanton and their children. "Mrs. Brooks is expecting their fourth child—from the looks of it, any day. Mrs. Stanton has two young children."

The captain nodded.

O'Malley continued to lay the groundwork. "They live too close to the stews for comfort. Their wives' clothing appeared to be worn and faded—thin at the elbows, with collars mended more than once. The children's clothing was not as worn, but definitely has seen a bit of wear."

"I've witnessed the same over the years, visiting with the families of my fallen comrades-in-arms," Coventry admitted.

"Some were too proud to accept any help." The intensity in his one-eyed gaze spoke volumes. "Others allowed me to help for the sake of their children."

O'Malley nodded. "I'm sensing that might be the situation here as well. Given her advanced condition, I'm thinking Mrs. Brooks may be easier to convince."

The captain shook his head. "I would not count on that. I seem to recall a very stubborn woman reminding me that she was more than able to care for her little one."

O'Malley grinned. "Ah, yer lovely bride?"

Coventry nodded. "I tried to discern the truth of Miranda Thompson's circumstances from my hospital bed all those years ago. Lieutenant Thompson—my good friend, Michael, had given his life for our country. He'd charged me with looking after Miranda and their two-year-old son before that last battle."

His voice trailed off and O'Malley sensed he was reliving that time in his mind. "And ye agreed."

"Aye. It was more than a decade ago. When I gave my word, I had no idea it would be the last time I would speak to him. That promise kept me from drowning in self-pity. I knew I was responsible for Miranda and their young son, but I'd been maimed in the Battle of Trafalgar. I'd lost one eye and injured my arm to the point I was not sure I would regain the use of it."

"I cannot imagine how ye managed to cope with yer injuries all the while knowing ye had a promise to keep to a young widow and her son who needed ye."

Coventry sighed. "It was right after I'd spoken with Miranda that I received the letter from my fiancée breaking off our engagement. Proof of her lack of faith that I would heal."

"She should have trusted in ye," O'Malley remarked.

The captain shrugged. "Thankfully, His Grace, the Fourth Duke of Wyndmere, had pledged to aid those of us injured—and those who'd fallen, while serving in His Majesty's military. He'd been visiting the hospital and, for some reason, stopped to speak with me."

"Ye'd never met him before?"

"No." Coventry slowly smiled, "But it was a meeting I never forgot. He gave me something I desperately needed to cling to if I were to keep my promise to Michael."

"What was that?"

Coventry's green-eyed gaze locked on his. "Hope. From that point on, I accepted the loss of my fiancée and concentrated on healing. The duke used his connections within the House of Lords and friends among those in the branches of the military and was able to help Miranda receive Michael's pension."

"His Grace is cut from a different cloth than his older brother, the Fifth Duke of Wyndmere, was."

Coventry agreed. "He is more like his father and grandfather before him."

"Where did yer money from the Royal Navy go while ye were recovering?" O'Malley prompted.

Coventry didn't bother to sidestep the question. He answered, "I sent money anonymously to Miranda. At least I thought she'd never guess who was behind the funds to help pay for their food and lodging."

"And after all this time, the two of ye married. Yer wife is an extraordinary woman, and I can say the same about yer new son," O'Malley told him.

Coventry beamed. "Michael will make a fine sailor."

O'Malley frowned. "Does yer wife know what ye're thinking?"

The captain chuckled. "Aye. She was there when Michael told her he wanted to join the Royal Navy like his father…like me, and not above reminding me. But back to the situation at hand. How do you propose to compensate Madame Beaudoine for the loss of Lady Aurelia's finished gowns—the materials and time spent creating them?"

O'Malley was about to speak when the captain continued, "Repairs to her shop, the injuries to Mademoiselle de Chauret and the fear you no doubt have seen in her eyes when she thinks no one is looking."

"I've been able to save a good part of me earnings," O'Malley told him. "Working for His Grace has its benefits...including room and board for me and me horse."

"How much do you send back home to your family?"

O'Malley wondered just how much to tell Coventry while the man patiently waited for him to answer. "Half," he replied. "More if I hear they—or one of me cousin's families have need of it."

"What if something occurred beyond your control? What if you, or one of your cousins or family, were injured and needed the money you're thinking of handing over to Mrs. Brooks and Mrs. Stanton?"

O'Malley had the overwhelming need to punch something— or someone...namely the bloody *arse* from the docks who'd fired the men for sharing a pint with their lunch before going back to their jobs. He slowly smiled. That idea had merit but would have to wait.

"Whatever you're thinking, it had best be above the law. His Grace does not suffer fools, nor does he approve of unnecessary violence."

"'Tisn't unnecessary."

The captain chuckled. "Best save whatever you're planning to do until after we help the women and their children."

Hope filled his heart to bursting. "Ye agree with me?"

"That the families need help? Yes." He paused for a moment, then added, "It's how *we* encourage the women to accept our help, and how we explain it to King and His Grace so they agree."

A thought occurred to O'Malley, recalling events when he was newly hired by the duke. He leaned forward in his seat. "His Grace was more than willing to help when Her Grace's lady's maid went missing."

Coventry did not deny it. "It was a difficult time for Her Grace. And then..."

O'Malley knew without a doubt where the man's thoughts

had gone. He was there at the time. "The duke stood beside Her Grace and made sure the young woman wasn't buried at the crossroads—"

"Aye, with a stake through her heart," Coventry added. "That poor young woman suffered enough at the hands of her abusers. The duke agreed and saw to it that she had a decent burial—not one reserved for those who take their own lives."

"The lot of us knew he accompanied Her Grace to the funeral."

"Sending shock waves through the *ton* at the time."

"The bloody *ton* could use a few more if ye ask me."

The look on the captain's face said the man agreed. "Before we decide whether or not we need to approach His Grace for assistance, tell me, how do you propose to convince Mrs. Brooks and Mrs. Stanton to accept our help?"

O'Malley noticed this was not the first time the captain had said *we*. "I'll see if I can have their husbands write a note, pleading with them to accept the coin I'll be paying."

"We'll be paying," Coventry corrected.

"Ye don't need to—"

"And there is where you'd be wrong. I know what would have happened to Miranda and little Michael if I'd not been there to lend a hand. God knows how long it would have taken for the Royal Navy to release the back payments and widow's compensation had it not been for His Grace."

O'Malley shook his head and the captain suggested, "Why don't we ask my wife?"

O'Malley was about to disagree when the captain added, "Having been in similar straits—without a husband or the necessary funds to keep a roof over their heads or clothe and feed her family—though not because Lieutenant Thompson was incarcerated," he clarified.

Coventry rose and O'Malley reluctantly followed suit. "Are ye certain ye should be involving yer family in matters such as this?"

The captain had already opened the door and paused to reply. "There are many aspects of my job that I would prefer to keep from my wife. Apparently, I solve difficult situations in my sleep."

O'Malley's eyes widened as they descended to the lower floor where Coventry and his family lived. "Do ye now?"

"Aye. At first when she told me, I was afraid it would give her nightmares, but Miranda is the salt of the Earth."

"I see."

Coventry opened the door and stepped aside to admit O'Malley. "Miranda, my love, we need a few moments of your time."

"Gordon?" She smoothed her apron and tucked a wayward strand of fiery hair back into its pins and smiled. "I did not expect to see you until our midday meal."

"O'Malley and I need your advice."

"Forgive me, Mr. O'Malley," she apologized. "I did not see you standing there."

For good reason, he thought, she only had eyes for her husband. "Not to worry, Mrs. Coventry. Oh, and it's just O'Malley," he gently reminded her.

"Of course. Would either of you like a cup of tea? I've a lovely gingerbread still warm from the oven."

O'Malley sniffed the air and smiled. "Thought I recognized the delectable scent." He glanced at Coventry who smiled and answered his wife. "We have time for a spot of tea."

"And gingerbread," O'Malley added with a grin. "Smells like me ma's."

"Please be seated. The kettle's hot. It'll only take me a minute." While she bustled about the kitchen, she asked, "How can I be of help to you?"

The captain gave her the details—very brief from O'Malley's point of view, of the situation while she poured their tea and served the gingerbread.

O'Malley's sigh of pure pleasure hummed in the air around them. Miranda was obviously pleased. "Don't be telling me ma," he confided, "from the scent alone, I'm thinking yers will taste better."

Coventry chuckled. "Good thing your mother isn't living in London."

"Aye." O'Malley agreed.

The captain stood to pull out the chair for his wife and seated her before returning to his seat. "What do you think?"

She took a sip from her teacup before setting it down to reply. "I feel for those women and their children." O'Malley noted the softness in Mrs. Coventry's gaze as she placed a scarred hand protectively to her stomach. She, too, had suffered at the hands of her would-be attacker but had rallied enough to toss a hot pot of stew to save herself. Unfortunately, she'd burned her hands when she'd grabbed hold of the pot. Those scars would never disappear though, in his opinion, they only added to her beauty.

About to ask when their child was due, he looked at the captain and noticed the look of shock on his face. Apparently, he did not know his wife was expecting.

Before either of them could speak, his wife continued, "Mayhap if I were to visit Mrs. Brooks and Mrs. Stanton, I could—"

"No!" Coventry and O'Malley barked at the same time.

She looked from one man to the other. "Whyever not? If they are in need of assistance, I'd like to lend mine."

Coventry chose that moment to rise from the table and walk over to his wife. Taking her hand in his, he asked, "Is there something you wish to tell me, my love?"

Her cheeks flushed, but she did not avoid the question or her husband, O'Malley noted.

"I was planning to wait until tonight..." her voice trailed off.

"I'd best be off," O'Malley interrupted. "I'm to meet with King. The man hates to be kept waiting."

Coventry gave a gentle tug on his wife's hand and pulled her to her feet and close to his heart.

O'Malley chuckled. "Don't bother, I can see meself out."

The last thing he saw when he closed the door was the captain placing his hand on his wife's still-flat stomach. The tug of envy caught him by surprise. He'd never given much thought to marrying, though his ma had been after him for some time. The vision of the woman he'd held to his heart the night before, while they rode on horseback through the streets of London, had him wondering if he should give it more than a passing thought.

He yanked his thoughts back to the job at hand, and the twists and turns his mind had taken since meeting the lovely dark-haired lass. Mounting his horse, he turned in the direction that would lead him to Bow Street and his meeting with Gavin King.

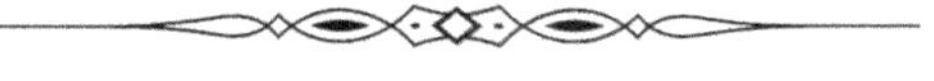

Chapter Thirteen

O'MALLEY ARRIVED ON Grosvenor Square worried that his meeting with King had all been for naught. King did not agree that the men who'd destroyed Lady Aurelia's gowns and the modiste's shop should be granted leniency.

He expected to have to convince King that these men were forced into the criminal act or let their wives and children starve. What he did not expect was to have his opinion and suggestions ignored. "Never thought he'd be so close-minded. Hardheaded. Stubborn."

O'Malley grumbled, "Reminds me of me family."

As he dismounted and led his horse around the back to the stables, he wondered why Jenkins had not greeted him on the sidewalk, as he usually did. The man must normally either have a footman stationed in one of the front rooms watching for visitors to arrive, or he was clairvoyant. He pictured the older servant consulting a crystal ball or staring off into space, seeing things no one else could, and smiled. The man had connections—far more than the O'Malleys and their kin.

Handing his mount over to the stable lad, he entered the town house from the side door and into bedlam. Two maids dashed along the length of hallway toward the sitting room where he'd last spoken to Mignonette. *His gut clenched.* He twisted to look behind him, and nearly dropped to his knees in agony. Drawing on his steely control, he let the pain wash over him, until it started to ebb. Finally, he was able to draw in a breath without visibly giving away the fact that he'd been injured. He'd have to make the time to tend to his own injuries.

Hand to his side, he stalked toward the sitting room. "I'll have me cousin's head if anything's happened to the lass—after he's wrapped me ribs."

Hand to the doorknob, he opened the door in time to hear Mignonette's tearful question. "Don't you understand?"

"Is there a problem here?" he rumbled. When no one immediately responded, he strode to the settee where the lass who'd captured his attention from the first sat with red-rimmed eyes. Sinking to one knee in front of her, he touched the tip of his forefinger beneath her chin, lifting it. "Lass, is it yer head? Are ye in pain?"

Troubled brown eyes awash with tears met his gaze. "No."

Relief speared though him. *Not her head…no pain.* "Who made ye cry then? I'll speak to the bloody bastard."

Her eyes widened in shock, but he had no idea if it was his language or the veiled threat that he'd take care of it. Placing a hand on his knee, he pushed to his feet. "Begging yer pardon for me language, Lass, but I'll not have anyone driving ye to tears."

Finding her courage and her voice, she replied, "No one made me cry." She couldn't hold his gaze for long. Once again, she stared at her tightly clenched hands.

He paced back and forth in front of her, wishing she'd confide in him. Was it because they weren't alone as they had been for most of the night before? She'd had no problem speaking to him then…well with a bit of prompting on his part.

Addressing the two maids who'd been speaking to Mignonette before he'd arrived, he asked, "Will ye leave us for a moment?"

One maid fled the room, while the older of the two frowned at him. "I cannot leave Mademoiselle de Chauret alone with you—unchaperoned."

He ran a hand through his hair. "Will ye at least give us a bit of privacy while I try to find out what's bothering the lass?"

The hard expression on the woman's face softened. "I'll close the door partway," she replied. Turning to Mignonette, she added, "If you need me, give a call, I'll be standing on the other side of the threshold."

He stood at attention, with his hands behind his back, waiting for the lass to respond, though he wasn't sure that she would. She surprised him by thanking the maid. Once they were alone, she lifted her gaze to meet his. "I do not belong in here, Monsieur O'Malley. I have tried to convince the housekeeper and the butler, but no one understands…no one listens."

She sounded so lost. Before he could speak, more tears gathered, magnifying the worry that replaced the warmth in her soft brown eyes.

"What would you have me do, Lass?"

She blinked and the determined lass from the night before returned. "I cannot move past the dread that someone will come calling on the duke and find me in His Grace's sitting room as if I had the right to lounge about instead of earning my keep."

He closed the distance between them. "The staff knows ye're here recovering. I've sent word to the earl and the duke. They know and agree with me. Ye do belong here."

She disagreed. "I do not. My stomach is tied in knots binding it to the point of pain. My head throbs, and I cannot close my eyes to rest."

The lass meant every word, and he had sense enough to realize there was no convincing her otherwise. "Leave it to me, Lass."

"*Merci,* Monsieur."

He prayed his ribs would hold, though without the binding to keep them in place, it was a risk. A risk he would take for the lass who'd turned his life upside down. He bent, swept her into his arms and strode to the door, kicking it the rest of the way open.

The maid jumped and spun around at the sound. "Where are

you taking her?"

"Where she'll feel safe enough to rest and recover."

The maid tried to keep up with him but couldn't match his stride. He'd apologize to her later. Right now, he had Mignonette's welfare to worry about. The lass' face was so pale, her eyes so red, he wondered if she'd made herself ill by letting her fears spin out of control. Did he have to worry about her contracting a fever, too?

As he walked, she tightened her hold around his neck and buried her face beneath his chin as he carried her past one of the footmen. Once they were a distance past the young man, a soft sigh escaped as she relaxed in his arms. He felt the warmth of her breath through his cravat and wished the bloody thing to perdition. Would her lips be firm or soft against his throat? *Eedjit! Ye don't have time for women!*

He stalked past the butler who stood for a moment with his mouth open before rushing to catch up to him. "O'Malley?"

Before he could open the door to the servants' side of the town house, the butler beat him to it. "Allow me."

"Thank ye, Jenkins."

The cook wiped her hands on her apron and asked, "What's happened, Sean?"

"Do ye have a spare blanket or two? I'm going to put the Lass in the room off the pantry—the one with the cot."

"Of course." She bustled past him, opening a large cabinet in the hallway between the kitchen and the rooms housing the butler's pantry and storage. "Let me place these on the cot before you set her down."

O'Malley watched the older woman smooth out the blankets, nod, and turn to face them. "You should be comfortable enough here—though it's not quite as soft and inviting as the settee in the main sitting room, or the bed we'd prepared for you upstairs."

Mignonette flushed with embarrassment. O'Malley took umbrage at the cook's words. Keeping his voice even, and not giving away the fact that he was angry on behalf of the lass, he remarked, "If we'd listened to her in the first place, we would have understood that in order to heal, she needs to be somewhere that won't cause her to worry and not rest." Briefly tightening his hold on the lass to reassure her, he relaxed his hold again to add, "'Tis on the lot of us for not listening to her."

"I'm sorry, Mademoiselle de Chauret," the cook apologized. "We were concerned for you and only wanted what we knew His Grace would insist upon."

O'Malley took pity on the woman he held against his heart, explaining, "She's never met His Grace. If she had, she would have realized he is not like the others in society."

"You are absolutely right, Sean." She frowned and he wondered if she was placating the lass.

The lass trembled in his arms. "What's wrong?" She shook her head against his chest and wouldn't answer him.

"Why don't you set her down while I see about a cup of tea and something sweet for her to eat."

"Will the doctor allow it?"

Mrs. O'Toole lifted her chin in defiance. "He isn't here, now, is he?"

O'Malley grinned. "Faith, ye sound just like me ma."

The older woman patted him on the shoulder. "If she doesn't want to lie down, take the folded blanket from the foot of the cot and place it on the chair in the corner. Be sure to wrap it around her so she doesn't catch a chill."

Watching the woman's retreat, he shook his head. "Reminds me of me ma every time she tells me what to do."

Mignonette's soft laughter had him smiling. An improvement already. Was it because she was more comfortable among the staff or the promise of a sweet confection and cup of tea? He'd ask her later. "Which do ye prefer, Lass. The cot or the chair?"

"The chair, *s'il vous plait.*"

"Grab the blanket and—" he twisted to allow her to reach it and felt his ribs shift.

His sharp intake of breath had Mignonette demanding,

"What is wrong? What's happened?"

"Nothing that cannot be seen to later."

"Please put me down," she entreated.

He drew in a breath and let it out slowly. He'd track down his cousin after he'd settled the lass, satisfied she would be more comfortable here.

"Shall I call for Mrs. O'Toole?"

O'Malley bristled at her question. When the lass got her grit back, it was with a vengeance. He didn't want to have to deal with the cook. She would demand to see to his ribs immediately. The woman would then feel honor-bound to tell Jenkins of his injury, who'd tell the earl. The last thing he needed or wanted was being told to rest while his ribs healed. He'd dealt with cracked and broken ribs before and survived. He would this time, too.

He placed her on her feet, keeping a hand to her waist to steady her. "Do ye need me to help ye to the chair?"

She picked up the blanket and placed it on the chair, sat down and wrapped it around her legs and smiled at him.

He shook his head at her. "Ye're used to being independent, are ye not?"

"*Oui*, Monsieur O'Malley."

"Do ye plan to continue to contradict me orders to the staff regarding yer care?"

She shook her head. "No. This room feels more like home. I do not have to worry and pretend to be someone I'm not. *Merci*."

"Now that's what I like to see," Mrs. O'Toole commented as she entered the room with a small tray. "I'm sorry we did not heed your words earlier." She placed the tray on the table beside Mignonette's chair and commenced pouring. "How do you take your tea?"

"As you poured it is fine. *Merci*."

The cook smiled as she handed the cup and saucer to Mignonette. "You are very welcome. Help yourself to a scone or two whenever you are ready. I have to get back to the kitchen. I have a few pans of bread ready to knead, if you'll excuse me." She paused in the doorway to add, "If you want anything, Mademoiselle de Chauret, please let me know."

Mignonette smiled. "I will. Thank you, Mrs. O'Toole."

"Will you stay with Mademoiselle de Chauret until she finishes her tea? She should lie down and try to rest."

"I am feeling much better," Mignonette advised. "The tea was just what I needed."

O'Malley replied, "I think we should listen to the lass, don't ye?"

The cook opened her mouth to say something, then seemed to think better of it. She nodded, turned, and left the room.

O'Malley chuckled. "I never thought to see the day when Mrs. O'Toole was at a loss for words. Emmett won't believe me when I tell him."

Mignonette's smile reached her eyes and erased the pinched look that had been there when he'd arrived. It would take time for the redness to fade around her eyes, but at least there were faint roses in her cheeks.

He would make a point to listen in the future, rather than ignore those in his care to do what *he* thought best for them. "If ye don't need me for anything else, I need to send word to Captain Coventry."

Dark eyes alight with merriment stared at him over the rim of her teacup. "And see to whatever injury you will not admit to having suffered?"

He rolled his eyes. "Aye, Lass. Since I've settled ye where ye're more comfortable, will ye do me a small favor?"

She set her cup on her saucer to reply, "*Oui*, of course."

"Don't mention it to anyone—especially Mrs. O'Toole."

"If you promise to see to your injury before you send word to the captain."

His sigh was loud and long. Finally, he agreed. "Aye, Lass."

"*Merci*, Monsieur O'Malley."

He shook his head as he left Mignonette sampling one of the

cook's specialties—scones. Although he was tempted to ignore her plea, he'd given his word. Heading to the left, and the door leading outside, he went in search of his cousin.

Normally when the duke was in residence, there would be four of the duke's personal guard stationed around the town house. When the duke returned to his estate in the Lake District, the two guards who'd arrived with the duke would return with him. It had been some time since he'd seen his cousin, Patrick O'Malley—head of the duke's guard. The current rumors flying about the *ton*—and the destruction of Madame Beaudoine's shop would keep him tied to London until the earl sent word that he was needed in Sussex.

Mignonette's lovely dark eyes and milk-white skin intruded in his thoughts. It was fast becoming a habit for his mind to wander where it should not go.

"No time for women," he grumbled.

Truth be told, he would not mind staying in London. Earl Lippincott and his wife were in excellent hands. His brother, Michael, and cousins, Dermott O'Malley and Aiden Garahan, were more than capable of handling whatever crises arose at Lippincott Manor in his absence. He and the earl had trusted one another early on and formed a friendship that had endured more than one attack on the duke and his family. Fighting alongside a man stripped away the outer trappings of rank and circumstance.

His da often reminded him it also revealed the heart of the man, and if he would have your back when it was against the wall. Da had his brother's back—no matter if he agreed with Uncle Patrick or not. The last time their backs had been to the wall, 'twas Uncle Patrick that saved his da…at the cost of his own life.

Lost in thought he didn't see the wall before he walked into it. Pain had him grinding his teeth as he reached out a hand to steady himself.

"Faith, I knew ye were distracted by the pretty seamstress, but I'd never have guessed ye'd lost yer heart and yer sight!"

Teeth clenched, he drew in air and slowly let it out.

"Easy now, Sean. Let me help ye—"

O'Malley let his hand drop to his side and squared his shoulders. "Just a twinge. I need to speak with ye about the lass."

"Did ye hit yer head since I last spoke with ye?"

He glared at his cousin. "Ye're about to hit yers against the wall," O'Malley warned.

"Well now, at least I know ye haven't lost yer sparkling sense of humor," his cousin jibed. "What ails ye? Ye'd best tell me before anyone else sees what I just did."

"I may have nicked a rib earlier."

"Did ye fall off yer horse?"

"Bloody hell, enough questions, Emmett!"

Their gazes met and held as understanding flashed between them. "Tell me how I can help, or I'll be sending a message to His Grace…and the earl."

O'Malley leaned his back against the wall. "Will ye wrap me ribs for me?"

"Do ye plan to rest?"

"When I'm six feet under and not before."

"An O'Malley to the core," his cousin remarked with a grin. "Mrs. O'Toole keeps a supply—"

"Can't," he warned, "she'll be telling Mrs. Wigglesworth—"

"Who will tell Jenkins. I understand. I stashed a small supply of linen strips in the stables."

"What about the stable lads?"

Emmett shook his head. "They haven't found it yet. Keep them busy and away from the tack room while I fetch what I need. We'll have ye wrapped and ready to ride in no time."

Trusting his cousin was like breathing. "Aye."

As they walked to the stables, Emmett asked, "So have ye kissed the lass yet?"

O'Malley didn't remember curling his hand into a fist, but he felt the impact reverberating up his arm when he delivered a right cross to his cousin's chin.

Emmett held him by the cravat and returned the favor with a

quick jab to his solar plexus. O'Malley doubled over as he heard the echo of something snapping as pain radiated through him.

"Bloody hell!" his cousin cursed. "Ye know better than to hit first and not expect a man to hit ye back."

O'Malley gasped, struggling to breathe past the pain. Pressing a hand to his ribs, he slowly straightened. "I won't be forgetting any time soon, Boy-o."

"I didn't mean to hit ye, Sean."

"Oh, I'm thinking ye did."

"Well," Emmett agreed, "I did, but I'd forgotten about yer ribs in the heat of the moment."

O'Malley shoved his shoulder into his cousin as they continued to the stables. "If I'd been in yer place, I'd have delivered a jab to yer throat, and then one to yer solar plexus."

Emmett nodded understanding the message. "Ye'd have left me stunned from the blow to me throat and gasping from one to me breadbasket. Sure and ye're the thinking man, Sean."

"Once me ribs heal, I promise to pound the living *shite* out of ye."

Opening the door to the stables, Emmett replied, "Ye're a man after me own heart, Cousin."

Distracting the stable lad was easy. All O'Malley had to do was express a worry his mount's gait had been off, and the lad was off to fetch the stable master. Making his way to the tack room, he was surprised at how organized the medical supplies were. "I'm thinking ye may have missed yer calling. Ye'd have made a fine physician."

"I'd have had to attend University and earn the blasted sheepskin, else they'd have strung me up from the nearest tree for practicing the black arts."

"We've had generations of wise women in our family," O'Malley reminded his cousin. "Each one learned the healing arts from their mother and mother's mother before them. 'Tis a gift ye should be proud to have inherited."

Emmett shrugged. "I'm thinking ye're trying to distract me from seeing how bad yer ribs are. Strip!" he ordered.

O'Malley unbuttoned his shirt but had to pause to take a breath after he tried to take it off.

His cousin watched, shaking his head when he saw the bruising. "Ye have to be in agony. Ye're bruised on both yer sides. Can ye lift yer arms over yer head?"

"I thought ye were paying attention when I tried to take me shirt off," O'Malley countered.

Emmett sighed. "We O'Malleys never like to admit that we aren't at our fighting best, do we?"

"I'm off to meet with Coventry."

"What about King?"

"Our Bow Street contact isn't in favor of me helping the men currently residing at Newgate. Me gut tells me the problem Mrs. Brooks and Mrs. Stanton face needs to be handled first. After I speak with their husbands—"

His cousin snickered. "What if their gaoler won't let ye have a word with his prisoners?"

O'Malley grinned. "I have me ways of convincing a man to talk."

Emmett frowned. "None of that now, Sean. Ye cannot be thinking to strike a man once ye're within the walls of Newgate Prison! Ye'll never see the light of day and be hanged for yer offense!"

O'Malley sighed. "I'll reason with the man. Ye need to have more faith in me."

His cousin finally inclined his head. "Mayhap I should...but the Sean I know—"

"Has changed," O'Malley interrupted. "I don't always punch first. I leave that to the Garahans," he quipped as he donned his shirt. It took him longer than it normally would. "Do ye think His Grace would be minding if I forego the bloody cravat?"

Emmett's laugh rumbled through the tack room. "I'm afraid he would. Let me help ye tie it."

O'Malley glared at his cousin. "I'll gut ye if ye try to choke me."

"Faith, I love ye, too, Sean."

CHAPTER FOURTEEN

"LIEUTENANT SAMPSON TO see you, Mademoiselle," Jenkins announced.

Mignonette smiled at the kindly butler and set aside the mending she'd convinced the housekeeper to give to her earlier that morning. "Thank you, Jenkins."

He inclined his head, but not before Mignonette noted a hint of a smile. Her heart lifted at the small victory—the duke's butler rarely showed any emotion in her presence.

"Mademoiselle de Chauret," the physician greeted her. "I understand you seem much improved since moving into this…er…location."

She didn't bother to hide the mending she'd been working on.

The twinkle in his dark eyes assured her he was pleased that she'd been feeling up to it. His words confirmed it. "Although I would have thought sewing would bring on a headache, given the head injury you suffered, it seems as if there are no aftereffects."

He walked over to where she sat in the room's only chair. "I am pleased to see you looking well and anxious to return home."

"I am."

"I do believe you to be well on the way to a full recovery." He paused and gestured to her arm, "May I?"

She nodded and held out her arm to him. He looked into her eyes. "Crystal clear." The tips of his fingers brushed against the inside of her wrist as he checked her pulse. "Excellent. I'm pleased with the way the abrasion on your face and cuts on your arms are healing without any sign of infection."

"Madame Wigglesworth and Madame O'Toole have been following your instructions and taking excellent care of me."

"I would expect no less, Mademoiselle. May I check the back of your head?"

"*Oui*, Lieutenant."

"You still have a slight bump, but nothing to worry about. I am confident that you may return home and will be reporting to Mr. King—"

"Mignonette!" Madame came to a halt just outside the small room and glanced at the physician who had turned to stare at her. "Who is this person with you, *ma petite*?"

"Lieutenant Sampson is Monsieur King's personal physician. He has been taking care of me since the night I was injured." Turning to the lieutenant, Mignonette introduced the modiste. "Madame Beaudoine is the most sought after modiste in all of London," she was proud to say as she introduced the two.

Mignonette noted the surprise in Madame's eyes, and the interest in the physician's. Madame rarely reacted to any of the gentlemen who visited her shop, arranging to have gowns created for the woman…or women in their lives. Except for Monsieur O'Malley—whose face and powerful form were hard to ignore. But the duke's guard had come to the shop for very different reasons.

Smiling to herself, Mignonette could not wait to share her observations with Yvette when next she saw her. They'd often whispered about the lack of a man in Madame's life. Mayhap with encouragement that could change.

"A pleasure to meet you, Madame."

Mignonette was happy to see the man's interest tempered with respect for her employer as he bowed over her hand.

What flashed in Madame's gaze was a bit more *risqué* as she inclined her head and slowly smiled. "Lieutenant."

"Mademoiselle de Chauret is well enough to return home, but I must ask if there will be anyone to take care of her should she suffer from any aftereffects. It is not uncommon with a head injury, even after a sennight."

"Mignonette will be returning with me to my home where I can assure you she will be taken care of."

The frown on his face surprised Mignonette. It seemed out of character with what she had come to expect from the lieutenant.

Madame was visibly irritated. "A frown is not a proper response, Lieutenant. Do you doubt that I or my servants will be able to care for her?"

He cleared his throat. "Not at all. I was merely going over possibilities in my head."

The modiste lifted her chin and stared at the physician. "You are more than welcome to follow us to my home, where you will be able to meet my staff and inspect my dwelling to ensure that it will meet with your approval."

Mignonette had heard Madame use that royal tone with difficult customers on more than one occasion and fought the urge to groan aloud. She did not want Madame to say something to injure the man's feelings after he'd taken such good care of her. "I do not think that will be necessary," Mignonette remarked. "Will it, Lieutenant?"

"On the contrary," Lieutenant Sampson rumbled, as he boldly stared at the modiste, ignoring Mignonette in favor of Madame Beaudoine. "I would be remiss if I were not able to assure Mr. King that you are in good hands, and in a setting conducive to regaining your strength."

"I shall speak with the duke's cook and advise her of our plans," Madame announced, stepping into the hallway.

A few moments later, Mrs. O'Toole appeared and looked from one face to another. "You wanted to see me, Lieutenant?"

"Ah, yes, Mrs. O'Toole. Madame Beaudoine has graciously

agreed to take Mademoiselle de Chauret home with her to recuperate. If you would kindly let Mrs. Wigglesworth know."

"I shall have her things brought down immediately, Lieutenant Sampson."

"Thank you, Mrs. O'Toole."

"What have you got there?" Madame asked, noticing the small pile of cloth on Mignonette's lap.

"Er…mending."

"For whom?"

"A few of the staff. I needed something to keep my hands busy and have no other way to thank those who have cared for me."

Her employer smiled. "You have a kind heart, *ma petite*. Are you certain you are ready to leave your safe haven?"

Her heart tumbled in her breast—leaving meant she would no longer see Monsieur O'Malley. *You have no right to expect to see a man of his importance—a member of the Duke of Wyndmere's personal guard.* Her brief time with the Irishman had proven her heart was not immune to a handsome face as Yvette often teased her.

Striving for an outward calm, while her very soul protested the idea of leaving, Mignonette stood and smoothed her skirts. Folding the blanket and placing it on the cot, she replied dutifully, *"Oui*, I am ready."

"After you, Madame, Mademoiselle," the physician intoned.

Madame slipped her arm through Mignonette's and walked along the hallway to the kitchen. There, they bid goodbye to the cook, who assured them that someone would meet them in the entryway with Mignonette's belongings.

With an efficiency Mignonette noticed and sensed was a part of the staff's responsibilities during her short stay at the duke's town house, she and Madame were ensconced in Madame's carriage and on their way to her temporary home.

"I am not surprised to find you in the servants' part of the duke's home. Were you terribly uncomfortable there?"

Mignonette sighed. She was grateful for all that Monsieur O'Malley had done to ensure she would be taken care of, but more…safe. It was not well done of her to bemoan what room he had deposited her in before he left. "I did not belong in His Grace's sitting room, Madame. I am a seamstress…not a high-born member of society. Why could no one understand that?"

"Are we speaking of the staff, or a certain handsome member of the duke's guard?"

Mignonette felt her cheeks heat with embarrassment. "Monsieur O'Malley had business elsewhere before I could tell him how I felt."

"Then it was the staff. Were they unkind to you?"

She shook her head. "They were very kind and went out of their way to care for me, which only added to the unease I felt."

"Mmmm, exposed." Madame nodded understanding what Mignonette had not said. "They were following instructions, and no doubt working hard to keep up with the added responsibilities your fierce guardian expected them to handle."

Fierce guardian? The light-haired giant of a man certainly appeared fierce when he had visited the shop that first day to speak with her. His temperament and actions the night he had come to her rescue forever endeared him to her. Though he seemed not to notice at the time, she had lost a piece of her heart to the man when he'd carried her off on horseback through the streets of London.

The ease with which he'd swept her into his arms, as if she were light as thistledown, had left her breathless more than once that night. But it was the sincerity and intensity in his light green eyes as he sought to assure her that he would protect her and have her injuries taken care of that added to her growing affection for the man.

She remembered the way his heart had pounded when she leaned against him. *Did he feel anything more than duty to her? Mayhap the tiniest bit of interest?* She sighed deeply. She would never know as he was duty-bound to the Duke of Wyndmere and his brother, Earl Lippincott. He did not have the time to visit with her, nor did she expect him to. The man had been kind and caring under highly unusual circumstances.

The steady clip clop of the horses' hooves over the cobblestones did nothing to soothe the growing ache in her heart. Blinking back tears, she turned her head to glance out the window. Her life had forever changed the night men broke into Madame's shop intent on destroying it, and her prayers had been answered by the Irish warrior who pulled her from the wreckage.

Without questioning where he came from or why, she'd put her life in his hands. His strength and size were intimidating, but she did not quail before him. She'd reveled in the strength of his arms, the width of his shoulders, and the breadth of his massive chest.

The safety of his arms soothed her, protecting her even in the darkness of the dreams that plagued her. How would she accustom herself to returning to her mundane existence?

A lone tear escaped, trickling along the curve of her cheek to disappear beneath her ear. She dare not wipe it away lest Madame know she was crying. Mignonette was strong. She'd had to be from the moment she'd lost her parents and became an orphan.

She had made her way from Orleans to London, found work she loved, and with the help of her benefactor, Madame Beaudoine, was supporting herself.

Dreams of being courted by the dashing Monsieur O'Malley were not meant for one such as she. He deserved more—a woman of higher status in life…not a lowly orphaned seamstress.

Her resolve stiffening her backbone once more, she turned away from the window. It was time she returned in her heart and her mind to the world she belonged to and accept the truth.

She would never see Monsieur O'Malley again.

CHAPTER FIFTEEN

Once more in control, now that his ribs were wrapped and supported, O'Malley mounted his horse. He needed to speak with Coventry about Brooks and Stanton before going to Newgate to speak with them. O'Malley dug deep to ignore the memory of visiting Da when he'd been incarcerated. The horrific conditions the prisoners had to endure was stamped upon his heart. The utter despair in Da's eyes was branded on his soul. The news that Da and Uncle Patrick would be released came one day too late. His uncle had perished from his wounds. Shoving the memories deep, he concentrated on seeking Coventry's advice. The captain would know the proper protocol at the prison.

O'Malley did not want to ask Gavin King to intervene unless there was no other alternative. Once the man's mind was made up, it was nearly immovable.

A carriage pulled away from the curb right in front of him. With practiced ease, he reined in his mount to avoid the wheels. If he hadn't been paying attention…*best not to go down that road.* One look at the elaborate crest emblazoned on the door had him grumbling, "The quality back home never gave a bloody damn about anyone but themselves either."

He didn't waste any time wondering who owned the carriage. He had no idea whose carriage it was, and truth be told, he wasn't going to do anything about the near miss. Drawing in a deep breath, he released it slowly. "What I wouldn't give to be home right now, lad," he rumbled to his horse. "Too many blasted carriages clogging up the streets of London."

When his horse lifted his head and whinnied, O'Malley chuckled. "Ye have the right of it. We'd be stuck in the middle of a flock of Haggerty's sheep right now instead of carriages!"

His heart lighter having the picture of home in his heart and on his mind, O'Malley rode the rest of the way, content to travel slower than either himself or his horse would have liked. As he had the day before, O'Malley dismounted and tied the reins to the hitching post outside the building where Captain Coventry resided, and had his office, on the corner of Hart and Lumley. It was late enough in the day that the captain should be in his office.

As he climbed the staircase, he wondered how the midnight-haired lass fared. She appeared much better after he'd carried her to the small room off the kitchen. When he'd held her against his heart, it felt as if a missing piece in his life had been returned to where it belonged. But what kind of a life could he offer her, when the bulk of his time was spent fighting to protect the duke and his family?

He never turned his back on his obligations, vows, or promises. He'd gratefully accepted the position with the Duke of Wyndmere, happy for the chance to work with his cousins and brothers. He could hold his head high knowing he'd be working for a member of the *ton* who had been raised with similar values. Leaving his position as footman for Lord Chellenham—a member of the *ton* reviled for living a life of depravity and having no morals, he felt clean…free.

He shook his head. "Get a hold of yerself, Boy-o. Ye're in no position, nor do ye have the time to court a woman." He frowned as he knocked on Coventry's door, mumbling to himself, "Ye'll be dancing attendance on the lass and spouting poetry when ye know ye haven't the time."

"O'Malley?"

Bollocks! Had the captain heard what he'd just said?

The two men stared at one another until the captain raised one eyebrow in silent question. "Have you suffered a blow to the throat rendering you mute?"

O'Malley's answering snort of laughter had the other man nodding his head. "Ah, not mute then. Come in. Together, we can resolve whatever is weighing heavily on your mind."

Coventry sat in one of the upholstered chairs in front of his desk. He motioned for O'Malley to do the same. When the Irishman sat, Coventry inquired, "Does this have to do with the earl and his countess?"

Firm in the knowledge that the captain would not judge him for his political convictions—at least he hadn't in the past, or his family background and those he called friends, all of whom were of the working class, O'Malley sighed aloud.

"You have my word that I will not repeat anything you say in confidence. Best to get it off your chest."

The captain's promise eased the worst of the tautness in his throat. He cleared it to speak. "'Tis more than that. I've just come from His Grace's town house and was surprised the lass did not look as well as when I'd left her in the care of the staff."

Coventry leaned forward in his chair, worry evident in his posture. "Has she been plagued with more headaches? Blurred vision?"

"Nay. 'Tisn't that, 'tis her worrying that she'd be discovered in the duke's sitting room, and the fact she'd been sleeping in one of the guest rooms that has her losing sleep and affecting her appetite and ability to heal."

Coventry sat back. "I see. I trust you remedied the situation before coming to meet with me."

"Aye. She's much more at ease in one of the small rooms off the kitchen." He shook his head, saying, "The room only holds a cot, small table and a chair." He relayed her immediate reaction to the room and how the fear in her eyes had started to fade by the time he'd left her.

"Well then, it would seem that she will improve thanks to

your timely intervention."

O'Malley reached up to rub at the back of his neck and ended up sucking in a breath to cover his gasp of pain. *Bloody ribs.*

The captain waited until O'Malley was able to conquer the pain and ignore it once again before speaking. "I trust you've asked your cousin to wrap your ribs and not attempted to do so without assistance."

"Aye. They do not plague me now that he has, but I keep forgetting not to lift me arms above me head."

"Have you seen His Grace's physician?"

O'Malley opened his mouth to speak, then quickly closed it.

"Ah. Not planning to have a qualified physician, one trusted by your employer, know that you've cracked, and probably broken a few ribs."

O'Malley shrugged and Coventry chuckled. "There has been more than one occasion in my past where I'd not admitted to an injury, not wanting the interference from well-meaning friends."

"Or an employer?" O'Malley queried.

"You could say that," the captain admitted. "However, my health is not in question right now," he stated. "Yours is. Will your ribs hamper your continued investigation into the matter of the vicious rumors surrounding Earl Lippincott and Lady Aurelia?"

"They will not."

"Or discovering who is behind this damnable business? The destruction of Madame Beaudoine's shop and Lady Aurelia's gowns?"

O'Malley shot to his feet, hands fisted at his sides, and vowed, "Nothing will keep me from unmasking whoever is behind these rumors and unwarranted destruction of the modiste's shop—and the injuries one of her seamstresses suffered."

"The two men responsible for Mademoiselle de Chauret's injuries—"

"Accidental," O'Malley interrupted. "Neither one of them struck her. In her haste to hide from them, she caused her own injuries."

"I highly doubt your rendition of what happened will free Brooks or Stanton from prison."

"It might," O'Malley countered, "if those charges were not levied against them."

"You and I both know that it would take more than that."

"What if the men vowed to repair her shop and repay her for the loss of Lady Aurelia's gowns?"

The captain shook his head. "Whenever high-ranking members of the *ton* are involved—in this case the earl and his countess, brother and sister-in-law to the Duke of Wyndmere, a prodigious amount of coin may be required."

"Does the truth matter?"

Coventry narrowed his gaze. "To His Grace, his brother, and me, yes. To you and your kin, yes."

O'Malley felt a huge weight begin to lift from his shoulders.

"We need irrefutable evidence as to who has orchestrated these crimes…not just the ones paid to perpetrate them."

Three loud, swift knocks had Coventry rising to his feet. "Excuse me."

O'Malley watched with interest as Coventry's face lost all expression before he answered the door.

"Captain." A tall dark-haired man with military bearing stood on the threshold.

"Come in, Bayfield. I'd like to introduce you to one of His Grace's private guard, Sean O'Malley. David Bayfield is a former captain in the Royal Navy."

O'Malley rose and walked over to where they men stood. "'Tis a pleasure, Bayfield."

Bayfield's lips twitched. "Be damned, another Irishman. Brother or cousin to Michael and Emmett O'Malley?"

"Michael's me brother, Emmett's me cousin."

Bayfield nodded. "That would explain your striking resemblance to them." He turned toward Coventry, stating, "I've urgent news."

Coventry informed Bayfield, "O'Malley has been working with me. He was present the night Madame Beaudoine's shop was destroyed, and one of her seamstresses injured."

Bayfield visibly tensed, then frowned. "Not seriously, I hope."

"She is recovering at the Duke of Wyndmere's town house."

"Excellent."

The man paused, and O'Malley wondered if he was remembering a similar circumstance. His cousin had confided what had happened when he'd been assigned to protect Captain Coventry's wife…how he'd heard the commotion and broken down the door, stepping into a volatile situation—right after Captain Coventry's wife had defended herself against attack.

Deciding to remind Bayfield, he remarked, "Me cousin, Emmett, spoke highly of ye. Though I'm not certain why he would when ye called the Watch on him."

Bayfield chuckled. "If you had walked in on what I had, you would have come to a similar conclusion. I wasn't about to take any chances when Mrs. Thompson appeared to be unconscious in your cousin's arms."

"Ye mean Mrs. Coventry," O'Malley reminded him.

"Aye, though she wasn't at the time."

O'Malley noted the intense emotion that flashed briefly across the captain's stoic features. "If you two are quite finished, we have more important things to discuss," Coventry reminded them.

Bayfield and O'Malley turned toward Coventry and waited.

"I believe you have something to report, Bayfield?"

"Brooks and Stanton are in the common area of Newgate," Bayfield relayed.

"How many areas are there?" O'Malley questioned.

"Two that I was able to see. Those committing petty crimes, theft, breaking and entering, and the like are chained and remanded to the common area. Those who are of a higher social standing and have the coin to support them while they are incarcerated would be taken to the state area."

"What of those who commit more serious crimes—murder?" O'Malley wanted to know.

"I believe there is a separate area on a lower level for those sentenced to death awaiting their execution," Bayfield advised.

"I'm quite certain I can prevail upon King to request a private tour of the prison if you'd like," Coventry told him.

O'Malley shuddered at the thought. "Thank ye, no."

"Wise decision," Bayfield told him. "I've seen horrors enough during battles at sea."

Coventry cleared his throat. "That we have, Bayfield. What else have you to report?"

He reached into his waistcoat pocket and withdrew two folded pieces of parchment. "Brooks and Stanton are grateful for the assistance of yourself and O'Malley. They've penned a note to their wives."

"Did anyone search you as you were leaving the gaol?"

Bayfield's rue smile had O'Malley wondering how he had avoided being searched.

"As you suggested, my friend," Bayfield told Coventry, "I removed my frockcoat and rolled up my sleeves."

"To most, that would signal you were getting ready to perform a task," O'Malley observed.

Bayfield nodded as he removed his frockcoat and laid it across the back of a chair. Rolling up his sleeves revealed a mass of scars covering his arms. The more of his arms he uncovered, the more devastating the scars.

Recognizing them as burns, similar to those Mrs. Coventry endured, he stated, "I take it yer scars distracted whoever would have been tasked to search ye."

Bayfield shrugged.

Before O'Malley could ask, Bayfield told him, "My ship caught fire during the Battle of Trafalgar."

O'Malley locked gazes with Bayfield. "Ye and the captain should have been lauded coming home from that battle, instead of shuffled off to a hospital where yer care was uncertain at best.

Thank ye for the honor of witnessing the scars ye bear from risking yer life for King and Country."

Coventry and Bayfield exchanged glances. "We survived," Coventry remarked.

"I'm thinking ye've more than survived. Yer battle scars are a testament to yer bravery and fortitude. If ye need me, me brothers, or cousins—at any time, send word. We'll have yer back."

Bayfield nodded. "Thank you, O'Malley. By the by, Coventry recently received a request from Captain Broadbank, who recently retired to assume the family title of Viscount Moreland, to join our ranks."

"'Tis always wise to have members of the quality assisting ye," O'Malley agreed.

Coventry chuckled. "I turned him down."

O'Malley was surprised. "Now why would ye be doing that?"

"He did not meet all of the criteria," Coventry advised.

Bayfield snickered. "He was not gravely injured during his time serving in the Royal Navy."

"Ah, so ye only hire those who were injured."

Coventry inclined his head. "Many of our comrades-in-arms in the other branches in service to the king were left with no way to support themselves or the families dependent upon them."

O'Malley's respect for the captain increased tenfold. "Ye may not show it often, Captain, but ye've a heart of pure gold."

"I cannot take credit for the idea of gathering former soldiers and sailors injured in battle."

"They work for ye, don't they?"

"Aye, but it was your cousin, James Garahan, who put the thought in my head."

O'Malley slowly smiled. "I remember now. 'Twas the night we were searching for information about the stolen *Chattsworth Emeralds*."

Coventry agreed. "Garahan planted the seed that night. After contacting a handful of trusted acquaintances, I approached His

Grace with the idea."

"Me offer still stands. If ye have need of me or me kin, just send word. Ye have me pledge that we'll be there, no matter the hour." Turning to Coventry, O'Malley asked, "Do ye need me to deliver the messages to Mrs. Brooks and Mrs. Stanton?"

"As you've already met and spoken with the women, I believe it would best."

"What if they ask how their husbands were able to send them a missive from prison?"

"Tell them the truth. We are working together to aid their families."

O'Malley hesitated, then asked, "And if they want to know why?"

"Tell them what you told me. I believe it will go a long way toward convincing the women that we are not helping them so that we can shout our good deeds to all and sundry," Coventry said.

"You and Coventry are helping them because you have been in similar situations in your own lives," Bayfield told him. "You both were fortunate enough to have the hand of providence reach out to you…to help you in your time of need."

"If that does not convince them," Coventry added, "you can change our offer to exclude the women and only help their children."

O'Malley nodded. "Wise plan. It would have convinced me hardheaded ma."

He shook hands with Bayfield and Coventry and took his leave. It was time to deliver the messages.

CHAPTER SIXTEEN

"COME IN MR. O'Malley." Mrs. Brooks paused to lift a blonde-haired waif the size of a faery onto her hip. O'Malley wondered if it was wise for her to be bending and lifting as far along in her pregnancy as she appeared to be.

He was about to voice his concern when he remembered how easily upset his ma had been before his younger brothers were born. Instead, he reached into his frockcoat pocket and pulled out two folded pieces of parchment, handing one to her. "'Tis from yer husband."

He waited for Mrs. Stanton to pull a little dark-haired boy onto her lap before handing her the second note. She inclined her head, and accepted the note, reading it immediately.

O'Malley waited while the women read, then discussed the contents of their messages, all the while noting how quiet the other three children were as they watched him like a hawk. Not a one of them looked to be over the age of four years.

"How do we know these are from our husbands?" Mrs. Brooks wasn't one to trust easily. He approved, knowing she was doing her utmost to protect her family.

Keeping his voice pitched low and soothing, he asked, "Do ye not recognize the handwriting?"

Mrs. Brooks frowned at the note in her hand. "It looks like Simon's hand, but it could be forged."

Taken aback, he asked, "Why would I do that?"

"We've only met you once before. We don't know you—or your family," Mrs. Stanton reminded him. "We trust one another, and we trust our families."

Her voice trailed off and O'Malley's gut told him she was wondering what would become of hers. It was important that these women trust him. He would give them what they needed to do so—the chance to learn more about him. He told of his family back home in Ireland, their struggles when Da had been imprisoned, and after his uncle's death the day before he and Da were to be released. O'Malley spoke of the difficult decision to travel to London with his cousins, seeking work to better support their families.

Mrs. Brooks placed a hand to the back of a rickety chair by the battered table in front of the hearth and slowly sat. "Then you do understand what it's like to worry over not having enough food for your children."

"And what it was like for your own mother," Mrs. Stanton remarked. "Knowing her husband was behind bars waiting for a sentence to be handed down. One that may very well have kept him locked away from all he held dear."

"The difference is that I wasn't a wee one like yer children. I was old enough to know the difference between right and wrong, being oppressed and being free." He paused to let his words sink in before adding, "If ye will not accept our help for yerselves, will ye do it for the sake of yer children?"

Mrs. Stanton reached across the table to grasp Mrs. Brooks' hand. He knew then he had swayed them.

Mrs. Stanton narrowed her gaze and asked, "What do you expect from us in return for your help?"

"Not a bl—" he paused before he blurted out the curse on the tip of his tongue. His ma would box his ears if he swore in front of women and children. Clearing his throat, he responded, "We don't require anything in return. All we ask is that ye have food in yer bellies and whatever else ye require to keep yer family safe and well cared for."

"You'd do this for us after—" Mrs. Brooks paused, wiping her eyes before she was able to gather herself to continue, "after what our husbands were paid to do to that poor modiste?"

"There are times in everyone's lives when they need help. It's not a shame to admit it or ask for it."

"But our husbands—"

O'Malley cut Mrs. Stanton off before she could finish. "Made the difficult choice to do whatever it took to feed their families. Me own da made that difficult choice. When I asked him if he would do it again, he told me he would…even knowing he'd nearly paid the ultimate price."

"But—"

He held up his hand and Mrs. Brooks fell silent. Reaching into his waistcoat pocket, he withdrew a small leather pouch. It jingled as he placed it on the table between the two women.

Their eyes rounded in disbelief, staring at the bag of coins.

"If ye'd rather not arouse suspicion among yer neighbors buying too much at once, I can bring food to ye in a sack. If necessary, I can borrow His Grace's carriage."

Mrs. Brooks' face lost every speck of color. He stepped closer to her in case she fainted.

"His Grace?" she rasped.

"Aye," he was quick to reply, pleased she seemed steady and not in danger of falling off her chair. "The Duke of Wyndmere."

Mrs. Stanton shoved the leather pouch toward him. "We cannot accept the money."

"It is not from His Grace," O'Malley told them. "'Tis from me family, two of me cousins, and Captain Coventry."

"Who is this captain?" Mrs. Stanton wanted to know.

"The best of men and associate who also works for the duke. He was severely injured in the Battle of Trafalgar but has not let that stop him from helping others, including his injured comrades—and the families of those who gave their lives in service to the Crown."

Mrs. Brooks collected herself enough to speak. "I am not certain it is wise to have this much coin in our possession."

Encouraged that she was no longer refusing to accept the money, he stated, "I will leave a handful of coins—ye can divide it between the two of ye while I see to the purchasing of supplies."

One of the little ones tripped and would have smacked his head against the chair leg, but O'Malley was fast on his feet and caught the boy in time. "Have a care, Boy-o," he warned. "Ye need to look after yer ma while yer da's away."

The boy stared at him for a few minutes before nodding. O'Malley set him on his feet, watching until he joined the others. "If ye'll tell me what ye need, I'll be on me way."

"You do not have to come back today," Mrs. Brooks said.

O'Malley glanced around him. "I noticed yer cooking pot is empty. Do ye plan to feed yer children today?" When the women stared down at their hands, he sighed. "I know 'tisn't easy to accept help from a stranger, but do ye think ye can begin to trust me?"

Not waiting for a reply from either woman, he stated, "I'll return with something that'll warm yer bellies." Reaching for the doorknob, he opened the door and paused in the doorway. "Ye have me word that I'll return with yer evening meal."

He closed the door behind him, satisfied he'd accomplished another difficult meeting with the two families. They needed him—whether they wanted to or not.

He mounted his horse and headed back toward Hart and Lumley. He intended to ask the captain's wife for help suggesting what to bring to the hungry families. Opening the door to the building, he stepped inside, pausing in front of the Coventrys' door.

He'd have to be very careful not to bring too much food at once. Someone might think the goods were stolen. The situation was more complicated than he'd thought it would be. Lifting his hand, he knocked, then stepped back.

The door opened and Miranda Coventry beamed at him.

"O'Malley! What brings you to our door?" She stepped aside and bid him to enter.

He smiled briefly as he closed the door behind him. "I need to ask ye a favor…and yer advice."

"The kettle's hot. Do you have time for a cup of tea and bit of gingerbread? I just baked another loaf—it's a favorite of Gordon's."

"Aye. Thank ye kindly." Uneasy with the situation and wondering if it might not be better moving the two families to a safer location, he began to pace.

Instantly on guard, Miranda set down the tea kettle. "You'd best sit down and get whatever is troubling you off your chest while our tea is steeping."

He sighed as he sat. "I was on my way back from visiting with Mrs. Brooks and Mrs. Stanton."

"You know I would love to help, but neither you, nor my darling husband, will allow me to meet with them."

"I haven't changed me mind as to that, but there is something ye could do."

She poured a cup of tea and set it before O'Malley along with a thick slice of warm gingerbread.

Distracted, he leaned close to the plate and inhaled.

Mrs. Coventry laughed softly. "Don't wait for me," she urged, passing the small crock of butter toward him. "Eat while it is still warm."

O'Malley spread a dollop of butter on his gingerbread and took a healthy bite. He closed his eyes as he savored the spicy treat.

She joined him at the table and asked, "Do they have enough food?"

"Nay. I was prepared to leave a small bag of coins with them, then remembered where they lived and thought better of it."

Taking a sip from her teacup, she remarked, "Wise decision. Did you leave them a few coins?"

"Aye. A handful apiece. Didn't want nosey neighbors or

shopkeepers asking questions."

"Did you have an opportunity to look in their cupboards?"

Mouth full, he shook his head.

Mrs. Coventry rose from her seat and lifted the lid on a large pot at the back of her cookstove. O'Malley rose to stand beside her while she stirred the contents.

"Why don't you take this pot of beef stew over to them for their evening meal?"

O'Malley lifted her hand to his lips, "Ye have a heart of pure gold, Miranda."

Neither one heard the door open...but they heard it slam shut.

O'Malley spun around, shoving Mrs. Coventry behind him, ready to defend her. When he relaxed, she peeked around his broad back and let go of the breath she'd held. "What on earth were you thinking, Gordon, slamming the door like that?"

He glared at O'Malley as he crossed the room, never letting his gaze shift until he was nose-to-nose with him.

"I take it ye have an explanation for scaring the bejeezus out of yer lovely wife."

Coventry clenched his jaw and growled, "Step away from my wife."

O'Malley knew when to stand his ground and when to back off. He raised his hands in the air and slid out from between Coventry and his wife. He was about to speak when the captain drew his wife into his arms and kissed her passionately.

O'Malley chuckled. "Faith, I'm thinking yer husband's jealous."

Easing the proprietary hold he had on his wife, he replied, "I have every right to be when I come home to find you cozied up to my wife, kissing her hand."

"You do know that I love you," Miranda whispered, laying a hand to his cheek. "Don't you?"

"Aye, though I am not used to arriving home to find another man in my kitchen, kissing my wife."

O'Malley did not want the situation to escalate. "Ye've every right to be angry with me—not yer wife. She'd just offered yer supper to those that have none. 'Twas me way of thanking her, kissing her hand."

Coventry shifted his hold, drawing her against his side. "From now on, a simple 'thank you' will suffice." He glared at O'Malley, warning, "Keep your lips to yourself."

O'Malley snorted, trying desperately to cover the laughter welling up inside of him. That the captain was jealous and overly protective of his wife wasn't a surprise. It was, however, the first time, he'd seen the man lose his composure since O'Malley had come to work for the duke. It was enlightening.

"Ye're a lucky man, Captain, and although yer wife is a beautiful woman with the purest of hearts, I've no intention of stealing her away from ye."

Coventry stared at him until Miranda pinched him in the side.

"What was that for?" he demanded.

She smiled at him. "It warms my heart to know that at my advanced age, you would be jealous of another man, especially one of the duke's trusted guard. You must know that I have loved you…and only you, for the longest time. My affections will never be swayed by another—no matter how handsome he may be."

Coventry's bark of laughter relieved O'Malley. "Minx! Just remember I protect what's mine."

"Yours?" she repeated. "Am I a mere possession?"

"Nay, my love." He drew her once more into his arms. "You are the better half of me." He kissed her forehead. "The love of my life," he rasped, before claiming her lips again.

"If ye're about finished kissing yer wife, she's helping me with the list of food I need to drop off for the Brooks and Stanton families."

Once more the epitome of the calm, clearheaded, man O'Malley was accustomed to, Coventry responded, "For the moment. I take it your conversation went well if you are bringing food to the families."

"Aye, but it took a bit of convincing." With a brief glance at Mrs. Coventry before continuing, O'Malley added. "Ye were right to suggest I ask if they'd accept help to feed their children."

Miranda glanced from one man to the other. "What mother would not put the welfare of their children before her own?"

"More than you know, Miranda love," Coventry replied. "More than you know."

A SHORT WHILE later, with the promise to return for the pot of stew, O'Malley mounted his horse and rode off to purchase the promised food. His thoughts kept returning to the way Coventry acted—totally out of character, seeing O'Malley kiss his wife's hand. He slowly smiled. Miranda Coventry was a lovely woman, obviously deeply in love with the man she had married.

How would his newly married cousin, Patrick, have acted under the same circumstances? Other than to punch first and ask questions later. He snorted with laughter…'twas the O'Malley way.

Would he ever react that way? His mind filled with the image of a sweet-faced lass with eyes the color of warmed chocolate and blue-black hair. What if a member of the *ton* overstepped the bounds of propriety while visiting Madame Beaudoine's shop? Imagining Mignonette backed into a corner, eyes wide with fear, as the lowest of rakes tried to force himself on her, he grew immediately angry.

His hands tightened on the reins as thoughts of pummeling anyone who laid hands on his lass filled him. His mount immediately reacted. "Easy, Lad," he soothed the now fractious horse. "I'm an *eedjit!*"

The answering whinny only proved his point. "Glad ye agree with me," O'Malley grumbled. It took more of an effort to clear his mind and return to the duty at hand. He had a promise to keep and a meal to deliver.

O'Malley wondered if Coventry would be waiting for him to return. "Mayhap, I'll be kissing the hand of the fair Mrs. Coventry again, if only to watch for steam coming out of the captain's ears." He wasn't above goading a reaction from the unflappable Captain Coventry.

O'Malley planned to stop at Grosvenor Square to see how the lass fared. Relief filled him at the thought of seeing her again. He missed her and looked forward to coaxing a few hesitant smiles from lips that were far too tempting for his peace of mind.

"Ye've a job to do," he mumbled aloud when his thoughts strayed too long wondering how her lips would give beneath his own.

"Ye cannot afford distractions."

CHAPTER SEVENTEEN

"WHAT IS IT, *ma petite?*"

Mignonette secured the needle in the garment she was hemming to reply. "I miss not being in the shop," she confessed. "When do you think we will be able to return?"

Madame Beaudoine stared at her for long moments before finally responding. "I cannot say for certain. However, Monsieur O'Malley sent word that the necessary repairs would begin tomorrow."

Mignonette felt the emptiness inside keenly. *She* had not seen or heard from Monsieur O'Malley. Oh, she knew he was attending to whatever duties the duke required of him, but what of his promise to visit with her? Why had he not at least sent word that he would be delayed?

Heart aching, but too proud to admit it to Madame, she sighed and picked up the garment once more intent on finishing the hem before attaching the lace their customer insisted would bring out the warmth in her daughter's skin tone.

Mignonette did not agree with the choice and asked, "Why did you not tell Lady Carstairs that the ecru lace would not enhance her daughter's coloring, it would only add to her deathly pallor?"

Madame's lips twitched. "Never say you do not agree with me, *ma petite!*"

Mignonette recognized the tone the modiste used as trying to appear shocked when, in fact, Madame was secretly crowing with laughter.

"Don't you think Lady Carstairs knows nothing short of a miracle could add color to her daughter's cheeks?"

Madame laid a hand to her breast, eyes wide. "Mignonette! Do you for one moment believe that Lady Carstairs would allow her daughter to appear in public looking so drab?"

Mignonette ignored the question, stood, and shook out the gown to show Madame. "I am ready to stitch on the lace. Can I not use the white instead of ecru?"

Her employer could not contain her amusement any longer, finally giving in to her laughter. "You should see the expression on your face, *ma petite*. So righteous in your indignation! Do you not wonder why a mother would care so little about her daughter's appearance?"

"*Oui*, Madame. Why?"

Madame motioned for her to regain her seat before speaking. "Did you not realize that she is her stepdaughter? Lady Carstairs married a widower with two daughters, promising to launch them on society when they were of age."

"Then why would she deny her husband's daughters the chance to shine at their debuts?"

Madame lowered her voice, claiming, "The woman practically blackmailed Lord Carstairs into marrying her."

"She was compromised?" Mignonette had no idea. Why would any woman go to such lengths to secure a man's promise of marriage?

"*Oui*—it was quite the scandal back then."

Mignonette could not contain her curiosity. "What happened?"

Madame's eyes practically glowed, and Mignonette knew the modiste could not wait to pass on the story. "I promise not to tell a soul."

The modiste inclined her head. "See that you keep your

word, or I shall deny ever hearing the *on dit!*"

"You have my word."

"I shall ring for tea while you hang up the gown you are working on. The tale I am about to tell will shock you! You would stick yourself with your needle instead of the fabric and bleed on the lace," Madame prophesized.

Mignonette did as she was asked, then settled once again on the settee in Madame's sitting room. When her butler, Jacques, appeared with the large tea tray, Madame smiled up at him. *"Merci,* Jacques."

Everyone who worked for Madame was expected to know her likes, dislikes, her every whim. Jacques was the glue that held Madame's household together. The one to remind the others beneath him what their employer wanted and at what time.

The butler set the tray on the sideboard and set out the tea service with the decadent pastries her cook, Pierre, was renowned for creating.

If asked, Mignonette could not say which she anticipated more, the tale of a young woman of questionable background snaring the illustrious Lord Carstairs…or savoring Pierre's pastries. It had been some time since she'd had the opportunity to indulge, and she planned to enjoy herself.

"Merci, Jacques," Madame murmured as she poured the two cups of tea. "Please extend my thanks to Pierre as well."

He bowed and replied, *"Oui,* Madame."

After he closed the door behind him, Mignonette noticed Madame's eyes sparkling with a cross between merriment…and devilment. She loved when Madame was in one of those moods.

"I do not believe you have met Lord Carstairs," her employer remarked.

Having just taken a bite of one of Pierre's flaky confections, she shook her head in reply.

Madame lifted her bone china teacup, sipped, and placed it on the saucer she held. "He is devilishly handsome. Although I have heard Monsieur Weston adds padding to the shoulders of the lord's frockcoats."

Mignonette was reminded of another devilishly handsome man…one who had no need of buckram added to *his* frockcoat. O'Malley's shoulders were broad, his frame powerful. She sighed remembering how it felt to be held against him, feeling the pounding of his heart as they rode through the night as if demons were nipping at their heels.

The modiste smiled. "It is not only our customers who require a bit of help now and then to show off their figures while enjoying the evening's entertainments."

Mignonette's attention snapped back to their conversation. "I had no idea."

"*Alors*! How could you, never having been courted by a member of the *ton*?"

"From all that I have observed since I have been in London, I do not look forward to any man paying court to me."

The look in Madame's eyes indicated the woman did not agree. "One day, a man will come into your life, and you will not be able to think of anyone but him. Your heart will rejoice whenever he is near. Your mind will play tricks on you, believing you hear his voice when you are running errands for me."

"I do not believe that will *ever* happen," Mignonette protested.

Madame did not agree or disagree as she delicately sampled one of the tiny, frosted teacakes on her plate.

"But what of Lady Carstairs?" Mignonette asked.

Lifting the linen napkin from her lap, Madame blotted her lips. "There was talk at the time that she somehow managed to wheedle the lord's comings and goings from his man-of-affairs. His weekly visits to Tattersalls and White's."

"That should not be considered a crime," Mignonette remarked. "Should it?"

The modiste lifted one shoulder in a dismissive shrug. "She would arrive at Tattersalls when Carstairs was there, asking his advice on various horseflesh for the fictitious purchases she planned to make. Whenever Carstairs arrived via carriage at White's, the woman would smile at him as he stepped down from his carriage. Sometimes stopping to speak with him about how she planned to use his advice when last they'd met."

Mignonette shook her head. "What harm could that have caused?"

Madame narrowed her eyes, staring at Mignonette. "Lord Carstairs found the schemer wandering on foot near his estate in Sussex, disheveled and disoriented as if she'd been thrown from her horse."

An uneasy feeling chilled her. "Where was her horse?"

"Her mount was never found."

Their gazes met and held. "You do not like her, do you, Madame?"

Madame's frown was fierce. "The man was ripe for the picking and never realized his peril until the rumors flying about the *ton* reached his estate. Tales of how he'd forced himself on her, sequestering her on his estate added fuel to the fire."

"I have never heard a word spoken against Lady Carstairs."

"And you will not. They married by Special License, and she has been treated like a princess ever since." Refreshing their cups, she sat back and sipped. "Carstairs proved himself a gentleman by his actions, his obvious affection for his second wife, and his insistence that his wife wear the latest fashions—no matter the cost."

"You do not believe he ruined the woman."

Anger radiated off the modiste. Madame's lips thinned as she pressed them together. "I do not believe he did—neither did his contemporaries."

"Why does he not chastise his wife for dressing his daughters in such horrid colors?" Mignonette could not believe a man such as Madame claimed him to be would do so.

"Like most married men, he leaves the cut and color of the gowns to his wife."

Mignonette smiled. "In other words, married men do not pay

attention to what their wives or daughters wear."

Madame laughed softly. *"Some* married men…not all."

Curious, she asked her employer, "Why have you not married?"

Madame stiffened for a heartbeat before setting her teacup and saucer on the table in front of them. "I would be Mademoiselle Beaudoine if I were not married."

Mignonette noticed the brief flash of gut-wrenching grief in the modiste's gaze before the woman blinked and it was gone. *"Pardon,* Madame."

Madame inclined her head but did not speak.

Mignonette would not normally pry, but having seen the pain in her employer's eyes, she did just that. "I am so sorry for whatever happened to Monsieur Beaudoine. Was he ill on your voyage over from France?"

Madame's gaze met hers. *"Non."*

From the expression on Madame's face, she was certain the woman would end the conversation with that one word. To her surprise, she did not.

She placed her teacup on the table between them and stated, "There was an influential man back home who thought he would be enough to lure me from my husband's arms."

Immediately wary, Mignonette asked, "What happened?"

"When I refused his attentions, he slandered my name publicly."

"Oh, Madame! What happened, what did you do?"

"I did nothing, and would have held my head high, but my Louis could not. He challenged him to a duel."

She did not need to ask what happened. Unsure if she should continue the conversation, or apologize, she was surprised when Madame drew in one steadying breath and then another to continue, "It was nearly ten years ago. I was so angry for the longest time."

"Surely not at your husband?"

"And why not? I would never have minded the slur to my

reputation as long as Louis was by my side. But he was adamant he would protect my name and that of his family. He aimed for his opponent's arm…the *diable* aimed for Louis' heart."

Unable to hold back her tears, Mignonette rose from her chair and knelt beside Madame's. "My heart aches for your loss, Madame."

Her employer patted Mignonette's arm and motioned for her to return to her seat. "I could do with another bit of tea."

Mignonette reached for Madame's teacup and refilled it with the still-warm brew. Handing it to her, she rasped, "Bidding a loved one goodbye is the single most difficult thing I have done in my life. I am so sorry for your loss, Madame."

Accepting the cup and saucer, her employer murmured her thanks. "I do not wish to speak of this ever again."

Mignonette's eyes widened at the proclamation. "Of course, Madame."

Sipping from her teacup, she continued to hold Mignonette's gaze. She set the delicate china on the table between them and stated, "You will not mention this to Yvette."

"*Je promets.*" Rising from where she sat, Madame Beaudoine inclined her head and took her leave, promising to have one of the footmen remove the remnants of their tea.

Mignonette now understood why her employer had never spoken of her husband. The memory was still fresh in the woman's mind even though it had been almost a decade since Madame had moved to London.

Would she still be holding on to the feelings she had for Sean O'Malley in ten years' time? Searching her heart, she knew without question that she would.

CHAPTER EIGHTEEN

"MEN, MEET O'MALLEY, one of the Duke of Wyndmere's personal guard." Turning to O'Malley, he introduced the men, "Dawson hales from Cornwall, Peters from Brighton, Holt from Sussex, and Hewitt from London."

The men Coventry hired appeared willing and able to get the job done. After a close inspection of the men, O'Malley had a suspicion they were former shipmates of Coventry.

"'Tis a pleasure meeting ye, lads. Tell me now, have ye ever served under the captain?"

The men started talking all at once. "We're all seasoned seamen," the oldest of the group, Hewitt, replied.

"Started out as serving as his cabin boy," Dawson added.

"Holt and I were midshipmen," Peters told him.

O'Malley listened to the men before adding, "I'm not certain that will aid ye today as we'll be cleaning up a mess of wood."

The men had similar reactions to O'Malley's words. Two shook their heads, disagreeing. One snorted to cover his burst of laughter, while the last man mumbled beneath his breath.

"If you'd ever been on shipboard during—and after a battle, you'd understand the reason for their reaction," Coventry informed O'Malley. "The destruction from cannon fire splinters wood and has been known to shred the mains'l."

"The mains'l?" O'Malley repeated.

"The largest sail on the ship."

"Ah. I've spent time in a much smaller boat—a *currach*." He grinned at the men. "Me grandda fashioned it after the crafts the ancient ones used along the coast of Ireland—though much smaller. If need be, a man could carry the boat over his head from creek to creek."

Before the discussion and comparisons of different watercraft could distract the men, Coventry interrupted, "Why don't we leave the discussion for midday, when we'll take a break to eat?"

The men readily agreed and listened intently while Coventry and O'Malley went over the instructions for the clean up and repair of Madame Beaudoine's shop.

They divvied up the tasks beginning with salvaging whatever wood, shelving, and furniture they could. True to their word, the men made short work of accomplishing the task. They moved on to the job of assessing what they'd sorted in order to plan what they would need to purchase in order to return Madame's shop to its former status.

By midday, the men were hungry. O'Malley had enjoyed working alongside the men for a change. The vast majority of his time was spent using his hands to defend...to protect. It was a welcome respite, though he was looking forward to returning to his daily routine.

The sound of a carriage carried in through the window openings—they were going to fit new windows in after they ate.

"Are you expecting visitors?" Hewitt inquired.

"Aye," O'Malley replied. "Give me a hand?"

O'Malley and Coventry had enlisted Mrs. O'Toole to prepare the midday meal for the men.

Hewitt followed him outside and returned a few moments later grinning from ear to ear as he hauled in one of the two large baskets.

O'Malley carried the other. "Now then men, Mrs. O'Toole has prepared a meal for us."

Hewitt opened the basket he was carrying while O'Malley

opened the other. Although not fancy by any means, the men's reaction confirmed what he'd surmised. The men were not accustomed to eating their fill. The men reminded him of Christmas on his family's farm. His da and his brothers always waited patiently to sample the delicious meal Ma had prepared, while he was the one who dared to pinch a bit of her Christmas pudding, getting smacked on the hand with her wooden spoon for his efforts.

He smiled as the men helped themselves.

"Are we expecting anyone else to join us?" Holt asked.

Coventry's expression showed the depth of the affection he held for those who served under him, but more, his compassion for those struggling as he had upon returning to their former lives.

"Sure and Mrs. O'Toole has fed more than one hungry man, working men at that," O'Malley told them. "She cooked enough for more than one helping. Eat yer fill, lads."

With whispered thanks, the men gathered around the first of the tables they'd repaired and dug in.

"These meat pies remind me of home," Dawson, the youngest man in the group remarked.

"I've not eaten this much in longer than I can remember," Peters managed around a mouthful.

"Please give our thanks to Mrs. O'Toole," Holt remarked.

Hewitt asked, "Does she have her own shop selling meat pies?"

Coventry shook his head at the question. "Mrs. O'Toole is the Duke of Wyndmere's London cook."

The men seemed a bit shocked. "Why would she cook for us?" Hewitt wanted to know.

O'Malley shrugged. "Because we asked her to."

Coventry packed the remnants of their meal back into the baskets, for the men to have at the end of the day. O'Malley was surprised at how little the men ate, though everyone seemed to be happy with what they'd eaten.

With the men paired to work in teams, they repaired more of the shelves and furniture. "If we work for a few more hours today," Coventry told them. "We should be able to finish by tomorrow afternoon."

O'Malley was not surprised at the enthusiasm or their willingness to work together. After serving in the King's Royal Navy, they would be accustomed to doing so. What was unexpected was their rigid refusal to eat before they left.

"Ye have to be hungry," O'Malley challenged. "Faith, I know I am."

As one, the men looked to Hewitt, their chosen spokesman. His gaze locked with one man after another before he spoke. "Please thank Mrs. O'Toole for us. The food filled our gullets to the brim."

"So ye'll not be needing the rest?"

Dawson poked Hewitt in the side, prompting the man. He cleared his throat to speak. "Would you mind if we brought it home to share with our families?"

Pride glittered in Coventry's eye as he responded, "Not at all."

O'Malley wondered why the captain did not ask or offer more. A glance at their military bearing, willingness to do whatever task required was all he needed to discern that the men were grateful for the work but would not willingly accept handouts. They'd be a fine addition to the O'Malley clan.

"One more thing, men." They paused to look to the captain. "We are expecting Madame Beaudoine and her seamstresses to stop by tomorrow to go over the repairs we've made and see if there's anything that still needs to be done."

"Aye, aye, Captain!"

The men smiled at O'Malley, who now knew why Mrs. O'Toole had provided a small supply of linen cloth. He wrapped the leftover food in it and divided it among the men.

They saluted Coventry on their way out the door, promising to return early the next morning.

"Ye've a fine group of men, Coventry. Will they be working with Bayfield and the others ye mentioned on the duke's behalf?"

"Mayhap in the future. At present, I do not believe there is enough work to support more than the few men I've already hired."

"The duke may have openings at Wyndmere Hall or Lippincott Manor. Are ye thinking to ask him?"

Coventry paused to stare at O'Malley. "I was mulling over that very thing this morning. After the day they put in, I believe they would be an asset, should the duke agree and hire the men."

"What do ye know about their families?"

"Hewitt has the largest family—five sons and three daughters."

"Ye'd best see about hiring him on first."

"I shall take it under advisement, O'Malley." The captain closed and locked the newly repaired door behind them. "You were quiet most of the day, O'Malley. Something on your mind?"

Meeting the captain's gaze, he shrugged. "How long do ye think the lass will be staying at the duke's town house?"

"A few days," Coventry replied. "At least until Lieutenant Sampson advises she is well enough to return to her normal duties."

"Ah, but she cannot do that until we've finished the repairs to Madame's shop, can she?"

Coventry paused as if considering O'Malley's words. "Would you like me to speak to the men tomorrow morning? We could break up their day, giving them ample time to do part of the work—but not all, extending their stay. Therefore, seeing that Mademoiselle de Chauret remains at Grosvenor Square for a few more days."

O'Malley nodded. "Do ye think that's possible?"

"If we speak to Jenkins and Mrs. Wigglesworth and gain their agreement, then, yes. I do believe it would be possible."

"I'll lock up," Coventry told him. "Make sure to thank Mrs. O'Toole for the men."

"I won't be forgetting. She'll enjoy hearing their reactions as they bit into her savory meat pies…and the surprise of her mouth-watering soda bread and buttery scones."

The two shared a smile. "A good meal goes a long way toward lightening a man's worries," Coventry murmured.

"Knowing he's earned the meal, working with his hands, adds to a man's feeling of worth."

"I'm glad you're here," Coventry remarked. "I've missed working closely with you, though I do not miss having to relive another round of rumor and innuendo involving the earl and his wife."

"We've uncovered a number of leads," O'Malley reminded him.

Coventry agreed. "We shall get to the bottom of who is behind this despicable verbal—and physical assault," the captain promised.

O'Malley nodded as they parted, mumbling, "Or die trying."

O'MALLEY'S MIND JUMPED from the men he'd worked with that day and their families to the midnight-haired lass he'd finally be able to see again. His mind snapped to attention, as he pulled up in front of the duke's town house and dismounted.

Running his hand along his horse's neck, he crooned, "Off with ye now, Laddie, for a bit of rub down and a fine meal of sweet hay with a handful or two of oats."

"I'll see to it myself," the stable lad promised.

O'Malley smiled as he thanked the young man, watching the pair as he led the horse to the stables.

O'Malley's heart picked up the beat, anticipation flowing through his veins at the mere thought of seeing the lovely lass who'd captured his attention. What burned in his gut was the desire to do more than speak with her.

The need to pull her into his arms and press his lips to hers nearly drove him mad, while the certainty that she stole a bit of his heart every time they were together tugged at his mind.

Thinking he may have met the woman Ma promised was waiting for the day their paths crossed to meet him, he greeted Jenkins on his way around the back of the town house.

"Time to see how the lovely lass fares today."

Chapter Nineteen

Emmett was waiting for his cousin when he walked in through the rear door to the duke's town house. "A missive arrived from his lordship."

O'Malley accepted the sealed note and continued walking toward the kitchen.

His cousin clapped a hand to O'Malley's shoulder to stop him.

Unease raked through his gut. "What's wrong?" O'Malley demanded.

"She's not here."

"Bloody hell! When did she leave? Where did the lass go?"

Emmett sighed. "Ye've met Madame Beaudoine," he remarked. "The woman is an unstoppable force."

Worry for the lass tangled with frustration. "Ye should have tried."

"She talked right over me as she swept the lass right out the door," Emmett grumbled. "Short of physically trying to stop the woman, there was no way to do so."

"Ye should have barred them from leaving!" O'Malley insisted.

"Bollocks to that," Emmett growled. "Ye weren't here!"

"And I trusted ye to see that Mignonette stayed put where she would be protected!"

"I did what I thought best," his cousin countered.

"Ye let the modiste talk around ye. Ye let her waltz out the door with the woman I swore to protect!" O'Malley's hands clenched at his sides. "As soon as me ribs are healed, I owe ye a broken jaw!"

Emmett relaxed his stance. "'Twould be yer right. Will ye buy me a pint before ye break me jaw?"

O'Malley snorted with laughter. "Aye. Now, tell me what happened. Where was Lieutenant Sampson?"

"The lieutenant arrived at the same time and declared Mademoiselle de Chauret was well enough to leave. 'Twas interesting though," his cousin added. "When pressed as to proper care for the lass, Madame challenged the lieutenant to follow them to her home to see for himself." Emmett grinned. "And he did!"

"Not one to back down from a fight during his time in the Dragoons, according to King," O'Malley replied. With a glance at the note in his hand, he asked, "Why did ye not open the missive from the earl?"

"'Twasn't addressed to me."

"Let's see what the earl has to say."

Breaking the wax seal, O'Malley read the note once. His blood boiling, he read it a second time, handing it to his cousin. "Whoever is behind these blatant attacks against the earl and his wife is not only trying to turn the tide of the masses," O'Malley stated. "They are trying to bury them so deeply in lies and innuendo they will never dig themselves out!"

"We have their backs! The duke and every blessed member of his extended family have their backs!"

"Aye," O'Malley agreed. "'Tis what's being said that turns me stomach. Given Lady Aurelia's current condition, we cannot let the earl issue a challenge when we discover who is behind this latest campaign to shred his reputation and his wife's."

"Agreed," his cousin echoed. "Ye've time before taking over the evening shift. Why don't ye pay a call on Madame Beaudoine...and a certain black-haired beauty that has yer guts tied up in knots."

O'Malley shoved his shoulder into his cousin's. "Have I mentioned lately that ye're a horse's *arse?*"

Emmett snorted with laughter. "More than once."

"I'll need to think of another insult for ye then."

"Tell the lass that I miss her smile!"

He paused with his hand on the doorknob. "Remind me to punch ye when I return."

Having the last word had O'Malley smiling as he stepped out onto the sidewalk.

The flash of a blade, out of the corner of his eye, had him bringing up his arm to protect his neck. Cold, sharp pain slashed through his forearm to the bone!

If not for his lightning reflexes, he'd be dead. God must have other plans for him. Fighting for his life, he kicked out with his foot, connecting with the side of his attacker's knee. The guttural cry of pain was music to his ears.

Digging deep to ignore the pain, blood flowing from the deep cut on his arm, O'Malley met his attacker's glare with a smile. "Ye've just unleashed the Hounds of Hell…I'd start praying."

The bull of a man shook his head as if he did not believe the man he'd attacked was still standing.

Straightening to his full height—two inches over six feet, he challenged, "Did ye not know we O'Malleys have nine lives?" His vision grayed. He shook his head to clear it, concentrating on remaining conscious until help arrived.

The battle cry of the ancient clan of O'Malley roared from behind him. Sean stepped to the side as his cousin launched himself at Sean's attacker. The two landed on the sidewalk— Emmett sitting on the man's back. The coward had turned tail and tried to run from the blood-curdling cry.

Emmett looked over his shoulder at O'Malley and grinned. "Grandda was right. Our battle cry still scares the *shite* out of an Englishman."

O'Malley could not feel the top of his head. A numbness

seemed to be slowly working its way down his body. Before he was rendered mute, he rasped, "I'm thinking ye'll have to pay a call on the lass for me."

His knees buckled and everything went black.

"COME ON NOW, Sean," a deep voice urged. "None of that now, or I'll be telling Aunt Eileen that her oldest has the constitution of a woman."

O'Malley heard the words and chuckled. "She'd box yer ears." The sound of a breath whooshing out had him opening one eye. "Worried were ye?"

Emmett denied it. "Nay, takes more than flaying open an O'Malley's arm to keep him down."

"Is it deep then?" O'Malley asked. "I don't remember passing out."

"Dropped like a stone," his cousin told him. "I was pulling a bit of rope from me pocket to tie up yer attacker, Sean. I'm sorry I couldn't break yer fall."

O'Malley nodded and winced. "Explains the pain in me head."

His cousin snickered. "Yer block head slammed against the sidewalk, nearly took a chunk out of it!"

"Me head?" Sean tried to lift his hand to his head but couldn't.

"The sidewalk," his cousin replied.

"Am I still bleeding?"

"Don't worry, ye've plenty left."

"Have ye no compassion for an injured man?"

"Not unless he's at death's door which, by the grace of God, ye don't appear to be."

"Sean!" The worry in Mrs. O'Toole's voice bothered him. She only worried when one of his family was badly injured. "I'm fine, Mrs. O'Toole," he assured her. "Just a scratch."

She leaned over him and, for the first time he could remember, her eyes glistened with unshed tears. "Don't cry over the likes of me. I'm fine."

"Not at the moment," a familiar deep voice remarked, "but thanks to my impressive skill with a sharp needle and boiled threads, you will heal…in time."

Finally able to keep both eyes open, O'Malley scanned those gathered in the small room near the kitchen…the same room he'd carried the lass to recently. Meeting Dr. McIntyre's direct gaze, he stated, "I'm not dead yet."

Emmett laughed. "Faith, ye're too hardheaded to die. If it had been a Flaherty, we'd be planning yer wake. We all know their heads are not as hard as we O'Malleys'."

"Thank ye for evening out the odds, Emmett."

"'Twas a pleasure—especially yer attacker's reaction. When he turned and tried to run."

"I understand a number of people went in search of the Watch, hearing the er…was it the Garahan or O'Malley battle cry?" Dr. McIntyre queried.

"O'Malley," Emmett and Sean answered at the same time.

The physician's eyes were filled with laughter—a good sign, O'Malley thought to himself. Dr. McIntyre would not be making light of the situation if O'Malley was in danger of bleeding to death.

"Thank ye for putting me back together."

"You're welcome. Although I would not recommend taking on another knife-wielding attacker anytime soon. You've lost too much blood, O'Malley. I've sent word to Coventry who will inform the others that you will require a fortnight—at the very least, to recover from your injury."

"I'm to return to Madame Beaudoine's shop tomorrow. Between the crew Coventry hired, we've finished half the repairs."

Dr. McIntyre shook his head. "A fortnight, O'Malley."

He ignored that last, telling his cousin, "Help me up."

"Slowly," the physician ordered.

With two pillows behind his back and his arm elevated on two more, he felt as if he'd gone three rounds with his eldest cousin, Patrick, and come out on the losing side. He tried to reason with the physician a second time. "I have a job to—"

Dr. McIntyre closed the distance between them. "You have lost enough blood that you are in danger of succumbing to fever and infection. If infection sets in," the physician warned, "you may still lose that arm."

His gut burned as bile rose in his throat. Emmett had seen him hurl more than once growing up, but he was unwilling to puke up his guts in front of Mrs. O'Toole or the doctor. He clamped his jaw shut and willed his stomach to calm, and the bile to recede.

O'Malley knew the sound of his retching could wake the dead. His family had reminded him of that often enough in the past. 'Twas his uncontrollable groans of agony while he heaved that usually had dogs howling and children running for cover.

"Ye're saying if I rest for a sennight, then I will be ready to return to me duties without fear of fever or..." he couldn't say it. Couldn't think of the possibility that he'd lose his arm. Reason returned with a vengeance as did his ability to speak. "I'm partial to both me arms. I'll be following yer advice."

Dr. McIntyre frowned at him. "A fortnight—not a sennight. And it's an order," the physician clarified. "Not advice."

Emmett glared at his cousin before speaking. "I'll personally see that me cousin follows yer orders."

"Excellent. I shall return to see how the patient is doing in the morning."

Mrs. O'Toole followed the doctor out of the room and O'Malley's stomach lurched violently. His cousin was by his side with a bucket before he could ask.

Relieving his stomach of the last meal he'd eaten, and then some, left him feeling wrung out. He'd rather suffer through being sewn back together a second time.

"Like it or not, ye'll do as Dr. McIntyre orders," his cousin declared. "I'll not see me favorite cousin lose his arm because he's too stubborn to listen to common sense and reason."

O'Malley's mouth felt as if he'd mucked out the duke's stables with his tongue. A glance at Emmett had him digging deep to control the aftershocks he always suffered through after retching. "Favorite cousin, is it?"

Emmett chuckled. "Aye, at the moment. If ye don't do exactly as the doctor orders, I'll be forced to be naming James as me favorite."

O'Malley wondered if Emmett was trying to get a rise out of him to distract him from the pain in his arm and ache in his belly. "But he's a Garahan!"

Squaring his shoulders, his cousin lifted his chin and replied, "As is your grandda on yer ma's side. Don't be forgetting."

O'Malley sighed. "Hearing ye bellow the O'Malley battle cry was music to me ears. Thank ye for capturing the bloody bastard who—" he paused to glance at the thick bandage on his arm before continuing, "did he truly flay me arm open to the bone?"

His cousin shrugged. "I was fully occupied tying his hands behind his back at the time. But ye did bleed like a stuck pig."

O'Malley nodded. "Did ye have a chance to question the man? Do we know who hired him?"

"I tied him up and handed him over to the Watch. Isn't that enough for ye?"

He was about to reply when Emmett growled at him, "I've never seen one of me own lose that much blood, Sean. Ye could have bled to death." Raking a hand through his hair, his cousin added, "Coventry is bound to show up now. Ye can ask him yer bloody questions!"

"Emmett, wait!"

His cousin smacked the flat of his hand against the door frame but did not turn around. "I'll not be the one telling Aunt Eileen and Uncle Sean how I failed to save their oldest son's life."

"I've already said I'd rest."

"See that ye do. I've nothing more to say to ye."

Alone, O'Malley let his ironclad control slip. Pain washed over him like a wave. Leaning over the side of the cot, he retched until his eyes teared, and his nose ran. Wiping his nose on his sleeve, he lay back against the pillows. "Ye're a bloody *arse*," he grumbled.

He closed his eyes and drifted off to sleep.

"I SEE REPORTS of your demise are premature."

O'Malley sighed. "Aye. Unless ye've met yer own and we're having this conversation in Hell."

Coventry chuckled. "And here I was hoping I would earn my wings."

O'Malley opened one red-rimmed eye. "Will ye tell me the truth?"

"Absolutely."

"Did the wound go clear to me bone? Will I lose me arm?"

Coventry had had more than one sailor under his command suffering from a similar wound, whether it be his leg or his arm and answered as honestly now as he had a decade ago. "Dr. McIntyre has been taking care of the last three Dukes of Wyndmere. His reputation for saving more lives than costing them is well-known. Follow his orders to the letter," Coventry advised. "And I would venture to say you will increase the chances that you will indeed keep that arm."

"I've a favor to ask of ye before I've got me hand on the knob of death's door."

"Though you do not appear to be anywhere near death's door, nothing in this life is set in stone, O'Malley. What is the favor?"

"I'll be needing a Special License."

"You're on the brink of succumbing to wound fever, and facing the distinct possibility of losing your arm, and you want to get married?"

"Aye...I wouldn't ask if it wasn't an urgent matter." Raising his good arm, he scrubbed a hand over his face. "'Tisn't me I'm thinking about, 'tis the lass."

"Ah," Coventry rumbled, "Mademoiselle de Chauret."

O'Malley nodded. "She has no family. I've more than enough

to spare…and share. I want to marry her before I lose me mind to fever or me life if they take me arm."

"You don't know what you're asking," Coventry insisted. "It's the blow to your head."

O'Malley snorted. "I've hit me head harder, and been hit harder in the head sparring with me cousins. I'll be asking Emmett to stand in for me—marrying the lass by proxy, if I'm unable to speak the words."

Coventry stared at the man who'd become a brother to him. Once before, he'd vowed to watch over his best friend's wife and young son years ago, never expecting his friend to die in battle. Would the same thing happen to O'Malley? Would he lose his life after Coventry promised to procure the Special License for him? Would O'Malley leave behind a widow?

O'Malley never looked away, never blinked, waiting for the captain to agree.

"I'll have to send an urgent missive to His Grace at once. With His Grace's written request, the earliest I would be able to obtain one on his behalf would be midday tomorrow."

O'Malley held out his hand. "I'll be thanking ye now, Coventry, and can rest easy knowing the woman who stole me heart will never be alone again."

"You're welcome, though you may change your mind when you recover and find yourself married to a woman you hardly know. Is there anything else you need?"

O'Malley's gaze met his. "Would ye mind sending me cousin in? I need to speak with him."

"Of course."

When the captain left the room, O'Malley wondered if his cousin would balk at the favor he would ask of him.

Emmett entered the room a few moments later. "Has the fever returned? Has the pain worsened?"

O'Malley shook his head. "I've a favor to ask of ye, but ye can't breathe a word of it within hearing distance of the lass."

"Whatever it is ye need, Sean, ye know I'll do it for ye."

Relief had him blowing out the breath he hadn't realized he held. Locking gazes with his cousin, he told him, "I don't want the lass to be feeling as if our vows were rushed to the point where that will be her only memory of them."

Emmett frowned. "The Special License is reason alone to understand yer vows will be rushed."

"Would ye send word to Madame Beaudoine that I'd like her to create a gown for the lass? I know we haven't much time, but tell Madame I'll pay whatever she asks."

"I don't want to leave, should ye need me," his cousin remarked.

"But—"

"I didn't say I wouldn't see to the task for ye."

"Thank ye, but that's not the whole of it."

Emmett snorted. "I should have figured that since it's ye asking. What else?"

"Would ye ask Mrs. O'Toole for another rose—"

"Another rose?"

"Aye, to match the one she picked for me to give the lass. I'd like Madame to find fabric to match the color of the rose."

Understanding filled his cousin's gaze. "Faith, ye're a lucky man to have found such a love. Rest now," he ordered. "I shall see to the task."

"Thank ye."

Emmett nodded and went in search of the duke's cook.

Knowing the request was in good hands, O'Malley relaxed against the pillows and closed his eyes.

Coventry entered the room again. He needed the man to stay awake until he'd at least had some of the promised broth. "Mrs. O'Toole has been caring for the duke's staff—and the various wounds they've received over the years—and more recently, you and the rest of the duke's guard. I'd say that only increases the odds in your favor."

Coventry watched O'Malley draw in a deep breath and slowly let it out. "Are you still nauseated?"

Before O'Malley answered, they were interrupted as Mrs. O'Toole bustled into the room, followed by one of the footmen with an empty bucket. She nodded to the footman, who set the empty bucket by the bed, and retrieved the other one. "You should feel improved after emptying your poor belly, Sean."

With her back to them, she lifted the pink and white ceramic pitcher and poured warm water into the large bowl. Wringing it out she walked over to O'Malley.

Coventry watched the kindly cook bathe O'Malley's face as if he were still a child, reminding him of the times the cook at Wyndmere Hall had done the same for him all those years ago. It was a testament to the way the duke and duchess treated their staff over the years that enabled their staff to show comfort and caring to anyone under the duke's far-reaching protection.

"Thank ye, Mrs. O'Toole."

"Rest now," she ordered. "I'll be right back with a nice cup of broth."

"What about a bowl of your renowned calf's foot jelly?" Coventry smothered his laughter at the look on O'Malley's face. "It certainly set the duke to rights after the earl broke his nose."

O'Malley visibly relaxed and so did Coventry. If he could convince the guard to give himself over to the care of the duke's staff, the man's chances would improve greatly.

"I'm quite certain both the duke and the earl reported the incident as an accident."

O'Malley chuckled and then groaned. The movement obviously pained him.

"Best lie still," Mrs. O'Toole told him as she stopped in the doorway. "Make sure he doesn't move. We don't want the bleeding to start up again," she warned.

"You have my word," Coventry promised. Turning to his patient, he rumbled, "Are you up to hearing your attacker's confession?"

"Ye have news already?" O'Malley questioned. "Just how long was I unconscious?"

"Longer than you realize," Coventry advised.

"Aye. What did the bastard have to say?"

Coventry locked gazes with O'Malley and told him, "He was hired by the same person who hired Brooks and Stanton."

O'Malley remained silent, waiting for Coventry to continue.

"The connection is there. We have the name of the man they worked for—before being let go. I've sent Bayfield to question the man. It may lead to who hired Brooks and Stanton."

"Why would he answer Bayfield? The man did not give a bloody damn when he fired the men, then blackballed them so they were not able to find work and feed their families!"

Concern that O'Malley was getting worked up and not resting, Coventry laid a hand on the man's shoulder. "Trust me when I tell you that Bayfield has a gift when loosening a man's tongue."

"Aye?" O'Malley perked up. "Torture?"

Coventry chuckled. "Nay. The man uses the power of words and the backing of powerful men in service to the king and among the *ton*."

O'Malley nodded. "If ye sent him, he'd have the backing of the Duke of Wyndmere."

"Aye," Coventry agreed. "Along with his brother, Earl Lippincott, and Lord Coddington, the earl's father-in-law, along with a host of the duke's contemporaries."

"Will ye tell me whenever ye learn more about the attacker?"

Coventry locked gazes with O'Malley. "If you suffer through another examination."

"I've already seen the duke's physician," O'Malley reminded him.

"Lieutenant Sampson served under battle conditions and saved more than one soldier's limb during that time. He has done, and will do, all in his power to save your arm."

O'Malley readily agreed. "Is that all ye require of me?"

Coventry cleared his throat to speak. "Through all we have had to face together protecting the duke and his family, you and your cousins have become more than my comrades-in-arms…you are brothers. I require your promise to do all in your power to abide and follow any and every dictate from both physicians in order to fully recover."

O'Malley's exaggerated sigh was loud and long. Coventry struggled not to laugh at his theatrics and was rewarded with his solemn promise.

"Excellent." Changing the subject, Coventry asked, "Do you have anything you'd like me to say to the men repairing Madame Beaudoine's shop tomorrow?"

"Aye," O'Malley said. "Tell them it pains me not to be able to work alongside them, but the captain forced me to take to me bed after receiving a paltry knife wound in the line of duty."

Coventry was chuckling when Mrs. O'Toole appeared in the doorway with a small tray.

"Here we are," she said with a smile. "The promised broth and calf's foot jelly."

When O'Malley grimaced, her smile widened. "Shall I feed it to you?"

"If Coventry moves that small table next to me good arm, I can feed meself."

She nodded to the men and left with the promise to return to collect the tray shortly.

"I've already sent word to Lieutenant Sampson."

"Before I agreed to yer terms?"

"Aye, Sean. You'll have to trust us."

O'Malley frowned, staring at the thick bandage around his arm. "I do…it's just—"

"Not easy *not* being in the thick of things. Righting wrongs and conquering evil," the captain finished for him. "I shall leave you in good hands, remember you gave your word."

"I'll not be forgetting," O'Malley replied. "Ye have me thanks for asking the lieutenant to look in on me, but do ye think it would bother Dr. McIntyre that ye have?"

"Not at all." Coventry moved the table and placed the small tray on it. "They are on good terms and have consulted one another in the past."

"'Twas a bit of a worry," he admitted, awkwardly lifting the cup of broth.

When he finished it, Coventry moved the bowl of jelly to within reach. "Finish this and I'll leave you to rest."

"*Bollocks!*"

"Shall I hold your nose for you?"

The bark of laughter was what Coventry needed to hear. He stepped closer and O'Malley waved him away, lifting the bowl—in favor of using the spoon, and downed the contents, shuddering as he swallowed. "Vile stuff."

"It is guaranteed to cure what ails you," the captain reminded him.

"So me ma used to remind me when I was younger."

"I shall return after I send the urgent missive to the duke and then meet with Bayfield. His report will be enlightening. Do you need anything before I go?"

"Aye. Did Mrs. Brooks and Mrs. Stanton get the food?"

"Rest easy. It has been taken care of. Your job in that regard is finished," Coventry admonished. "You are to rest and recover."

O'Malley let go of the breath he held, and the worry that the two families would not be taken care of as he had promised them. "Aye. Thank ye."

Coventry inclined his head. "You are welcome." Striding to the door, he inquired, "Would you like this closed?"

"Leave it open, people coming and going will be a distraction from me staring at the ceiling when I tire of the walls."

Pleased with O'Malley's sense of humor returning, he bid him goodbye. He spoke with Jenkins about the missive and was relieved to have that handled for O'Malley. He hoped he wasn't consigning Mademoiselle de Chauret to widowhood should his friend perish from his wound.

Shaking his head to clear it of such negativity, he went in search of Emmett before leaving to meet with Bayfield. Once he had the name of the bastard that hired the men involved in ransacking the modiste's shop and the knife-wielding assailant, he intended to see that the man behind the assault be made to pay for ordering the attack. The duke's cachet would guarantee the bloody blackguard would know how it feels to lose everything.

CHAPTER TWENTY

MIGNONETTE HEARD A commotion coming from the entryway but paid little attention to it. Madame was given to dramatics, although she had to admit, it was entertaining.

Heavy footfalls approached the sitting room where she was setting sleeves in yet another ballgown for one of their many customers. She carefully set the gown on the settee and hoped it would be Monsieur O'Malley who'd finally come to call on her. She had not been expecting him, but she'd been hoping.

Jacques appeared in the open doorway. "Monsieur O'Malley to see you, Mademoiselle."

Something was not right. Jacques never clenched his fists or his jaw. Was he worried or angry? *"Merci,* Jacques."

"Ye've got to come with me," Emmett O'Malley proclaimed, striding into the room. "Sean's lost so much blood—" the big man paused to clear his throat.

She noticed his skin had a deathly pallor to it, and his eyes were red-rimmed. Had the man been crying? She shot to her feet. *"Oui!* Tell me what happened."

"On the way. Ye need to hurry, Lass. He's burning with fever, calling for ye."

Madame slipped the shawl from her shoulders and wrapped it around Mignonette, instructing, "Send word if you need me."

Mignonette nodded as Emmett tugged on her arm to get her

moving again.

"Remember—send for me, and I shall come at once!" her employer promised.

When she noticed one of Madame's footmen holding the reins to a horse, she wondered if all the O'Malley cousins and brothers preferred riding a horse to a carriage.

Without warning, she was lifted off her feet and plunked down atop the horse. Emmett vaulted on behind her, took the reins from the footman, and slid his arm around her. "Hang on!"

There was no time for questions. He urged the horse from a walk to a canter and then a fast trot through the streets of London.

Praying to God in Heaven, and all his angels, to keep the man she loved safe, she concentrated on the sound of the horse's hooves pounding on the cobblestones eating up the ground between Madame's town house and the duke's.

Emmett dismounted and whisked her off the horse, not bothering to set her down as he strode through the open door, past the pale-faced Jenkins and scattering of servants loitering near the door to the servants' side of the town house.

"I can walk," she insisted.

He ignored her and used his shoulder to open the door between the privileged and the working class.

The deep timbre of O'Malley's voice reverberated through the hallway. "Mignonette? Lass! Where are ye?"

"He's never been like this…" Emmett's voice broke and so did her heart. That the imposing man would be near tears told her how close she was to losing the love she'd only just found. "Whatever you need, I shall do!" she vowed.

"She's here!" Emmett called out, making his way down the short hallway between the kitchen and the butler's pantry.

There were too many people in the room, was her first thought. They all stepped to the side, revealing the horrific sight before her. The Irish warrior—the man who'd cradled her to his heart, protecting her, thrashed about on the same cot he'd placed her on but a few days earlier.

"Monsieur O'Malley?"

He did not answer.

She called to him, louder this time. "Monsieur Sean?"

"Lass?"

"*Oui.* I am here!" Emmett set her on her feet, and she rushed to Sean's side. "Who did this to you? What happened?"

Lieutenant Sampson's deep voice revealed, "He was attacked as soon as he stepped outside."

She did not look away from the drawn man who lay bathed in sweat when she asked, "Who attacked him?" Worry clutched at her heart, making it hard to draw in enough air to breathe. Finally, she managed to do so and asked, "Have they caught him?"

"Aye, but not the man who hired the assassin," Emmett replied. "I heard Sean curse and then his grunt of pain and knew it had to be bad. Me cousin never complains when he's injured…he laughs."

Letting the shawl slide off her shoulders, Mignonette asked for a damp cloth and was immediately handed one. As she gently bathed the sweat from O'Malley's brow, she spoke to him in low, soothing tones.

"Ye're here," he murmured.

"*Oui, mon coeur,*" she crooned. "I am here and will not leave you."

Within minutes of arriving, she'd calmed him to the point where he ceased to thrash on the cot. His breathing slowed.

"What does *coeur* mean?

"Heart."

"I'm yer heart?"

"*Oui, mon amor,*" she soothed as she continued to bathe his face with cool water.

"Amor, means love?" O'Malley asked.

"*Oui.*"

He was struggling to keep his eyes open when he asked, "I'm

yer heart and yer love?"

"*Oui, mon coeur et mon amor.*"

A hint of a smile appeared as he asked, "Ye promise ye won't leave me?"

"*Oui, je promets,*" she soothed as she continued to bathe his face with cool water. "I promise."

Finally convinced, he closed his eyes. She watched his breathing settle into a slower pattern and one of the hundred knots in her belly loosened. "He is asleep, but his fever worries me." She dipped the linen cloth into the bowl someone had placed on the table at her elbow.

"It is the cause of the fever that is a concern," Lieutenant Sampson advised, coming to stand beside her. "May I speak with you?"

"I cannot leave him. I gave my word I would not leave him."

"You aren't. If you would move to the other side of the room, our voices will not rouse him."

"Let me take over for you," Mrs. O'Toole urged.

Grateful, Mignonette slowly rose to her feet, letting the lieutenant take hold of her arm and guide her over toward the door. "The wound is deep."

"How deep?"

"Down to the bone. His fever was not unexpected, but the assailant's knife may have nicked the bone of his forearm."

Mignonette wanted to weep but did not dare show weakness in front of the men who had sought her help. She needed to stay strong. She still did not know what they expected of her, or what they needed her to do. "It is dangerous?"

"Very," the lieutenant agreed. "If the fever continues to rage, and we cannot bring it down, the infection will kill him."

Not could...*will.* She swallowed against the lump of anguish trapped in her throat. Nodding that she'd heard and understood, she waited for the physician to tell her what they wanted her to do.

"If the infection has taken hold, the only way to save

O'Malley is to remove his arm."

Her hands flew to her mouth as every ounce of air flew out of her lungs. Her mother's voice whispered in her heart, *Etre fort, mon ange—Be strong, my angel.*

Oui, Maman. "Does he know? Have you told him?"

The lieutenant nodded. "Dr. McIntyre, Captain Coventry, and I have spoken to him at length."

"Was he fevered at the time? *Mon Dieu!* What if he wakes with only one arm and doesn't remember your conversation?"

The lieutenant frowned at her. "He was lucid at the time. He'll not bloody likely forget our conversation."

Anguish filled her. *What would the proud warrior fighting against the raging fever do if the wound he received caused him to lose an arm?*

She gripped her skirts in both hands, needing to hold on to something—anything, as memories filled her. *Would he accept God's will as his own?*

Would he lash out at his family and those who love him?

She had seen firsthand what happened when a family friend had returned from war with one leg. He had withdrawn from his family and friends. He'd hurled insults and obscenities at her when she'd visited with him. The loss of his limb tortured him until one night he'd put a pistol to his head to end his torment.

Needing confirmation that Sean knew and understood the risk he faced once his fever took hold, she glanced at Emmett who walked toward them.

She reached out to him. He took her hand in his and held it tight. "Sean asked Captain Coventry to do him a favor—it concerns ye."

"I hope the captain will do as he asks."

"He already has seen to the first part of the favor. 'Tis up to ye to do the rest. Do ye swear to uphold yer promise to me cousin?"

"I do not give my word lightly, Monsieur. Whatever he asks of me. I promise to do!" she vowed.

"We're counting on ye."

Turning to the lieutenant, she remarked, "Not that I do not believe you, Lieutenant Sampson," she said by way of apology before turning back to Emmett, "but you are certain Monsieur O'Malley heard and understood the risk he faces if the infection sets in and his fever refuses to break?"

Emmett clenched his jaw. "Aye, he heard and understood," he confirmed.

"And he will not despair? He will not be consumed with what he can no longer accomplish with only one arm, until he can learn how to fully use the other?"

He dropped her hand. "What do you know?" Emmett demanded. "Who have you spoken to?"

She shook her head, not wishing to add to the turmoil that awaited to engulf them.

"From what Mademoiselle de Chauret is not saying," the physician remarked, "I would venture to guess she has personal knowledge of someone who faced such a challenge. Is that correct?"

"*Oui*, back home," she rasped. "He was a friend—a good friend, who fought to defend our country. Before I lost my parents."

"Was?" Emmett queried.

"*Oui.*"

"Losing a limb killed him?"

"No." She pushed the memory of that terrible time to the back of her mind. "He could not endure his new life...so he ended it."

"War is hell," the lieutenant murmured.

"Tell me what I need to know to prepare," Mignonette whispered. "I know what I have experienced but believe Monsieur O'Malley to have a stronger will to live than my childhood friend."

Emmett glanced over his shoulder to where his cousin was sleeping and cleared his throat. "Ye haven't known me cousin long, but ye'd be right. We O'Malleys have a zest for life, heads as hard as granite, hearts as big as our homeland, and will fight to the death for our family and those we have sworn to protect."

She let go of the breath she held. "*Merci*. I needed to hear you say it."

"Healing ointment needs to be applied and his bandages need to be changed daily," the lieutenant stated.

"I can do that," she assured the physician. "What do we give him for the pain?"

"Laudanum. I will write down the dosage, but do not administer it unless he asks for it. Too much is not good, too little will not take away the pain."

She nodded. "And for his fever, other than bathing his face with cold cloths?"

The intensity in the lieutenant's gaze threatened to drag her under, like a wave after a storm crashing on the shore. "His bandage must not get wet. Emmett will see to his care. I cannot in good conscience allow an unmarried woman to do so."

"I am more than capable of bathing his face—"

"What of the rest of him?" the lieutenant interrupted. "When the fever is at its worst, you'll need to bathe his face and more—his chest, torso, legs. His position within the Duke's Guard makes him fodder for members of the *ton* with nothing more to do than spread rumors to all and sundry. Your reputation will be in shreds if anyone finds out. O'Malley would not want that for you."

"I have been the object of ridicule before. After my parents died, I was alone. More than one man thought to take advantage of me. When I refused their offers of *protection*, they spread lies to anyone who would listen…it is why I left my home and came here."

"And Madame Beaudoine hired ye," Emmett added.

She nodded. "She saved me from a life of drudgery—or worse." She locked gazes with the physician, challenging him, "But know this—no one…not you, Emmett, or even the duke will keep me from his side!"

He opened his mouth to speak, but the rage simmering inside of her let loose. "If you try," she warned, "I will raise bloody hell!"

"I think the lass knows what she is about, Lieutenant. I, for one, agree with her."

When the physician looked as if he were about to refuse, Emmett added, "Do not forget me cousin's plan to protect her. Trust him." With a glance at Mignonette, he ordered, "Trust her."

The physician grumbled. "I do not agree willingly, but will concede as he has a plan to ensure her reputation will not suffer for nursing him back to health." He turned to Mignonette and stated, "Send for me at once if you notice any swelling, inflammation, putrid matter, or foul smell."

"I will. Thank you, Lieutenant Sampson."

She held out her hand and he grasped it, holding it for a few moments before letting it go. "O'Malley is strong. The next few hours are crucial. Whatever you do," he warned, "do not give up on him."

"I won't," she told him.

"Send for me if his condition changes—no matter the hour."

"*Je promets.*"

He inclined his head, accepting her promise. He checked on the patient once more, then took his leave.

Emmett did not follow after the lieutenant as she expected him to. He moved to stand beside the cot and stare down at his cousin. "Sean's the oldest of the Wexford branch of the O'Malleys. Patrick is the head of our branch, the Cork O'Malleys. We grew up depending on the oldest in our families for more than setting the example."

Turning to face her, he rasped, "He will pull through—he has to! No matter if he loses his arm or not, Sean will pull through! The fabric of our lives would forever change. Please," he urged her, "help me get him through this nightmare. Promise you will do as Coventry asks when he arrives."

"*Je promets.* It is not just your life that would forever change.

My life changed the moment he stepped through the door to Madame's shop. His moss green eyes drew me in. The way he protected me made me feel as if I mattered. When he realized I was injured, he took care of me—a seamstress far below his station in life as part of the duke's private guard."

Mignonette locked gazes with Emmett. "Between the two of us, we will do our utmost to see that we keep his fever in check and be vigilant in caring for his wound."

Emmett seemed relieved. "If I were to ask ye to add a poultice and herbal draught to Sean's care, would you?"

"Will it help him heal?"

"Aye, it has worked for the last few generations of O'Malleys."

"A family recipe?"

Emmett's face flushed. "Ye could call it that."

Her eyes narrowed as she stared at him, as if trying to pull the truth from his soul. "Back home in France, our family visited a wise woman who knew which herbs would break a fever, which herbs reduced swelling and inflammation. I would be foolish not to agree if you have such knowledge, Emmett."

"Ye may be questioned closely by one, or both physicians, if they discover what we're about."

She lifted her chin and met his intense gaze. "I have stood firm in the face of disapproval more than once over the years. I am no coward. If it will help Monsieur Sean, you have but to ask."

Emmett wrapped his arms around her for a brief hug, then set her aside. "I need to speak to Mrs. O'Toole. She may have a few of the herbs on hand. If not, she'll know where to purchase the herbs we need—and quickly." He strode from the room.

Leaning over O'Malley's sleeping form, she placed the back of her hand against his brow. Concern filled her. "Warmer than before."

She dipped a clean cloth into the cool bowl of water and wrung it out. With great care, she bathed his face and his neck with the cloth. Dipping it in the bowl again, she lowered the sheet, surprised to see his torso bandaged. "His ribs? Stubborn man," she murmured. "Why could he not admit to being injured?" A dark thought filled her. *Had it happened when he rescued her from the wardrobe?*

Shaking her head, she tried to unwrap the bandage, but she needed Emmett's help lifting Sean to do so. Mindful of his injury, she bathed what she could reach of his chest and his torso, then bathed his arms—careful not to get too close to his bandage.

She repeated the motions again and again, whispering to Sean all the while of her promise to care for him no matter what happens. One arm or two, her love for him would not waver.

Sean became more and more restless as she cared for him. She was just getting ready to call out for Emmett when he returned, carrying a tray. Mrs. O'Toole followed behind him.

"Let's start with the herbal draught," Emmett stated.

"We need to remove the bandage around his ribs," Mignonette stated. "Would you help me?"

"Sean's ribs were injured?" Mrs. O'Toole inquired.

"'Tis nothing," Emmett remarked. "I'll lift, you unwrap it. Quickly now. We need to give him the herbal draught!"

Working together, Emmett lifted the semi-conscious Sean, while Mignonette removed the bandage and then coaxed him to swallow the herbal mixture.

Mrs. O'Toole tut-tutted over Sean's bruised torso but collected herself enough to appear satisfied when he'd finished the cupful and sent one of the footmen to bring fresh water.

Mignonette pressed her lips to his forehead, his cheek, his jaw, whispering prayers for his healing over and over while Sean's fever climbed. A few hours later, they roused him again, coaxing him to sip from another cup of the herbal draught. Finally, his fever broke.

"We need to change the bedding," Mrs. O'Toole told them. "He'll catch a chill lying on these damp sheets."

"Then his fever has broken?" Coventry asked from where he

stood in the doorway.

"Just now," Emmett informed him. "Have you spoken to Bayfield?"

Coventry nodded, frowning at the sight of O'Malley's bruised torso. "I will relay what we discussed after I speak to Mademoiselle de Chauret. She must be made to understand."

Emmett nodded.

Mrs. O'Toole interrupted. "First, we need your assistance lifting O'Malley. We cannot let him linger on sweat-soaked sheets." Turning to Mignonette, she asked, "I need you to remove the sheets. I'll place dry ones on the cot."

"*Oui*, Madame."

With the four of them working together, they settled O'Malley on dry bedding to ensure he did not get chilled. Relief speared through her that his fever finally abated. She poured water from the pitcher one of the footmen delivered along with a supply of clean cloths.

"He seems calmer," Mignonette rasped. "The herbal concoction is working."

"Aye, Lass," Emmett agreed.

His use of Sean's name for her soothed her. Their voices were similar, though not the same. She looked forward to hearing Sean calling for her when next he woke.

Coventry laid a hand on her arm, calling her attention to him. "Mademoiselle de Chauret, O'Malley has charged me with a favor that involves your participation."

She tilted her head to one side, waiting, wondering what that favor would entail. "I have promised to do whatever will aid in Monsieur O'Malley's healing. Tell me what you require of me, and I will do it after I help Emmett rewrap his broken ribs."

Emmett spoke up. "Until we're certain his fever had completely broken, we'll not be wrapping his ribs."

"Are you certain that is wise?"

Emmett chuckled. "Is this ye being difficult, Lass?"

She ignored his question. "Very well, do not wrap his ribs, if you are certain that is what is best for Sean."

"Aye, bedridden, he'll need to breathe without restriction or risk an ailment of the lungs."

The captain interrupted their conversation. "I need you to pay attention to what I'm about to say to you."

Mignonette turned her full attention to the captain.

"A Special License will be arriving by messenger midday tomorrow."

Disappointment swept up from her toes, but she buried the emotion deep. "Ah, I understand. You need me to stand in as proxy for the woman Monsieur O'Malley intends to marry."

"You have half of it right," Coventry rumbled. "You'll be standing beside O'Malley, but *you* are the woman he intends to marry."

Shock arrowed through her, while concern for his injury battled with elation that he wanted to marry her. *"Moi?"*

"Aye, Lass," Emmett replied. "'Tis no secret he's fallen head over heels for ye."

"O'Malley asked me to procure a Special License—through His Grace, to marry you. He did not want the woman who stole his heart to be without a family."

Fingers to her lips, she whispered, "Stole his heart?"

"His words, Mademoiselle, not mine."

"'Tis the God's honest truth once ye marry Sean, ye'll be surrounded by O'Malleys, Garahans, and Flahertys. We'll protect ye with our lives—no matter if Sean has one arm or two."

"Or if he gives his most precious gift in service to the duke and the earl," Coventry added, "his life."

Her tears fell unbidden. Mignonette was too overwhelmed by Sean O'Malley's request. How could she not honor what could be his last wish—to marry him?

"It would be my honor to marry Monsieur Sean. But I warn you, I will not be a biddable wife! I have a mind and I am not afraid to speak it."

Emmett pulled her into a fierce but brief hug, then set her

from him. "Ye'll be a welcome addition to the family. We Irish always fall for the hardheaded lasses."

Coventry nodded. "Thank you, Mademoiselle."

"Mignonette," she urged.

"Thank you, Mignonette. Whatever the outcome, you shall not lack for family or friends. O'Malley is the best of men."

"Lass?" Sean called out. "Where did ye go?"

Mignonette rushed to his side. "Here I am. I was speaking with Captain Coventry and Emmett."

"Ah, then he's told ye of the favor?"

"*Oui.*"

"Will ye, Lass?"

"Will I what?" she rasped, hoping he would ask her.

"Will ye marry me?"

"Before I agree, I have a confession to make."

His eyes widened. "Do ye now?"

"I am not marrying you as a favor to you, your cousin, or the captain."

"Why are ye agreeing then?"

"I am marrying the man who rescued me. The man who protected me. The one who saw that my injuries were taken care of before his own…the man who stole *my* heart."

O'Malley lifted his hand to her cheek. "Ye won't regret it, Lass. I'll make it up to ye."

"Make what up to me?"

"However long ye have to spend helping me recover. I'll see that ye've a roof over yer head, food in yer belly and…"

"And?"

"Show ye how much love I have inside for ye."

Undone by his declaration, she leaned closer until their lips were a breath apart. "You will recover, and I will be by your side every step of the way…no matter how long it takes."

Strengthened by his declaration of love, she pressed her lips to his. Tentatively, softly, sinking into the kiss.

She gasped when a strong arm banded across her back, pulling her flush against him as he plundered her mouth with the promise of passions untold.

"Well now, it seems me cousin isn't quite ready to leave this world, Coventry."

The deep chuckles coming from behind them did not deter O'Malley from shifting his hold, to cup her cheek. "Ye'll not regret it, Lass," he rasped. "Once an O'Malley gives his word, he keeps it from this life into the next."

"You should rest now, Sean," Emmett remarked from where he stood by the door. "Ye'll need every ounce of yer strength to fight against what yer body will be putting ye through in the next few hours."

Mignonette shifted so she could sit on the chair beside his cot. "Rest now. I am not going anywhere. Until tomorrow when I will need to change my gown before we marry. Do you have a favorite color?"

"Aye," O'Malley rasped.

She held his hand to her breast. "Which color?"

"Whatever one ye're wearing."

CHAPTER TWENTY-ONE

A FEW HOURS later, Mignonette's vow would be put to the test. Sean's fever raged again as she continued to soothe and bathe him with cool cloths until her arms ached. Through the long hours of the night, she refused to leave his side or rest.

Every few hours, Emmett lifted his cousin, supporting him, while she coaxed the herbal draught past Sean's lips. They noticed a difference in how quickly they brought his body temperature down when Emmett lifted Sean so she could bathe his back. Adding this to what had become routine, she finally agreed to let Emmett spell her, taking turns bathing his cousin.

Through the endless night, they fought the fever that had its grip on the man she loved. She no longer tried to hold back her tears. At one point, she began to wonder if the salt of her tears aided in bringing down his fever as his skin began to cool beneath her ministrations. But then the fever would build again, until the next dose of Emmett's herbal treatment, and the cycle would repeat again…and again.

Sometime just before dawn, Mignonette no longer wondered if the man she pledged to marry would make it until tomorrow— she knew he would. Exhausted, she knelt beside his cot, his hand grasped tightly in hers, so he did not move his injured arm.

The lass sighed in her sleep but did not waken as he swept the hair from her face to gaze upon it. "She didn't leave."

"Ye asked her not to," Emmett said as he moved to stand beside him. "The lass gave ye her word."

"I can't feel me fingers or me hand."

Emmett chuckled. "She's wanting to keep ye, I'm thinking. Do ye want me to move her?"

Sean sighed. "No…and I don't want her to marry me out of obligation."

"Don't ye believe that she could love ye?"

"I don't know. What if she feels obligated to marry me for protecting her?"

"*Eedjit*," Emmett grumbled. "If she believes that ye love her…why can't ye believe she loves ye back?"

Sean's rumbling laughter filled the room. "One minute I'm minding me own business, the next, I'm rescuing the lass." He stroked the tips of his fingers along the line of her jaw. "When I held her in me arms—against me heart, I knew she was the woman Ma promised was waiting for me."

"Aunt Eileen's never wrong," Emmett agreed, then added, "unless she argues with me own ma."

When Sean shifted on the bed and moaned, his cousin asked, "How do ye feel?"

"I've felt better. Are ye planning to unwrap the bandage again this morning?"

"Aye. We were planning to do so once you woke. I've a poultice that I asked Mrs. O'Toole to prepare for me, though I'm thinking not many physicians would approve."

Sean's eyes met his. "If it's something ye've learned from yer ma or yer grandma, I know it will work. I have faith in the old ways."

When Emmett inclined his head, Sean added, "No matter the outcome, I trust ye."

Mignonette shifted, groaned, then stilled. Lifting her head, she gasped. "You're awake! How do you feel?"

His eyes lit with humor. "I've felt better. Me cousin promised to unwrap the bandage again this morning as he's a poultice to apply to it."

She gripped his hand as she asked, "What of Dr. McIntyre's ointment?"

"Ease up, Lass. I cannot feel me fingers."

She immediately let go and began to stroke the back of his hand. "Forgive me. I was dreaming that I'd lost you…but then I found you. I knew if I let go, I'd never find you again."

"I'm right here. Can ye stand? Yer knees must be paining ye for having been on them all night."

"Not all night," she corrected as she slowly unfolded her legs to stand. "Emmett and I have been taking turns cooling you down and making you drink the herbal concoction he had Mrs. O'Toole prepare. It is what kept your fever from raging out of control…that and the cool cloths."

The first beams of sunlight broke through the clouds, streaming in through the window. His light hair glowed as if he wore a halo, adding to what she already thought of the man—he was *her* guardian angel, sent down from Heaven to protect her.

Drinking in the sight of him as the sun caressed the breadth of his shoulders, she felt her cheeks heating. Her breath caught in her throat.

"Whatever ye're thinking must be interesting," Sean commented, watching her. "Care to share yer thoughts?"

She opened her mouth to speak, but instead of words, a strangled gasp emerged.

"Me intended is speechless in the face of me naked glory."

Her sharp intake of breath had Sean and Emmett breaking into laughter. "You are not naked!"

The devilment in his gaze tugged on her heart, though she'd never tell him that. "The sheet has covered you from the waist down all night." As if of their own volition, her eyes shifted to take in the glorious display of his pectoral muscles…and lower to those banding across his abdomen. She swallowed as moisture gathered in her mouth. *Mon Dieu!* She was practically drooling over the sight of Sean without a shirt—what must he think of her?

Would he worry that she was a woman of loose morals?

"Have a seat, Lass."

When she made no move to regain the seat she'd abandoned during the night, he sighed. "Emmett, help the lass sit before she falls on her face."

Mignonette tried to steady herself, but her legs refused to cooperate. Emmett made the decision for her and gently braced a hand beneath her elbow as she sat. "*Merci*, Emmett."

"Me pleasure." With a wicked grin, he asked, "Do ye need me to toss the sheet over his manly chest to preserve yer tender feelings?"

Sean's sharp bark of laughter echoed in the room.

"Well now, that's a sound I've missed," Mrs. O'Toole remarked. She entered carrying a small tray, followed by two footmen carrying larger ones. She set the tray on the sideboard and walked over to Sean, placing the back of her hand against his forehead. "Still warm…but not hot. Do you think you can swallow a bit of broth?"

Sean frowned. "Is that all I'm allowed? No crust of bread soaked in milk?"

His quip brought a smile to the cook's face that brightened the room. "You *are* feeling better. We'll start with the broth—"

"Don't be forgetting the calf's foot jelly!" Emmett reminded her. She nodded and hurried from the room to fetch it.

"Horse's *arse*," Sean grumbled.

"Monsieur Sean!" Mignonette gasped. "How could you call your cousin such names after he helped me to care for you all night?"

He wasn't given the opportunity to reply as she continued, "It is his knowledge of herbs that has been keeping your fever from raging out of control! Without his strength, I could never have lifted you up to bathe your back."

Knowing he'd be married to the lass before the end of the day, he decided to see how far he could push her before she lost her temper with him. "Ye expect me to apologize to him?"

She folded her hands beneath her breasts and frowned at him. "*Oui!*"

Swallowing the expletive poised on his tongue, he acquiesced. "Do I have to mean what I say when I apologize?"

Her face flushed a delightful shade of peach, reminding him of the roses in his ma's garden. She frowned at him. "Do you often say things you do not mean, Monsieur Sean?"

Faith, the lass has spirit! He could not help prodding her further. "Aye, depending on who I'm speaking to and if it serves me purpose."

She drew in a breath and held it to the point where he wondered if she'd burst. Finally, she blew it out and pointed a finger at him. "You should always say what you mean. To lie is a sin."

The lass was close enough that he reached out to grab hold of the finger she pointed at him. He tugged and she fell against his chest. "There are times when a man has to make the decision to bend the truth to expose a far greater lie that would bring down the ruination of those he's sworn to protect."

Her lips were a breath away. Plump, soft, tempting him to take what would soon be his. Passion simmered in the depths of her warm brown eyes, pulling at him until he gave in. "Temptation be damned," he rasped, cupping the back of her head as he tasted, savored…and then plundered.

She sighed and kissed him back with a hint of the passion he now knew lay in wait for him to unleash it. If ever a man had a reason to recover—quickly, teaching his wife to trust him with her heart, her soul, and her body was his.

He eased his hold on her to change the angle and deepen the kiss.

"If ye're through mauling yer intended, Sean," his cousin prompted, "we need to change yer bandage and apply the poultice."

With a sigh of regret, he released the lass, placing a kiss to the tip of her nose as he caressed her cheek. "I will never lie to ye about how I feel, and ye won't lie to me." He slowly smiled. "Yer kisses will tell me the truth, no matter what yer mind urges yer lips to say."

She harrumphed and straightened. "I have no intention of lying to you—ever. I will say what I feel, when I feel it," she declared. Turning to Emmett she squared her shoulders and asked, "Shall I unwrap the bandage while you ready the poultice?"

"Aye. Mind ye don't move, Cousin."

Sean nodded. He knew without question that it would be painful uncovering the raw wound.

"Mrs. O'Toole left what we need right here. I just need to sterilize me knife in case we need it."

"Knife?"

Sean watched the color leach from the lass' face. "Catch her!"

Emmett was quick on his feet, bracing his arm around Mignonette's waist, steadying her. "Have a care now." He eased her onto the chair beside his cousin. "Did ye not know that inflammation can be eased by lancing a wound?"

"I thought the poultice was for that."

"Aye, but if the inflammation warrants it, we will have to draw out the infection first."

"With a knife?"

"We O'Malleys always carry a knife in our boots. Ye never know when you'll be jumped from behind. The surprise of it has won more than one fight."

"Shouldn't you wait for the physician? He may have a lancet."

Sean snorted out a laugh. "There's been many a time we've been involved in a fi—er, situation," he clarified, not wanting to upset the lass, "when one of me cousins or I was wounded. Do ye think we carried a surgeon's tool with us?"

Mignonette shook her head and admitted, "No. But if we wait for the lieutenant—"

Emmett's eyes glittered with purpose. "We run the risk that the infection takes hold. If that happens, we're already too late." Meeting her gaze, he asked, "Do ye understand the urgency?"

Sean watched as tears welled in her eyes, but she did not let them fall. The lass blinked them away. He knew in that moment that he'd been right to follow his heart. She was the one—the woman meant for him alone. "The lass understands, don't ye?"

She nodded. "Forgive me. My father never carried a knife. I'm not used to such." Brushing a strand of hair that slipped from its pins behind her ear, she drew in a fortifying breath and stood. "I'm ready." She placed a hand to Sean's shoulder. "I will be as gentle as possible, but I may still inadvertently hurt you. Know that I wouldn't do that unless I had no choice."

"Aye, Lass. Go ahead."

True to her word, Mignonette carefully unwrapped the length of bandage. Her indrawn breath had him bracing for what would come next.

"Sean?" Emmett's expression reeked of concern. "I'll send for the lieutenant, but we won't be waiting for him to arrive. I have to drain it now!"

He nodded and turned to Mignonette. "Are ye up to holding me hand still, or should we call for one of the footmen?"

She lifted her chin and replied, "I'll hold you still."

Emmett moved to the doorway. "I'll have Jenkins send for Lieutenant Sampson. Mrs. O'Toole's got the fire going in her cook stove. I can use that to heat the blade."

Sean chuckled. "Don't be running with a hot knife now."

His cousin shook his head at him. "Bloody *eedjit*."

"Watch yer words in front of me bride," Sean warned.

"She's not yer bride, yet," Emmett shot back.

"Aye," Sean admitted as his gaze met hers. "But she will be."

"I keep my promises," Mignonette reminded him. Looking into his eyes, she whispered, "Did I hurt you?"

He shook his head. "Nothing that I cannot handle, Lass. 'Tis what comes next that'll be a challenge."

"Mayhap we *should* ask one of the footmen to be on hand. I may need help keeping your arm immobile."

He did not want her to worry. He had no intention of showing weakness in front of her—by giving in to the pain and moving his arm. "If it will ease yer worry, ask. There should be someone stationed in the entryway, just outside the kitchen."

"I shall be right back!" she promised. She practically flew out of the room.

Alone, O'Malley nearly gave in to the overpowering need to howl in pain. Mrs. O'Toole's smiling face returning with the small bowl in her hands had him grunting instead. "I see ye didn't forget."

"You can either spoon it up, or drink it down as you did yesterday," the cook informed him. "Mark my words, you will swallow every bit of it."

"Would ye hold me nose? I'm not supposed to use me right hand."

She was laughing as she handed him the bowl. "If you really want me to."

He shook his head. "Nay, I just love the sound of yer laughter. It reminds me of me ma."

Sean lifted the bowl to his lips and gulped it down, shuddering at the noxious smell and taste. "Me family has a small farm back in Ireland. We raise sheep, have a couple of chickens, a milk cow...and a few pigs. The scent of the jelly reminds me of butchering time. Once it was done 'twas time to cure the meat and use every bit of the pig. Ma boiling those feet had me running for the bucket she kept just outside our cottage door."

"Poor lad," Mrs. O'Toole said accepting the empty bowl. "Why don't you lie back down? Emmett will be a few minutes more."

Sean thought about it, then refused. "I want to make sure the blasted jelly stays in me gut, if ye don't mind."

Her eyes twinkled with laughter. "A wise decision."

"Monsieur Sean!" Mignonette called to him. "I did not find the footman, but Jenkins assured me your visitor is more than up to the task."

"Visitor?" He craned his neck to see past Mrs. O'Toole and

the lass into the hallway.

"I see I've arrived just in time, O'Malley."

"Yer lordship!" The earl was the last person Sean expected to see. "What brings ye to London?"

The earl's eyes met his. "Need you ask?"

"Ye aren't here to issue a challenge are ye?"

"Challenge, your lordship?" Mignonette queried.

"'Tis an expression, Lass. Don't be worrying about it."

As if she didn't hear him, she asked the earl, "Isn't it illegal to engage in a duel?"

"O'Malley misunderstood my meaning. He must have hit his head when he was attacked," Earl Lippincott proclaimed.

"Which time?" Mignonette asked.

The earl cleared his throat, swallowing a laugh. "I see nothing has changed. How many times have you been injured since leaving Lippincott Manor?"

"More than once," Mignonette answered for him. "Would you like to hear what happened?"

Sean noticed she did not look at the earl when she spoke, but knew she wasn't being disrespectful, she was busy placing a thick layer of linen beneath Sean's arm and arranging the bowl of hot water and linen squares to within reach.

The earl smiled indulgently. "I would—" he paused and looked over his shoulder as Emmett returned. "Later. Mademoiselle, why don't you sit here and hold O'Malley's hand. I'll stand behind him and brace his shoulders."

Sean felt the weight of the earl's strong hands on his shoulders and relaxed. He would not have to worry that he'd embarrass himself by jerking his arm away from the gut-wrenching pain he knew the hot knife to swollen flesh would cause.

When the lass had a firm grip on his hand, he looked to his cousin. "Have ye washed yer hands?"

Emmett's lips twitched, but the concentration glittering in his gaze never wavered. "This may prick a bit."

Sean nearly closed his eyes, not wanting to watch, but heard a tiny gasp. "It would be best if ye look at me face and not me arm, Lass."

Her eyes held a mix of worry and fear that faded when her gaze met his. "I've got you, Monsieur Sean. I won't let go."

The strength in her hand and vow on her lips washed over him, eclipsing the pain the knife piercing the swollen skin on his forearm caused. Sweat broke out on his brow and trickled down the sides of his face. He clamped his jaw and willed his gut not to rebel.

"Monsieur Sean?"

He tilted his head to one side in silent question. If he opened his mouth, he'd lose the fight against the bile bubbling up his throat.

Her expression fierce, her voice firm, she promised, "I won't let go."

Relief filled him at her words. He won the battle and the bile receded.

Her vow twined with the one she'd pledged the night before—to marry him, filled his heart.

His vow to protect her, keep a roof over her head, and food in her belly, added to the bonds that tied them together.

The connection already forged between them would bind their hearts and their souls from this day forward. Speaking their pledges before the minister later would bind them legally. O'Malley prayed he would have the strength to seal their union. Because no one—no one would tear them apart.

The pain left him by degrees as he felt his body reacting to the poison leaving his system. Without looking, he asked his cousin, "Were ye in time?"

"Aye. 'Twas infected to be sure, but not the worst I've seen any of us suffer in the past. Ye'll be right as rain if ye follow me instructions."

Sean sighed. "Yers, too? What of the lieutenant's and McIntyre's?"

"Ye'll have to follow them as well. But mine are more important as I'm thinking I've just saved yer arm."

CHAPTER TWENTY-TWO

"M ONSIEUR SEAN?"

"If we're to be married in a few hours, do ye think ye can call me Sean?"

Mignonette slowly smiled. "*Oui*, Sean."

"Much better."

"Your color is returning to normal, and your arm is not warm to the touch above the bandage."

"I told ye, ye had no need to worry, Lass. Emmett's the gifted healer in the O'Malley clan. We've been blessed with one every generation."

"You are so lucky. If we'd had one…" she didn't bother finishing her sentence. They did not have a gifted healer to heal her mother or father. No point in reliving that devastating time. It nearly destroyed her the first time.

"Ye're thinking of yer parents?"

The understanding in his gaze was a soothing balm to the ache in her heart. "*Oui*."

"I still remember feeling helpless when Da and me Uncle Patrick were wrongfully imprisoned."

She waited for him to continue, knowing it would be one more conversation that drew them closer together. Trust did not happen at first glance—love could, and in their case had.

"They were eventually vindicated when the truth emerged."

Mignonette tried to discern the reason he hesitated. Taking a chance that he only needed to be prompted, she stated, "That must have been a relief to your mother and your aunt."

"Me Uncle Patrick never walked through those prison doors a free man." He swallowed visibly. The anguish in the depths of his eyes pulled at her. "He breathed his last an hour before they released them. When the jailor unlocked the door, he found me da cradling his brother to his chest. Tears on his face and vengeance in his eyes. Da's never forgotten...nor will he ever forgive those who lied to put them behind bars."

Mignonette did not know what to say, but her heart knew what to do. Easing to her knees, she placed her head on Sean's broad chest and placed her hand to his heart. "*Maman* vowed to see *mon papa's* attackers punished for causing his death."

Sean stroked her head. His touch encouraged her to push past the hurt to let him know she understood. "The blow to his head did not kill him immediately."

"Why were ye not worried when ye'd suffered the same? I know I was."

A warm glow filled her breast at his concern. "I did not feel the blow."

"Mayhap ye were hit hard enough that ye blacked out."

"I don't—"

"Ye'd best get used to listening to yer husband, Lass. I know what's best for ye."

She jerked upright. "Will you listen to your wife, Monsieur O'Malley? Do you agree that I know what's best for you?"

The soft green of his eyes darkened and, for a moment, she thought he would disagree and become angry with her. His laughter belied that worry.

"Faith, if ye're not all that Ma promised the woman I was meant to marry would be."

"Oh? And what is that?"

"A woman who knows her own mind, like me ma. A woman who is not afraid to stand toe-to-toe with her husband and tell him when she thinks he's wrong."

"Like your *maman?*"

"*Oui,*" he teased, "Like me ma."

His words softened the edges of her irritation with the hard-headed Irishman. "*Maman* said I would find love one day."

She sighed remembering that long ago day, listening to *Maman* while she sipped from her cup of rich chocolate—a special treat to honor the day her body changed from a young girl to a young woman. A time to celebrate, her mother had told her, as she assured her change never came without pain. She was a de Chauret, her mother had reminded her, but she was also a Dubois. Her lineage may not be royal, but she was descended from strong and honest men and women.

Sean reached for her hand and confessed, "I love ye, Lass, and promise to for the rest of me life."

Tears filled her eyes, but she did not bother to blink them away. She would not hide her emotions from her husband-to-be. "I love you now. I will love you always."

Their lips were a breath apart when a deep voice rumbled, "I do not remember kissing being a part of O'Malley's wound treatment."

Sean pressed a swift, but potent kiss to Mignonette's lush mouth. He would have time later to kiss her more deeply. "Ye should be adding it to yer list of duties for a nursemaid to perform. It cured me."

"Emmett was outside standing guard when I arrived," Lieutenant Sampson told them. "I could tell from the look on his face that you were much improved, though from the missive I received, I expected to find you in far worse shape."

Mignonette glanced at Sean before speaking. "Emmett said he had to lance the wound immediately. He could not wait for you."

Approaching the couple, the lieutenant demanded, "Let me have a look at your arm, O'Malley."

The physician noticed the poultice, but did not comment on it, simply removed it, and set it aside. "Your coloring has returned. Emmett's quick thinking may have spared you from the threat of further infection."

"Aye, but 'twas me self-prescribed kissing that put the color in me cheeks."

Shaking his head, the lieutenant unwrapped the bandage and inspected the stitches the duke's physician had used to close the wound. He studied the three small incisions where it had been drained. "I won't ask if your cousin sterilized the blade. Any soldier or seaman worth his salt would know what to do."

"Mrs. O'Toole can vouch that me cousin held his blade to the fire in her cookstove."

"I know the duke's physician prescribed an ointment to use on the wound," the lieutenant said. "I grew up on a farm. We did not have the luxury of a physician nearby. My mother learned how to care for wounds, fevers, and the like from her mother— who learned from her mother before her. I would never advise against using a poultice—or herbal draught when I've grown up more accustomed to the old ways myself."

"Well now, I thought I'd either have to convince ye that Emmett knows what he's about—or wait until ye left and follow what me cousin advised."

The lieutenant chuckled. "You still need to rest for at least a sennight," he instructed, using a fresh bandage to wrap O'Malley's arm. "Unless the fever returns. In that case, you rest and recuperate for a full fortnight."

"Aye, Lieutenant."

"Try to avoid heavy lifting, using that arm to wield a blade— or to ward off an attacker."

It was Sean's turn to chuckle. "Aye."

Lieutenant Sampson smiled at the couple. "I hear congratulations are in order. I trust that you will be cautious when engaging in any…shall we say…marital activities."

Sean's bride-to-be flushed from her neck to her forehead.

"I know me limits, Lieutenant. Have no doubt of that."

The physician ignored Sean. "I advise caution while he

sleeps," he told Mignonette. "No pressure is to be applied to that arm until the wound is fully mended. There is still a chance that infection could set in—and with it, fever. He must follow either my instructions, Dr. McIntyre's, or his cousin's."

"I promise to heed your words and do my utmost to ensure that he does not injure his wound further."

Bowing over Mignonette's hand, he replied, "I could not ask for more, Mademoiselle. As I said before, do not hesitate to send for me should his condition change."

"Thank you, Lieutenant Sampson. Monsieur Sean and I are grateful for your excellent care."

"You are most welcome. Goodbye."

"*Au revoir!*"

"Goodbye," Sean murmured as the physician departed. "Are ye hungry, Lass?"

"Not especially."

"Do ye think ye might be in a quarter-hour from now?"

She slowly smiled. "Mayhap."

"Me gut is empty. Have pity on a starving man. I'm too weak to charm a bit of bread and butter—or a couple of Mrs. O'Toole's scones from ye."

"I shall ask your cousin permission. I do not want you to suffer a setback from setting aside your invalid's diet."

Sean blew out a breath. "Why bother asking him? I'm not an invalid. He and I both know that."

She cupped his face in her hand and pressed her lips to his forehead. "Your fever is gone, and your wound has vastly improved from last night. I would suggest you heed your cousin."

"Ye know he'll insist on broth...and the blasted calf's foot jelly." He visibly shuddered.

Tracing the tip of her finger along the line of his jaw, she soothed, "Mayhap since you are so improved, Emmett may allow you a bit of bread with your broth."

"Fine then. But I won't be the one whose conscience is smarting when me patient is writhing in pain from an empty gut. 'Twill be on yer head."

Mignonette's eyes sparkled with light and love as she replied, "I'll risk it if it will help you heal fully."

"Are ye sure ye haven't met me ma?"

Her soft laughter trailed after her, but O'Malley wasn't irritated. He offered up a silent prayer to his Maker, marveling at the fact that the lass cared enough to want him to heal. But more, that the lass loved him in return, praise God!

O'Malley found himself anxious for the arrival of Coventry and the Special License. He was ready to get married.

Chapter Twenty-Three

I T TOOK ONE more day to ensure O'Malley would be able to stand on his own to say his vows. The fever, blood loss, and lack of food had taken more of a toll on her intended then either of them would have suspected. Although O'Malley was insistent that they marry right away to protect her, he was adamant that he stand by her side when they did.

Mignonette appreciated the gift of time and did not waste it, watching over her patient like a hawk, waiting to pounce if he so much as deviated one tiny bit from the wound treatment prescribed—his diet, or activities. She had been blessed the day he strode into her life, and she did not intend to lose him when it was within her power to save him.

Mrs. O'Toole and Emmett insisted she take frequent breaks while caring for her grumpy patient. Although she hated to leave his side, Mignonette knew his belligerent attitude was a sign that he was improving. During one of her breaks, Madame and Yvette arrived with a gown they stayed up all night creating at O'Malley's request.

Standing before the looking glass in Mrs. O'Toole's quarters, she sighed. "It is like a dream, Madame! Oh, Yvette!" she gushed. "Look how the gown dances around me when I twirl!"

Madame laughed softly as she watched Mignonette turn this way and that, admiring the gown they'd conspired with her husband-to-be to create as a surprise for her.

"I will have to work very hard to earn the cost of this gown." Tears filled her eyes studying the gift of their time and talent. "I will pay you back for the material and your time, Madame. I know how much a gown such as this would cost one of our customers."

Madame walked over to stand beside Mignonette. "*Ma petite*, you owe me nothing. Your Monsieur O'Malley is the one you need to thank for the gown, and the lovely color, although he was wise enough to ask me and Yvette to create it. We all want you to look your best when you stand beside Monsieur O'Malley and say your vows."

"*Oui, mon ami*," Yvette chimed in. "A bride deserves to look her best."

Mignonette wrapped her arms around Madame and Yvette and held tight. "I have missed working with you so much. Our chats while our fingers were busy sewing seams, creating dream gowns for others." She eased back and smiled at the two women. "Especially our lively discussions where we plotted to convince overbearing *mamans* to try a more pleasing color palette for their daughters."

Madame agreed. "Without telling them their sense of color was skewed."

"Shouldn't our customers rely on our expertise regarding the color and cut of their gowns?" Yvette asked.

"*Ma ous.*" Madame's sigh was heartfelt. "Though we can only suggest and encourage our customers. One must also remember, the one who has the coin to pay for the gowns is correct— whether or not they know the difference between ecru and white."

Mignonette stared at her reflection. "Do you know," she remarked, "this shade of warm rose reminds me of the one I received as a gift earlier this morning?"

Yvette winked at Madame. "Was it from Monsieur O'Malley?"

Mignonette felt her cheeks fill with warmth at the mention of his name, realizing he'd asked Madame to find fabric to match that rose to create a gown for her. "Mrs. O'Toole smiled at him, as if they shared a secret," she replied.

"I do not believe Monsieur O'Malley to have a bashful bone in his body," Madame declared.

Mignonette remembered the kiss they shared just moments before she left his side. Her lips tingled, her breath hitched, and an unaccustomed warmth spread up from her belly to her breast.

Yvette sighed aloud. "From the look on your face, *mon ami*, you know it to be true."

Mignonette struggled to put her emotions and feelings into words. She wanted to share her newfound love and joy with the mother—and sister…of her heart. "It is as if I have been be-witched when I look into the depths of his moss green eyes." She placed a hand to her breast and confessed, "He is regaining his strength and is not afraid to use it to tempt me. When he pulls me close, it is all I can do *not* to beg him to kiss me again. I am afraid that I have lost my will completely and will never get it back. Is it normal to feel this way, Madame?"

Madame slowly smiled. "*Oui, ma petite.* It is how it should be when one is deeply in love. Enjoy every moment. Love can be fleeting—or last beyond the grave."

Mignonette recalled the heartfelt conversation she'd had with the modiste recently. Madame had married young…and lost the love of her life when he fought to protect her honor more than a decade ago.

"Yvette, help Mignonette out of her gown. She has plenty of time to change back into it before the vicar arrives to perform the ceremony."

Dressed once more in one of her serviceable work gowns, Mignonette hugged Madame and Yvette. "I have been gone too long. Monsieur Sean will worry. You will return to bear witness to our vows?"

Yvette nodded and Madame smiled, replying, "*Mais oui!*

Promise you will allow Mrs. O'Toole and other members of the duke's staff to help you take of care Monsieur O'Malley—especially today."

She nodded and Madame patted the side of her face. "You want to be well rested," she advised.

"I shall join you momentarily, Yvette. Please close the door on your way out." With a wave of her hand, she shooed her from the room. After the young woman departed, Madame inquired, "Did your *maman* explain what to expect on your wedding night?"

Mignonette shook her head. "She did not have a chance to before she died."

Madame nodded. "Come, sit, and I will tell you of the beauty two people in love share with one other."

"Oh, but I already have shared my love with Monsieur O'Malley," she protested.

Madame raised one eyebrow. "I see, you have anticipated your vows and given yourself to him?"

Mignonette frowned. "If sharing the splendor of his kisses while he held me to his heart is giving myself to him," she replied, "then, yes. I have."

Madame nodded. "There is more to making love than sharing stolen kisses with the man whose very presence fogs your brain and makes the blood rush through your veins."

Mignonette's eyes widened. "Please, tell me what to expect."

MIGNONETTE'S BREATH SNAGGED in her breast as her heart skipped a beat before pounding furiously in her breast at all that Madame told her. "And this is possible for a man and a woman to join this way?"

"*Oui*. Do not be afraid. There is brief pain, your first time. But with the right man," she confided, "you will soar to the heavens and float back down, wondering when you will be able to soar again."

"You make it sound so beautiful," Mignonette whispered.

"It can be. Trust Monsieur O'Malley to be careful with your body and your heart."

"I must be gentle with him, too and to watch that he does not strain his arm while it is healing." She felt the warmth of her face flushing as she added, "Lieutenant Sampson warned me to be not to add pressure to his arm during what he called marital activities and while we sleep."

Madame rose to her feet and pulled Mignonette into her arms. "Trust your love to know what he is about, and he will reward you with pleasures untold."

Mignonette was unsure if she would be able to do the same for him. "Before you leave, will you tell me how to please him?"

Madame opened her mouth to speak, then shook her head as if changing her mind.

Mignonette urged, "Please? I do not want him to be sorry he married me."

"*Ma petite*, you have no fear of that. But, I will say this, ask him. He will either tell you how to please him, or if I am right…he will teach you how to please him. Now go. Yvette and I shall see you later."

"*Merci*, Madame! *Je t'aime.*"

"*Je t'aime, ma petite.*"

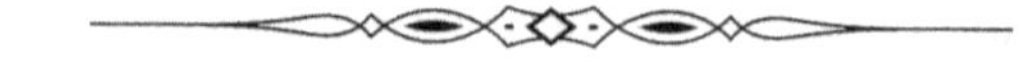

CHAPTER TWENTY-FOUR

Lady Kittrick paced in front of the hearth. She'd been about to mount her horse for her morning ride in the park when she'd been interrupted. Her daily routine was part of what kept her fit, as her partners often remarked as they lay spent, tangled together.

With each step, her frustration twined with the anger bubbling below the surface of her calm, threatening to spill over.

She paused and glared at the ragged messenger as he leaned on his crutch, not bothering to let her distaste for him show. "You are certain you did not mishear the conversation?"

"I *ain't* deaf," the man spat out. "Now, do I get the coin you promised, or do I take what I heard to Grosvenor Square."

She flew across the room, raising the riding crop she carried and slashed the man across his face. "You will do no such thing! I have been planning the social ruin of the earl and his countess for over a year. No one will interfere!" She raised the crop, threatening to lash him a second time. "Do you hear me?"

The man did not flinch…did not show any outward sign that he felt the pain of the crop, though it left a raised welt on his cheek.

He stared at her until her stomach quailed and for the first time dealing with those who made the docks their home, she felt a frisson of fear race up her spine. "You will limp back from whatever dank crevice you crawled out of on the docks and never return."

"I am not leaving until you pay me."

He did not look away when she stared at him. Most of her staff and those she delt with on the docks and in the underbelly of London never dared to meet her gaze. The man was not afraid of her. What did he know? Who else paid him to do their dirty work? Someone of a higher rank among the *ton*?

Before she could ask, he straightened, until he was no longer leaning on his crutch. His height surprised her. The lack of emotion in his pale eyes worried her. Who was the man? Was he another of the men England sent off to battle in the name of the king only to return a shadow of their former selves?

His gaze met hers as he took a step closer, his hand extended outward.

Lady Kittrick was not used to being approached by any member of the lower class—or rabble as she thought of them. She slapped at his hand, then wiped it on her skirts.

The beggar's reaction was not what she expected. He stared at his hand, curled it into a fist and glared at her. The angry gleam in his cold blue eyes promised retaliation. He wouldn't dare strike her…would he?

"You will leave at once!" she commanded.

He made no move to do so.

Her shock was complete when he took a step forward.

A glance was all it took to seal her fate. She was too far away from the servants' bell pull. She could not discretely summon help. Her insides trembled. Though she fought against showing fear in front of the enraged man towering over her, she drew in a breath to scream.

He reached out to touch her and the scream died in her throat. The last thing she remembered before losing consciousness was how clean his hands were.

"BLOODY HELL!" BAYFIELD grumbled. He kicked his crutch out of the way and caught the woman before she hit the floor. He carried her over to the settee and dumped her there. Striding over to the bell pull, he tugged on it and opened the doors to the sitting room.

"What happened?" the butler demanded rushing over to his mistress. "I shall summon the Watch!"

Bayfield snatched the frayed cap from his head and tucked it in his ragged coat pocket. "Do not bother, my good man," he intoned, pleasantly. "I shall summon them for you."

"Who are you?"

"Bayfield. Retired captain in the King's Royal Navy, at your service."

"What did you do to Lady Kittrick?"

"I merely asked for the payment she promised for information I delivered." Bayfield turned so the butler could see the injured side of his face. "I caught her as she fainted."

The butler swallowed audibly as he glanced about him.

"If you are looking for the lady's riding crop, I believe she dropped it over there." He pointed toward the hearth.

"The Watch won't believe you did not harm my mistress," the butler informed him.

He slowly smiled. "That will not be a problem. Captain Coventry is well aware of the situation and that I intended to call upon Lady Kittrick this morning."

"I do not know Captain Coventry."

Bayfield shrugged. "Mayhap you recognize the Duke of Wyndmere's name?"

The butler's eyes goggled at the mention of the duke. He nodded.

"Coventry is the duke's London man-of-affairs. Any other questions?"

"Did you strike her?"

"Do you see any marks on the lady?"

"You could have hit her where it wouldn't show," the butler rasped.

"I have never in my life hit a woman, although I have hit below the belt more than once in my youth—before I became an officer, sparring while our ship was becalmed."

The older man hesitated and before he asked another question, Bayfield reached into his waistcoat pocket and retrieved his card. "Should you need to contact me, I would be more than happy to speak with you."

"You do not act or speak like a beggar from the docks."

"I would have been reduced to doing so returning from the war after I recovered from my injuries if not for the kindness of a friend and his employer the duke." He handed the card to the butler and waited while he read it.

"You would do well not to trust anything your mistress has to say about others."

"Aye, Captain Bayfield. Thank you for the warning."

"If you find yourself in need of new employment, please contact me. I shall be happy to recommend you to either the duke or his brother, Earl Lippincott."

The lone moan coming from the settee had the butler nodding at the captain. "I shall take care of Lady Kittrick. You'd best be gone before she rouses."

Bayfield was reaching for the door when the butler rasped, "Don't forget your crutch—and use the side door to the alley."

He retrieved it, nodded to the older man, and left. As he stepped onto the sidewalk, he resumed the character he'd adopted while working at the docks, leaning on his crutch. Pleased the lady's butler was adept at reading a person's character—more adept than the woman who employed him. Then again, it was part of the butler's job…and the lady had not expected one of Coventry's newly hired men to be working on the docks in the guise of an injured beggar.

Time to report back to Coventry. He'd be interested in this latest turn of events.

CHAPTER TWENTY-FIVE

"**Y**OU MAY KISS the bride," the vicar intoned.

O'Malley slid his good arm around his wife's slender waist and held her to his heart for a moment, gazing into the warmth of her soft brown eyes before lowering his head to meld his lips with hers.

His kiss sealed his vow to love, honor, and protect her for the rest of their lives. O'Malley ached to give in to the passions he held at bay with an iron will…time enough for that later. He relaxed his hold, unable to believe the woman who'd stolen his heart with one glance was now his wife. "Ye're beautiful, Lass. The roses in yer cheeks match the gown ye're wearing. I hope ye like it. I gave Madame Beaudoine a rose to match the color."

She sighed and reached for his hand. Holding it, she confessed, "No one's ever given me a rose before—or a gown."

He frowned. "Ah, then mayhap 'twas a daisy."

She shook her head.

"Wildflower?"

Again, she shook her head. "No flowers."

"'Tis their loss, Lass," he rasped, trailing the tip of his finger along the curve of her cheek, the line of her jaw. "Ye deserve flowers, and to be dressed in gowns befitting ye."

"May I kiss yer bride?"

Before O'Malley could tell his cousin, no, the *eedjit* swept

Mignonette into his embrace, kissed her, and set her back on her feet next to him.

Mignonette's eyes blinked twice before her mouth finally closed.

Emmett's laughter reverberated through the room. More than one person shook their head at his antics. "Faith, ye're bloody lucky, Sean."

"Give me one good reason not to knock yer hard head off yer shoulders!"

His cousin grinned. "'Twas like kissing me sister. Ye've nothing to fear from either of us."

Mignonette put her arm around her husband and her cousin-in-law. "The two of you are more like brothers than cousins." She lifted to her toes to press a kiss to Emmett's cheek, saying, "If I had a brother, I imagine your kiss would have reminded me of him."

"Ye wound me, Lass," Emmett confided. "I'll be going now, I've duties to see to." With a nod to O'Malley, he reminded him, "Ye've duties of yer own now. I'm betting ye'll have a son as hardheaded as yerself."

O'Malley locked gazes with his bride, answering, "I'm hoping for a daughter with blue-black hair and deep brown eyes."

Emmett smiled and clapped him on the shoulder. "As me ma would say, a healthy babe from her nose to her toes."

Coventry smiled as he and his wife congratulated them, followed by Gavin King and Earl Lippincott.

The earl smiled as he walked toward them. "Congratulations, O'Malley...and Mrs. O'Malley. Aurelia and I have a wedding gift for you, but I left it back in Sussex."

"*Merci*, your lordship."

He flashed a grin at O'Malley before asking her, "Don't you want to know what it is?"

She hesitated, before blushing and responding, "*Oui*, if you wish to tell me."

"I have set aside a parcel of land on my estate and have commissioned a house to be built for you."

O'Malley felt the bottom drop out of his stomach and swayed on his feet. Quick to react, the earl reached out to steady him. "I take it you are thrilled with our gift," the earl drawled.

"Overwhelmed by yer generosity, yer lordship," O'Malley managed. "Ye didn't have to—"

"My brother and I are firm in our decision to offer a home to those within my brother's guard who marry. We cannot possibly repay you for the number of times you have already saved our lives and the lives of our families."

"What of the quarterly rotation of the guard?" O'Malley asked. "How are ye planning to manage that? I'm not liking the idea of leaving me wife behind for four months at a time and cannot imagine packing up our wives and our lives to switch houses."

The earl laughed and shook his head. "If you'd like to continue to participate in the rotation, I am certain my brother will consider it. Although Jared recently sent word," the earl informed him, "that the married men—at the moment yourself and your cousin, Patrick, will no longer be expected to rotate their positions among his other estates and those of our cousins and their wives."

O'Malley held out his hand and the earl grasped it. "Thank ye, yer lordship. I never expected to receive a gift—let alone such a grand gesture from ye or the duke."

"You are most welcome." The earl glanced at the new Mrs. O'Malley and noted how pale she was. "Are you feeling all right, Mrs. O'Malley?"

"*Oui*, a bit tired is all," she rasped. "*Merci* for your kindness, your lordship. Please extend our gratitude to His Grace as well."

"It will be my pleasure." The earl smiled as Madame Beaudoine and Mademoiselle Augustin approached. "Mrs. O'Malley is radiant wearing your latest creation, Madame."

Mignonette's employer beamed. "She is the beauty that inspired us, is that not so, Yvette?"

"*Mais oui*, Madame." Turning to the couple, Yvette beamed. "*Bonne chance*, Mignonette and Monsieur O'Malley. We shall miss you."

Mignonette nodded and hugged Yvette and then Madame Beaudoine.

O'Malley thought it odd that she did not speak until he noted the unshed tears glistening in her dark brown eyes. *What had upset her?* Moments ago, she was smiling.

He bent his head and whispered to her, "Are ye unwell, Lass?"

She shook her head but still did not speak.

"If ye'll excuse us for a moment, I need to speak with me bride." With her hand in his, he gave a gentle tug to get her moving.

Mrs. O'Toole stepped in front of the sitting room doors. She frowned and crossed her arms in front of her. "You cannot leave before your wedding supper. I slaved for hours preparing it."

"'Tisn't what ye think, Mrs. O'Toole," O'Malley informed her. "Something is bothering me wife, and I intend to get to the bottom of it."

"Have you asked her?" the cook inquired.

"I'm not an *eedjit*, Mrs. O'Toole," he reminded her, "of course I asked."

The cook glanced at Mignonette, and then O'Malley. "May I borrow your bride for a few moments? We shall be right back."

O'Malley sighed. "Aye, but if ye're not, I'll be coming to fetch me wife, meself!"

Mrs. O'Toole gently guided Mignonette through the doors and into the hallway. With a nod at the two footmen, they stepped away to give them privacy. "Now then, Mrs. O'Malley, can you tell me what happened? What has you on the verge of tears?"

When she did not answer, Mrs. O'Toole urged, "Mignonette?"

She sighed and met Mrs. O'Toole's gaze, admitting, "The earl and the duke's gift."

"Ah. It was a surprise to me as well. But how wonderful a surprise, wouldn't you say?"

"But it isn't in London."

Mrs. O'Toole nodded. "I think I understand what is bothering you. Have you ever been to Sussex before? The countryside is beautiful—the lush green of the trees and meadows."

Mignonette blinked away her tears. "Madame's shop is in London."

"Did you and Sean discuss where you would live after you married?"

She shook her head. "With all that has happened, we have not had the time, though I thought we would be staying in London—he is here now, is he not?"

"He is," Mrs. O'Toole replied, "but he is currently stationed in Sussex and is on loan here working with Captain Coventry and Mr. King."

Mignonette grasped her hands to her waist. "I see."

"Talk to Sean. He is very understanding and would not want you to be unhappy. This is the beginning of your new life. Start it off with an open mind and loving heart and you will never regret it."

"How long have you been married?" Mignonette asked.

Mrs. O'Toole smiled. "Forever it seems, though my darling is no longer with me."

"I am so sorry…he left you?"

Mrs. O'Toole put her arm around Mignonette, prompting her to return to the sitting room. "Not willingly. He lives in Heaven now, but I still talk to him, argue with him, and will always love him."

Mignonette wrapped her arms around the cook and hugged her. "Thank you for your kind words and advice, Mrs. O'Toole."

The older woman stepped back and beamed at her. "Now, go and assure your husband that all is well and that he has nothing to worry about."

"*Oui*, Mrs. O'Toole. I shall tell him all is well…and that I love him!"

"An excellent start. Please let him know the wedding supper is ready to be served."

O'Malley was pacing just inside the doorway when his bride entered. The first thing he noticed was that Mignonette's smile reached her eyes—*dry eyes*. Relief speared through him. "Where is Mrs. O'Toole?"

"She said to tell you our wedding supper is ready to be served."

Sliding his arm around her waist, he beamed at those gathered. "Won't ye join us in the dining room? Mrs. O'Toole has prepared a supper, and I'm famished!"

The group moved as one to the dining room where china, crystal and silver shone beneath the glow of the candle-lit chandelier.

As he guided Mignonette to her seat, he felt her trembling. O'Malley leaned down, pitching his voice low so only she could hear, he asked, "What's wrong, Lass?"

"It is so grand," she whispered, glancing at the elegant place settings. "Too grand. Will someone arrive demanding I be removed from the duke's dining room?"

He squeezed her hand in his, awed when he remembered the strength he knew resided beneath the softness of her skin. "Faith, I know what ye mean. The first time I met with the duke on *this* side of his town house, I was waiting for the Watch to drag me away in chains."

Edward, Earl Lippincott, cleared his throat to speak. With the wave of his hand to encompass the group, he announced, "Please be seated," though he remained standing. With a nod at one of the footmen he waited while the guests' glasses were filled with champagne.

O'Malley stared at his glass, then watched the way his wife's eyes widened as the sparkling liquid was poured into hers. He'd suffer through one swallow to make his wife happy. His stomach would not tolerate more than that.

"I'd like to propose a toast," the earl stated, raising his glass. "To Sean and Mignonette—Mr. and Mrs. O'Malley. May their lives be blessed with love, health, happiness…and half a dozen children."

O'Malley grinned at the earl. "Thank ye, yer lordship, but I'm thinking a dozen is more like it."

Mignonette's soft laughter reminded him of faery bells at dawn in his ma's garden back home. O'Malley found it wasn't so hard to swallow the sip of the vile stuff after all. Though he'd rather have three fingers of the Irish…or a tankard full of ale!

It was highly unusual for an employee of the Duke of Wyndmere to be sitting down to a meal in His Grace's dining room in the company of Earl Lippincott, Gavin King of the Bow Street Runners, Captain Coventry and his wife. Mignonette bravely conquered her fears, how could he not? With her by his side, he enjoyed the meal and the company.

When Coventry asked O'Malley to stay for a meeting, involving Coventry, King, and the earl, he protested, "It's me wedding night."

"This will only take a few moments of your time," Coventry advised. "We've news from Bayfield."

O'Malley's gut clenched. "Let me escort me wife—"

Coventry chuckled. "If I do, we won't see you until tomorrow afternoon." Turning to his wife, he asked, "Miranda, love, would you accompany Mignonette to the upstairs sitting room? I need to have a word with O'Malley."

Mrs. Coventry readily agreed, leaving O'Malley to wonder if his contracting wound fever had delayed the meeting. Either way, he could not in good conscience refuse to meet with his employer's man-of-affairs.

"Lass, I promise to keep the meeting short, but I must attend."

"*Mais oui*, Sean. I shall wait upstairs for you."

"Mrs. Coventry will keep you company…in the upstairs

sitting room."

Unsure of what to expect, given the fuss his wife put up demanding she stay to nurse him back to health, he was relieved when his wife graciously agreed. Lifting her hand to his lips, he tilted it toward him, inhaling the subtle scent of wild roses. He brushed a whisper-soft kiss to the back of it. Turning her hand over he pressed his lips to the middle of her palm. Locking gazes with her, he traced her lifeline with the tip of his tongue, savoring her intoxicating flavor.

"Wait for me, Lass," he murmured. "I'll make it worth yer while."

Heart in her eyes, she laid a hand to her breast and nodded.

Unable to resist, he drew her in for a swift kiss, set her aside, and followed the men from the room.

CHAPTER TWENTY-SIX

"BAYFIELD WAS HIRED by Lady Kittrick," Coventry told O'Malley.

O'Malley glanced at the earl before nodding. "As a man-of-affairs, working for ye?"

Coventry smiled. "No, not as yet. The men I hired need to meet with His Grace first. Arranging our schedules is taking a bit longer than anticipated as we will be meeting at the duke's estate in the Lake District."

O'Malley's curiosity was aroused. "How did Bayfield manage to meet with her?"

"We have discovered the woman has connections throughout the underbelly of London and on the docks."

"His disguise is quite convincing," King interjected. "I did a double-take when he came to meet with me before going to the docks the other day."

The earl had been silent up to this point. O'Malley glanced at him, raising his brow in silent question. The earl responded, "Tell O'Malley what happened this morning."

Coventry clenched his jaw, then relaxed it to speak. "Lady Kittrick hired him to uncover information, and apparently did not believe Bayfield when he delivered the information. She questioned him."

"She didn't pay him," O'Malley rumbled, "did she?"

"When he threatened to go to Grosvenor Square with his information, as we'd planned, the bloody—" Coventry closed his eye, drew in a deep breath before letting it go to continue, "The *lady*—and I use that term loosely, slashed him across the face with her riding crop."

"What did Bayfield do? How did react?" O'Malley wanted to know. "I've been slashed across the shoulders, and it ached. Across the face must have stung like a son-of-a-bitch."

"Bayfield, staunch seaman that he is," Coventry remarked, "showed no outward reaction."

"From what I've witnessed," the earl stated, with a glance at O'Malley, "once unleashed, she has a wicked temper."

"Aye," Coventry agreed. "Bayfield and I were counting on her temper. After she struck him—"

"She confessed," Earl Lippincott interrupted. "She's been planning the social ruin of me and my wife for over a year." Shaking his head, he told the men, "I never did more than dance with the woman and accept her invitation to tea the following day. A short time in her company was more than enough to last a lifetime." He slowly smiled. "My heart had already been stolen by my Aurelia."

O'Malley knew that to be a fact. "Garahan and I witnessed when one of her scullery maids was booted out the door."

"They brought her here to Mrs. O'Toole, who doctored her injuries. The maid, Mary Kate, accompanied my brother, his wife, and our sister to Wyndmere Hall. Shortly thereafter, she accompanied Lady Calliope to Chattsworth Manor as her lady's maid after Lady Calliope married the viscount."

"It is well known among those seeking employment that you and His Grace treat their servants fairly—and well, and pay them in a timely manner," King said.

Coventry brought the conversation back to what Bayfield had reported. "According to Bayfield, after she confessed, she raised the crop over her head a second time."

Revulsion filled O'Malley. "I've met men who were evil to

the core, but never a woman." He shook his head while he went over everything he'd been told. "What I'm wondering is why would me marrying the lass be of concern to her?"

"I have no bloody idea," the earl replied.

"Surely she cannot think yer lordship or His Grace would forbid me brothers, cousins, or me from marrying while in the duke's employ."

"I cannot pretend to know what the woman thinks," Coventry replied.

"She has a black heart," the earl stated. "That the woman would dare to slash him across the face—no matter if she knew his true identity, or not, is unconscionable!"

King agreed, and Coventry added, "Bayfield has suffered enough for King and Country."

"Aye, and he carries the scars to prove it," O'Malley rasped. "What will ye have me do?"

"Nothing," the earl responded.

"We wait," King told him.

"She'll likely add to the damning rumors she's already planted among her contemporaries," Coventry remarked. "We'll give her enough information—"

"To trip her up," O'Malley said with a nod. "What if she goes after her ladyship again?"

The earl's eyes gleamed with deadly intent. "I shall see to it that she lives to regret it."

"We've kept you long enough," King intoned. "Your bride is waiting," he added with a smile.

O'Malley's heart lifted at the thought. "What do you suggest I tell her about our meeting?"

"The usual," King stated.

O'Malley wished he could tell her at least part of it. "None of it?"

"If anyone should overhear your conversation with your wife..." Coventry began.

"'Twould jeopardize our mission," O'Malley finished. "I will not fail ye."

"We're counting on that fact," King told him.

"Take tomorrow to regain your strength," the earl said.

Coventry's eyes glittered with laughter when he added, "If you don't overexert yourself tonight."

O'Malley shook his head. "I'm not daft, and I won't be making any promises."

The men were chuckling when their meeting disbanded.

O'Malley followed Coventry to the main staircase. They ascended in silence. The weight of the truth that the brash woman had planned to ruin the earl and Lady Aurelia since they married had been a shock.

His ma's words echoed in his head as Coventry knocked and then opened the door to the sitting room. *"There are good people in this world, Sean…and bad. Ye'll likely recognize the good right off, but the bad have a way of hiding the evil in their hearts."*

"Miranda? Are you ready to leave?"

Coventry's wife rose. "Thank you for the tea. It was just what I needed to perk me up after that champagne."

When the lass rose beside her, O'Malley smiled, watching as his wife reached for Miranda's hands. "You are most welcome. Thank you for keeping me company. I hope to see you soon."

"I'd ask you to tea tomorrow," she said with a smile, "but know you will be otherwise engaged."

The blush on his wife's face gladdened O'Malley's heart. He may have to deal with the dregs of society—and he did not mean those of the working class, he meant those who were privileged and chose to use their positions to their own ends and the detriment of others. Coming home to a woman with such a pure heart would be the balm he needed to help him forget until he had to bid her goodbye the following day to deal with evil once again.

"We'll see ye out." O'Malley offered his arm to his wife.

Coventry followed suit and the couples descended to the entryway.

Jenkins opened the door with a flourish, motioning for their waiting carriage. The couples bid one another goodbye with Mrs. Coventry promising to call in a few days.

Closing the door, Jenkins turned to O'Malley and his bride. "May I offer my felicitations, and that of the staff, on your marriage?"

"Aye. Thank ye, Jenkins."

The older servant inclined his head. "If you require anything, no matter the hour, we shall be happy to be of service."

O'Malley held out his hand and Jenkins took it. From the look on the butler's face, it was not expected but pleased him, nonetheless. Arm around his wife, they bid him goodnight.

Ascending the stairs, O'Malley wondered what was preying on his wife's mind. Was it the prospect of sealing their union, the meeting he had been called to attend or something else entirely? He had a feeling he would have to get to the bottom of whatever it was before he could begin to soothe his bride's hesitation toward their marriage bed.

⇥⇥⟫✕⟪⇤⇤

MIGNONETTE WONDERED WHAT the men had discussed while she and Miranda shared a pot of tea. There was little doubt in her mind it had to do with whatever brought Sean to London from the earl's estate in Sussex. She could ask him outright, but would he confide in her?

The door closed quietly behind her husband. She looked into eyes swirling with emotion. Mignonette recognized frustration and worry—was it because of his healing injury, and the fact he would need her help until he regained the full strength and use of his arm? Was it something she had done, or simply his meeting? Only one way to find out. "Have I done something to displease you?"

"Nay, Lass." He slipped his arm around her and confessed,

"Every time I put me arm around ye, I'm reminded how delicate ye are. I hope ye know I would never willingly hurt ye."

She slid her hand to cup the elbow of his injured arm and lifted it until she was fully wrapped within his arms. Unsure if he would be happy for her assistance, she glanced up, surprised by the depth of emotion and searing warmth in his beautiful green eyes. *"Oui, mon coeur,"* she whispered.

"Mo chroi," he countered.

"What does that mean?"

"My heart."

Staring at her lips, he rasped, "I may not have the full use of both me arms at the moment, but I'm strong enough to brace meself on me elbows." His smile was rakish as he added, "The rest of me is ready, willing and able to seal our union."

She nodded, wondering what the flutter in her belly meant.

His moss green eyes locked with hers. "I've been thinking about making love to ye since Coventry told me about the Special License."

"I haven't."

He stared down at her as if trying to understand why she hadn't. She smiled and placed a hand to his heart. "If that means what happens in the marriage bed, Madame told me what to expect."

"Did she now?"

She hesitated. *"Oui,* and she said to trust you and to ask you to teach me how to please you."

Sean leaned down and captured her lips. *"Mo chroi."*

Her heart stuttered in her breast at the timbre of his voice, understanding the beautiful sentiment.

He cupped the back of her head and traced the rim of her mouth, tempting, tasting. *"Mo ghra."*

Sparks of desire tingled from the top of her head to the pit of her belly. Trembling, she moaned his name.

"Go deo," he rasped a heartbeat before he plundered.

He sipped from her lips with soft, sweet kisses that had her floating. The devastating, hungry kisses that followed whipped her up to heights she feared but craved. Mignonette could not keep up with the staggering emotions he demanded from her.

As if he sensed her worry, he soothed her lips with a tender kiss and relaxed his hold.

Bereft, she whispered. "You make me ache…hunger for what I do not understand."

He brushed a strand of midnight silk from her eyes. "Do you trust me, Lass?"

"*Oui.*"

He slipped one arm free from his black frockcoat, then blew out a frustrated breath. "Can ye help me?"

She blinked and, for a moment, wondered what happened to the passionate man who kissed her senseless. "What can I do for you?"

He frowned at his injured arm. "Tug on the sleeve of me coat, so I can take it off."

Mignonette gently tugged on his sleeve as he shrugged out of his coat. Should she ask how he was able to turn off the feelings still rioting inside of her? Would he laugh at her inexperience…or walk away and leave her body churning with needs she'd never felt before.

"Bleeding, buggering *eedjit!*"

She hadn't heard that particular curse before, but she recognized the angry, frustrated tone of his voice. "I am sorry for whatever I said or did. I'll send your cousin up to help you undress."

Hands shaking, she yanked open the door.

A large hand slammed it closed. "Don't leave."

Tears stung her eyes, but she refused to cry in front of him.

"Lass…"

She did not answer him.

"Mignonette," he drawled. "Why are ye leaving?"

Frustrated that he would ask, when he should know why— suddenly Mrs. O'Toole's words echoed in her head. *"Talk to him."*

She spun around, tilted her chin up and bit out, "It is not my fault that I have never kissed a man before! Is it normal for your kisses to leave my limbs weak, my insides quaking, and my heart trembling?"

Tears welled in her eyes, and she furiously tried to blink them away. When that did not stop them, she wiped at her eyes with the backs of her hands. "I am sorry you were injured, Sean, but do not take your anger and frustration out on me."

When he stared at her without speaking, she hung her head, staring at her feet. "This is a mistake. I should not have let my heart rule my head." She turned and reached for the door again.

"Open that door, and I'll toss ye over me shoulder."

"You would not treat a lady that way," she shot back at him.

Her gasp of shock echoed through the room as she was weightless for a heartbeat before her breath whooshed out as she was hauled over his shoulder. A hint of fear sprinted through her as she landed on her back on the bed.

His rumbling laughter had her springing to her feet. They were nearly eye-to-eye, so she raised her fists. "You dare to laugh at me?"

"God in Heaven but I love yer spirit, Lass! I'm not laughing at ye. 'Tis relief that has me laughing, realizing how blessed I am that I pulled ye from the wreckage of that wardrobe."

His eyes were a clear, soft green once more.

She dropped back down onto the bed. "Blessed?"

"Aye. Did ye not hear me words before?"

"I heard you murmuring words I did not understand."

He cupped her cheek in his hand, brushing his thumb across her kiss-swollen lips. "Ah, ye understand *mo chroí*?"

"*Oui*, my heart."

His strong hands were twice the size of hers, yet so gentle. She sighed. Mignonette did not remember climbing into his lap, though she slipped her arm around his neck so she would not tumble off it.

"*Mo ghra*," he rasped, pressing his mouth to hers. "My love."

"*Mon amor?*"

"Aye, Lass, *mo ghra.*"

His words soothed her worry. Needing to show him she trusted him, she brushed her lips across the warmth of his, trembling at her body's reaction. "*Mon coeur,* you taught me how to love you with your lips. Would you teach me to love you with my body?"

He groaned and pulled her against him and, once again, she helped support his injured arm to wrap it around her. "I promise to go slowly. Ye must promise to tell me to stop if ye're unsure. I'll try to explain what I'm feeling so ye know ye aren't alone as yer body erupts with pleasure that will set fire to yer blood and have yer heart singing."

"*Oui, je promets, mon amor.*"

For a big man, her husband moved quickly. One moment she was sitting on his lap, the next they were standing beside the bed, and he was unfastening her gown, mumbling to himself as he fought to complete the task. Lifting it over her head, he told her, "I'll need yer help undressing."

His boyish grin caught her by surprise. She wouldn't have thought such an imposing man would still have that quality. Though she stood before him in her whisper-thin chemise, the look on his face smoothed out her nerves.

He tried to unbutton his waistcoat and kept fumbling. She gently brushed his hand aside. "Let me."

She did not need to look at the buttons to unfasten them, she did so by touch. Standing on her toes, she slipped his waistcoat off his broad shoulders. Before he could ask, she was helping him with his cambric shirt, tossing it aside to reach for the placket on his trousers.

His hand stilled hers. "Wait."

Confusion filled her, and she dropped her hand.

"If ye take me pants off now, I may not be able to uphold me promise to go slowly."

She was about to ask why when he yanked her against him.

She felt the heat pouring off him as he pulsed against her belly. "I hope Madame is right."

"Madame?"

"Aye. She explained how we would fit together, but I was not certain I believed her."

"Come with me, Lass." He took her hand and drew her to the bed. Lowering her to the mattress, he moved next to her. "Yer body is meant to fit mine. Let me show ye."

With whispered words and honeyed kisses, he slowly removed her chemise, delighting in her soft moans and strangled cries as he sampled, savored, seduced. "That's it, Lass," he encouraged as he drove her higher with lips and teeth and tongue.

"I can't," she rasped, afraid to let go…afraid of the unknown.

"Ye can," he promised. "I'll not let ye go alone."

With her whole heart, she trusted and let go. She clung to her husband as she shot over the peak into oblivion.

"Hang on, Lass," he urged, nudging her thighs apart, poised at the very heart of her.

Heart still hammering, she opened her eyes. *"Mon coeur,"* she rasped. *"Mon amor."* Surrendering to the desire and passions he held in check while he taught her to fly.

"Mo chroi," he murmured, fighting against the need clawing at him to drive into her, seeking release.

Sweat broke out on his brow as he slowly eased into her, the pure pleasure of her warmth surrounding him. *"Mo ghra,"* he rasped, "trust me." He felt the moment she relaxed beneath him, sweetly offering herself to him. Her body stretched, accepting the length and breadth of him. He plunged and withdrew as she lifted her hips, meeting him thrust for thrust. She tightened around him a heartbeat before she cried, *"Mon Dieu!"* as she shattered apart.

With one last thrust, he emptied himself inside of her, holding her to his heart as he whispered, *"Go deo."* Still joined together, he rolled onto his back, settling her on top of him, exhausted from bracing his weight on his injured arm.

When she shifted as if to move, he placed his hand on the sweet curve of her backside, anchoring her to him. *"Mo chroi, mo ghra, go deo,"*

"My heart, my love," she echoed. "Go deo?"

"Forever," he rumbled. He pulled the blanket over them and sighed. For the first time in his life, he loved and was loved in return. The exhaustion he'd been holding at bay tried to drag him under, but he held out until he felt her body relax. When sleep claimed her, he finally gave in and followed her under.

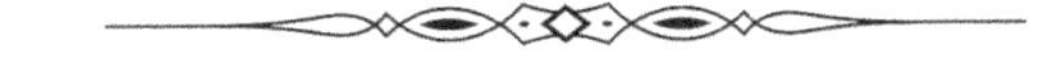

CHAPTER TWENTY-SEVEN

O'MALLEY STARED DOWN at the beauty in his arms. She'd put her trust in him completely last night. With every stroke…every kiss, their bodies had laid claim to one another. They were well and truly one—in the eyes of the law, the church…and God.

She shifted until the curve of her backside was nestled against that part of him that always woke up first. His low moan of pleasure roused her. If he hadn't felt her stiffen against him, her squeak of shock would have told him she was awake.

He leaned close and whispered in her ear, "Morning, Lass."

"Morning, Monsieur—"

His rumbling laugh had her shifting away from him. "After making love to ye more than once last night, do I have to remind ye 'tis Sean?"

When she did not reply, he reached out to pull her back where she belonged…in his arms.

"I was not laughing at ye, *mo chroi*."

"No?"

"I was teasing ye, there is a world of difference."

"So you say."

"I'm pleased ye've got yer grit back," he told her. "I would not want ye to fear me, Lass."

"I do not fear you," she grumbled.

He noticed she was no longer trying to put any space between them. Time to let her know he would be returning to his duties tomorrow. They had not had the opportunity to discuss what either of them expected or wanted in life, or how their lives would be changing now that they were wed. He was concerned that he had so little time to talk to her about it now, but would muddle through it, hoping she'd be reasonable.

"I need to report back to me duties tomorrow. If ye need me, ye can ask Emmett to send a message to me. I'll be in London, so ye won't have any trouble tracking me down."

His wife was out of their bed, and vibrating with indignation, like a shot! "But you need to rest! To heal!"

"I've done nothing but rest since that bloody bastard sliced me arm." Staring into her warm brown eyes, he added, "I do not have to work today. We can spend the day together doing whatever ye wish. Where would ye like to go, Lass?"

She stared at him for long moments without speaking. Finally, she drew in a deep breath and slowly let out. "Anywhere."

"Anywhere?" he repeated.

"*Oui*…as long as it is not here."

"We can go for a ride in the park or take a carriage ride along Bond Street and visit the shops. What do ye say?"

"Is it common for newly married couples to be shopping the day after they wed?"

"Who in the bl—" O'Malley shook his head. "I beg yer pardon. It'll take some getting used to."

"What will?" she asked.

"Watching me words around ye. I've never had to do it on me own time before."

"Are you implying that spending time with me will be as if you were at work?"

"Ye might say that."

"I did say that," she told him. "What I'm asking is, would you say that?"

"Aye." O'Malley noticed his wife was avoiding looking at

him. He got out of bed and stretched, amazed that despite his injury, and a few muscle aches, he hadn't felt this good in weeks. Must be making love with his wife just before dawn that had him so relaxed. She was frowning at him. *Was it something he said?* He'd best be asking the lass. Thinking he knew what was weighing on her mind would not be wise. He'd start with a simple question. "Did ye sleep well?"

Eyes the color of melted chocolate narrowed as she stared at him.

He had to fight the urge not to shift from foot to foot while he waited for her answer. No woman had ever had him second-guessing himself. *What was wrong with him?*

"Oui. Merci."

And then it occurred to him, she had to be sore from their lovemaking. Though he'd tried to go slowly, he knew there was a point when he'd stopped thinking at all. Walking toward her, he extended his hand—palm up. The wait had his stomach roiling, but he was patient. Finally, she placed her hand in his.

So soft. How could someone who worked as hard as she did with her hands not have rough skin? About to ask how it was possible, he remembered the question he needed to ask. "Did I hurt ye last night?"

Her cheeks flushed that delightful shade of rose again.

"Lass," he prompted. "I need to know if ye need tending this morning."

She spun around, placing her back to him, but not before he noticed how her face flamed with embarrassment.

Placing his hands on her shoulders, he drew her back against him. "Ye need to tell me how ye feel and when something is wrong or bothering ye, Lass. How else can I fix it?"

"You cannot fix me," she grumbled, struggling to get free.

"Never a step ye'll take until ye've told me what's wrong."

She lifted her shoulder, trying to hide from him.

"I can wait all day," he told her. "But ye'd best know I'm feeling a bit weak from hunger."

Mignonette spun around, concern etched across her face. Her embarrassment forgotten, she slipped her arm about his waist and led him over to the bed, easing him onto it. She placed the back of her hand to his forehead.

"I don't have a fever."

Instead of the retort he expected, she leaned close and pressed her lips where her hand had been. "*Oui*. You are right—no fever. *Maman* always kissed my forehead to see if I was feverish."

"Ye're me own guardian angel." He waited for her to speak, then resigned himself to wheedling the truth of her discomfort later. "Me stomach aches from lack of food."

Her smile bloomed slowly, like a rosebud unfurling in the warm spring sun. "I shall ring for breakfast."

"No need." He reached for her hand and pulled her onto his lap. "Mrs. Wigglesworth said she'd be bringing our breakfast along with water for a hot bath."

"If we do not ring for her, how will she know we are awake?"

O'Malley chuckled. "Mrs. Wigglesworth has her ways. If ye don't want to be seen in yer nightrail, ye might want to put on yer dressing gown."

Mignonette stared at their joined hands and confessed, "I do not have one."

He rubbed his hand in circles on her back to soothe her. "We'll have to see that ye have one—as well as a few new gowns."

"I do not need any gowns," she protested.

"We'll be making the trip to the earl's home, Lippincott Manor, soon. While we are there, we'll visit one of his distant cousins, Viscount Chattsworth and his wife, at Chattsworth Manor. I'd like to see ye in a new gown when we visit his lordship and introduce ye to his countess, Lady Aurelia. She has something in common with you," he told her. "She lost her parents, too. But she was fortunate that her uncle took her in. Lord Coddington is a good man, one ye'll want to have at yer side—or guarding yer back in a fight."

Leaning against him, she asked, "Do you measure all of your life by the times you've had to fight someone?"

Her question caught O'Malley off guard. *Did he?* If he admitted it, would that upset her? The only way to know was to ask. "Would it bother ye if I did?"

She shook her head. "No. Just curious. My life used to be separated into two parts—while my parents were still alive...and after their deaths."

"I'm more than happy to share me family—and every one of me blasted cousins with ye. They're going to love ye, Lass...but not nearly as much as I love ye."

She threw her arms around his neck and pressed kisses to his cheeks, his nose, and his chin, all the while thanking him.

"Ye'll be meeting one of my brothers, one of Emmett's brothers, two of me Garahan cousins, and one of the Flahertys when we go to Sussex."

"They all work for the earl?"

He chuckled. "Nay. Me brother, Michael, is taking me place in Sussex. He's normally stationed here. Emmett's brother, Dermott, and Aiden Garahan and I work for the earl. James Garahan and Seamus Flaherty work for Viscount Chattsworth."

Placing the tip of his finger to her chin, he angled it up and stole a swift kiss that pinkened his wife's cheeks. "Lady Aurelia and Lady Calliope are good friends. They have big hearts, though I have heard the earl and the viscount mention their wives are a bit on the stubborn side. The earl's staff—"

The knock on the door interrupted their conversation. "Come in," O'Malley rumbled.

Mrs. Wigglesworth was smiling as she bustled into their room. "Good morning! I trust you slept well?" Not expecting—or waiting for an answer, she motioned for the footmen bearing pitchers of hot water into the room. "Start filling the tub, if you please."

The men did as she bid them while two maids entered, one carrying their breakfast and the other, the tea service.

The housekeeper beamed as she had the maids set out breakfast for two on the small table by the window. "Now then, you two eat every bite while I see that you have everything you need for your bath."

Smiling indulgently at the couple, she waited for them to be seated before pouring their tea and serving them. "Now then, I shall return shortly—after you've eaten of course, to see if you have made plans for today and whether or not you need anything."

"You have been most kind, Mrs. Wigglesworth," Mignonette remarked.

"It is not only my pleasure, Mrs. O'Malley," she replied with a smile, "but part of my duties."

O'Malley grinned. "Ye never make it seem as if ye're doing yer duty. Ye make everyone who comes here feel as if they are special guests of His Grace."

"What a lovely thing to say, Sean. Thank you."

With her hands at her waist, she waited for the last pitcher of hot water to be poured into the tub. "I have a bit of dried rose blossoms to add to the water—I hope you don't mind, Sean."

"'Tisn't me ye should be asking, 'tis me wife."

Mrs. Wigglesworth looked as if she wanted to say something but changed her mind. She waited a beat before asking, "Would you like to freshen up in one of the other guest rooms while your wife bathes?"

O'Malley's gut clenched at the thought of the petite beauty immersing herself in a tub of fragrant water and had to bite the inside of his cheek to keep from groaning. "Thank ye, but no. I'll be taking on the duties of a lady's maid. If we need ye, we'll let ye know."

With a nod to the last of the footmen, he preceded her. "There is nothing like it," the housekeeper said with a sigh.

"What is?" O'Malley inquired.

"Young love. I'll leave you to finish the rest of your meal and enjoy a good long soak."

When she closed the door behind her, O'Malley walked over to the door and locked it. Blowing out a breath, he remarked, "Faith, I thought she'd never leave." With a wicked grin, he asked, "Now then, I'm thinking ye're a bit overdressed for yer first bath as me wife."

Mignonette was laughing as he plucked her off her chair and carried her into the dressing room. The scent of wild roses wafted toward them from the steam rising off the surface, luring them closer. "Now then, Lass, if ye don't want me to inspect every inch of ye as I remove yer nightrail, ye'll be telling me what's wrong."

Her hesitant smile and silence pleased him. "Well then, let me help ye undress. I've a lot of curves to inspect."

Dark brown eyes watched him as he slipped her sleeping gown off one shoulder and then the other. She did not hide from him as the gown pooled at her feet. She was perfect, from the top of her head to the tips of her toes...*and she was his.*

Resolving to ignore the desire tearing his insides to shreds, he dug deep, finding the will to do as he said. He brushed his hands along the curve of her spine. Where his hands touched, his lips caressed.

He jolted, noticing the faint marks on her wrists and hips. He traced them with the tip of his fingers. "Why did ye not tell me I'd hurt ye?"

"You didn't."

He lifted her hand. "But these marks—"

Staring at her wrists, she shrugged. "I was too lost in the splendor of your touch."

Her words, and her body pulled at him until he felt his control fraying. "I know I promised to inspect all of ye, but I don't know if I can without making love to ye again. Ye'll be taking to yer bed for the rest of the day if I do."

Locking gazes with him, she lifted to her toes and fitted her curves against him.

His groan of anguish ripped at the tatters of his control. "Don't. I will not hurt ye again."

"Madame explained there would be pain the first time." She tugged his head down and pressed her lips to his. "She also said it would take practice to learn the touches and textures of one another—and there would be joy in the learning."

"Praise God for Madame!" O'Malley banded his arm around her and supped from her lips until they were both weak. "Into the tub with ye!" Lifting her into his arms, he slowly lowered her into the tub.

"Now then, Lass. Have ye ever shared a bath before?"

Desire swirling in the depths of her warm brown eyes, she bit her lip and shook her head.

His gaze riveted to hers, he undressed, stepped into the tub, and reached for her. "Now then, Lass, if ye're careful not to get me bandage wet, I've neglected the softest parts of ye." His grin was full of promise. "Let me make it up to ye."

THEIR BREAKFAST WAS cold by the time they'd managed to climb out of the tub, dry off, get dressed and change the bandages on his wound.

True to her word, Mrs. Wigglesworth returned to find out their plans for the day. "The earl left strict instructions that we were not to intrude unless you rang for us. He also suggested a cold collation be laid out in the conservatory at half past one. You can eat whenever you are hungry. He suggested we serve your evening meal in the garden at eight o'clock unless you wish to eat later. Does that meet with your approval?"

"His lordship has thought of everything," Mignonette marveled. "We are so grateful to his lordship and yourselves. *Merci.*"

"I've never eaten in a garden before, Lass. What do ye say, would ye like to?"

"*Oui!* That sounds so romantic. Er…what about the midday meal in the conservatory?"

O'Malley slowly smiled. "I'm thinking we might be otherwise engaged."

His wife's lovely lips rounded in a small "o", delighting him.

Mrs. Wigglesworth suggested, "I can have one of the footmen leave your meal on a table outside your door. Would that suit you?"

"Aye, it would. Thank ye, Mrs. Wigglesworth. Please let Mrs. O'Toole know breakfast was delicious."

Mrs. Wigglesworth motioned for the serving maid to collect the remnants of their breakfast and retreated, pausing in the doorway. "Enjoy your day." With an indulgent smile, she closed the door behind her.

"I've never in me life felt like royalty before," he confessed. "We'd best enjoy it, but not get used to it."

"It has been lovely, but I must tell you it makes me uncomfortable. I'll feel better when we are not being treated as the duke's guests."

"Aye, I prefer being a member of the working class." O'Malley walked to the door, locked it, and turned back to his wife. Holding his hand out to her, he rasped, "I've a need to hold ye, Lass."

Hands entwined, he led her to the bed. "I'm thinking a short rest will do us both wonders."

She frowned at him. "I am not sleepy."

His low, rumbling laugh filled the room. "Ye will be, Lass."

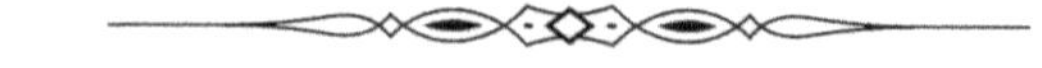

CHAPTER TWENTY-EIGHT

MIGNONETTE WOKE TO the sound of her husband grumbling. "Blasted meeting, bloody *buggering*, privileged class."

"You are up early, *mon coeur*."

"I did not mean to wake ye, Lass."

"You cannot get dressed until I have changed your bandage." She slipped out of bed and walked over to where he stood by the washstand. "Do sit down, *mon amor*. You should not move your arm until I have finished."

She washed her hands and brushed a lock of sunlit hair out of his eyes. Hoping to soothe his frustration while the strength in his arm returned, and what she recognized as ruffled pride, she kept her voice low, peppering her words with the language of her youth.

"I don't understand a word ye're saying," O'Malley groused.

"*Pardon*," she murmured. "Whenever I was frustrated and cross as a child, *Maman* would soothe me with words I was too young to understand but I recognized the love behind them."

"Love, *mo ghra*?"

"*Oui—mon amor*." Mignonette gently cleansed and bandaged his arm. "I must ask Emmett for the herbs he used in his poultice. From what I have gathered you and your family are accustomed to the injuries you receive as part of your job." Gently drying his arm, she noted, "Your wound is healing without infection."

"Aye. Emmett will be happy to share it with ye. More than two generations of O'Malleys have used its healing powers. He dropped off a jar of ointment for ye to use before ye wrap it up."

She opened the small jar, sniffed it, and dipped the tips of her fingers in it, applying it to his injury. The silence between them was easy—not forced, as if they had known one another all of their lives and were at ease in one another's company.

Bandage in place to her satisfaction, Mignonette lifted his hand to her lips and kissed the back of it. *"Fini."*

He tilted his head, watching her closely.

She laughed and told him, "Finished. Now, let me help you dress. I would not want your sleeve to rub against the bandage. It may irritate your wound—and undo all of the healing. Lieutenant Sampson warned—"

"Ye don't need to remind me. I'll not be forgetting his warning."

"Would you do me a favor?"

He stared into her eyes, and she remembered every kiss, every touch, treasuring them and the man who so patiently shared his body with her as he taught her to fly.

His words belied the look she thought she understood. "I'm not going to like doing this favor, Lass. Am I?"

Without a doubt, but would he resist? She shrugged, then explained what she wanted him to do. "I can fashion a sling for you to wear beneath your frockcoat so that the sleeve will not constantly rub against your injury. *S'il vous plait,* wear it for me."

When he did not immediately respond, she reminded him, "Captain Coventry wears a sling."

"Aye, *over* his coat."

"His wound has long since healed. Yours is raw." He hesitated, and she added, "I will ask Mrs. Wigglesworth to send for Lieutenant Sampson, if you do not heed me."

O'Malley glared at her, but she would not back down. *"S'il vous plait? Je t'aime,* Sean."

The moment his shoulders slumped, she knew he would

agree. *"Merci!"* Before he could change his mind, she helped him into his waistcoat and pulled out the sling she'd fashioned the night before. "You see, it is black to match your imposing uniform."

He bent down so she could fasten it around his neck. Her husband would not use his arm and injure it further if he kept it in the sling. Satisfied, she placed her hand over his heart.

Eyes the softest shade of green stared down at her. The mix of emotion in his gaze—frustration, worry…desire, drew her in. At the last moment, she remembered what she wanted to tell him. "Do not take that sling off the moment you are out of my sight!"

O'Malley snorted in laughter and yanked her against him, kissing her deeply. Ending the kiss, he asked, "Bossy, aren't ye?"

"When it is important. Promise me?"

He sighed and rested his chin on the top of her head. "Aye, *mo chroi.* Ye have me word."

"Let me help you with your frockcoat." She held it out for him, listening to his mumbling, loving him all the more for acquiescing to her request when she knew he did not want to.

She reached for the buttons. He stayed her hand before she could take care of the task for him. "I never button me coat."

"Then do not wear it."

He started to shrug out of it when she inquired, "What will His Grace have to say when he learns one of his guard is not properly attired?"

He scrubbed a hand over his face. "Fine! Button the blasted buttons. I'll be late if I don't leave now."

She did as he asked. When he turned to leave, she grabbed the back of his coat.

"What?"

The sharp tone of his voice did not bother her. He had done as she asked. "Be careful, *mon coeur.*"

The hard expression on his face softened as he lifted his hand to cup her cheek. "I will, *mo ghra.* Thank ye for yer help, Lass."

He was gone before she remembered to ask what time he would return. Would he be off to do the captain's bidding once the meeting was over, or would he return to Grosvenor Square? Should she stay and await his return, or use the time to visit with Madame and Yvette?

"I should have asked. Mayhap Emmett will know." Washing and dressing quickly, she made the bed and straightened their room to go in search of her husband's cousin.

"Good morning, Mrs. O'Malley," the cook called out as Mignonette entered her domain. "Are you ready to eat?"

"Good morning. Not yet. I need to speak with Emmett. Have you seen him?"

Mrs. O'Toole stopped kneading the bread dough. "Is something wrong?"

"Everything is fine. Sean left a few moments ago to meet with the captain."

"And you are wondering when he will return?"

"How did you know?"

"Your worry lines are showing. Jenkins will know where Emmett is at this hour."

"Thank you!"

"What about breakfast?"

"I am not hungry."

Mignonette rushed out of the room with Mrs. O'Toole's reminder to eat ringing in her ears. The need to question Emmett had her hurrying along the hallway. Jenkins was speaking with one of the footmen when she opened the door to the servants' side of the town house.

"Good morning, Mrs. O'Malley. May I be of assistance?"

"*Oui*, Monsieur Jenkins. Do you know where Emmett is?"

"He should be standing guard on the north side of the house. Shall I fetch him for you?"

"No, thank you. Is there a side door I can use?" She did not want to explain why she hesitated to use the front door. Fortunately, Jenkins did not ask. He merely told her where the door was.

Emmett O'Malley glanced over his shoulder as she opened the door. Was he expecting one of the footmen?

"Is something wrong, Lass?"

"Mayhap," she replied. "Sean left early." She hesitated, unsure of how much to confide in her husband's cousin.

"He needed a bit of help mounting his horse."

She sighed. "My husband was most unhappy with me, but I had to insist he wear the sling. You understand how easily his wound could become infected, don't you?"

"Aye. I'm grateful ye insisted he wear one. Me hardheaded cousin refused earlier when I told him to. Coventry's missive and early morning meeting had him rushing off."

"Do you know how long Sean's meeting with the captain will be?"

He smiled down at her. "Anywhere from half an hour to three hours. Depending on the outcome of the meeting, he will be doing the captain's bidding. Is there something I can help ye with?"

She sighed. "I was hoping to visit with Madame and Yvette today. The shop should be open."

His hesitation surprised her. "Am I not allowed to leave?"

"Unescorted, ye may not. However, if I were to accompany ye, Sean would not mind."

"Oh, but I do not want to take you from your duties."

"That's fine then. Mrs. O'Toole and Mrs. Wigglesworth would enjoy yer company today."

"I did not agree to stay here all day."

The man grinned at her. "Ah, but ye meant to, didn't ye, Lass?"

"I would not—"

"Want me cousin to worry while he's seeing to the protection of the duke and the earl," he finished for her. "Would ye?"

Defeated by the smooth-tongued Irishman, she sighed. "I would not."

"Would ye like me to send a message to Sean for ye?"

"Will it interrupt whatever he is doing?"

"Family is the glue, Lass. He would not mind and, in fact, would be frustrated to arrive home knowing ye worried about him all day."

"Then let us not worry him at all. Mayhap I can catch up on my mending."

"Thank ye for understanding, Lass."

Mignonette wished she could have asserted herself, demanding to know when her husband would return. But what would that accomplish other than having him wonder if he married a shrew? Best to wait and ask him what his days were like, and plan accordingly, when she saw him this evening.

Resolved to be patient, she went in search of Mrs. O'Toole and the promised meal.

⇻⟫⟫⟩⟨⟨⟨⇺

O'MALLEY PACED IN front of Coventry's desk. His gut iced over at the anger the man tried to conceal. "Does his lordship know?"

"I sent word to him early this morning and would not be surprised to see him in a few hours."

"What of Lady Aurelia?"

"She will be safe if she remains in Sussex."

O'Malley nodded. "His lordship may insist she stay at Chattsworth Manor. Ye know he'll balk at having one of the men accompany him to London."

Coventry agreed. "The duke will have our collective hides if he finds out the earl is traveling without protection, given the threats and rumors."

"With Lady Aurelia at Chattsworth Manor, there will be four guards—five if the earl decides to ignore his brother's advice."

As if Coventry knew the sliver of fear snaking into his heart, the captain added, "Emmett and King's men will guard your wife while you are away from her."

O'Malley's heart hammered in his chest. "I thought it best not to worry her with the latest vicious rumors…even though she is tangled in this web of deceit."

"It might be wise to tell her, so you can assure her we have the matter under control."

"How do I tell me wife her name is being dragged through the mud—in a tryst with me and the earl's wife?"

"With as few words as possible…and a glass of brandy at the ready," Coventry advised.

"Mayhap I'll have a bit of the Irish on hand," he quipped though his guts were turning inside out. "She's an innocent, Coventry. Her mind may not be able to wrap around the meaning of the insult."

"You do not have to go into detail. Simply tell her the latest *on dit* involves the two of you and Lady Aurelia."

"And if she asks?"

"Tell her that is all you heard."

"Aye, but the meaning is clear."

"Don't spoil her *naivete* if you can help it," Coventry advised.

"What of the earl? Ye know he'll be bent on avenging Lady Aurelia's honor."

"As you will no doubt want to avenge your wife's."

O'Malley sighed. Coventry was right. "Me aim isn't as true with me left arm."

"That will not stop you. Will it?"

Righteous anger swept up from his feet. "Nay. Nothing will stop me from killing the bloody bastard who'd sully me wife's reputation to satisfy whatever twisted reason he has." Meeting the captain's steady gaze, he demanded, "Tell me his name and I'll be on me way."

"I have a better idea," Coventry replied.

O'Malley didn't want to listen but had no choice. Trying to deflect Coventry's interest in his mindset, he asked, "Does it involve someone getting shot?"

Coventry shook his head. "Given all the duke and the earl have been through, it would be best to avoid a dawn meeting at Chalk Farm."

"What if it was yer wife?" O'Malley countered. "What would ye do?"

The captain drew in a calming breath, and then another. "I'd keel-haul him, then I'd hang him from the yardarm…but that's just me."

"Do ye have access to a ship?"

Coventry's green eye glittered with anger. "At a moment's notice."

O'Malley did not have to feign interest when he asked, "Can I watch? I've never witnessed a man being keel-hauled."

The snort of laughter was what O'Malley hoped to hear. He'd distracted the captain. His next words would get an honest reaction from the man, "Ye'd do the same bloody thing I'm wanting to do. I say we uncover the name of the person responsible for this latest atrocity, and we back him into a corner until he confesses."

"The idea has merit."

"Do ye have proof of the lie?"

"Aye," Coventry responded. "A friend of mine, Viscount Moreland, overheard Lippincott's name and your own while at White's last night."

"Idle talk, though I can't think why me name would merit attention."

"Other than your connection with the Duke of Wyndmere?"

O'Malley shrugged. "Did yer viscount friend have anything else to say?"

The captain nodded. "Moreland stayed long enough to confirm what he'd heard before passing along the information to me. He read the wager in White's betting book."

"Wager?" O'Malley clenched his jaw and curled his hands into fists, ready to pummel the blackguard responsible. "Why didn't ye mention that first?"

The captain stared at him, waiting for O'Malley to calm down. "I anticipated your reaction—you did not disappoint me."

"Does the viscount know who placed the bet?"

"Aye, the man was bold enough to leave his title after his initials."

"Why the devil would he? Is he asking to be challenged?"

Coventry nodded. "You have the right of it. Obviously, he is emboldened by his claim and must believe it to be true—either that or he stands to earn a sizable bag of coin for his troubles."

O'Malley paused to consider the possibilities. "Do ye think this wager will lead back to Lady Kittrick?"

"I do."

"How can we prove it if she denies it?"

"Confront the man and offer him more money than Lady Kittrick has. By the by, I have asked Viscount Moreland to meet us at White's this afternoon."

Keeping an outward calm while his insides raged with anger and frustration was a skill he'd adopted working for Lord Chellenham. It came in handy now. O'Malley inclined his head. "Will that be all? I'd like to speak with me wife."

"King is expecting us. He'll need the particulars and will be interested in your thoughts as well. Why don't you pen a quick note to your wife? I'll have it delivered for you."

"She won't like what I'll be asking her to do."

"Oh, and what's that?"

"To bloody well stay put until she sees the whites of me eyes."

"I see your point. Best to wait until after meeting with the viscount."

CHAPTER TWENTY-NINE

O'MALLEY WAS RELIEVED to see King's men standing guard on either side of the duke's town house when he rode up. Emmett appeared out of the shadows. "Ye're late."

He handed the reins to his cousin and frowned when Emmett held out a hand to help him dismount. "I can bloody well get off me horse without yer help."

He swung his leg over and dismounted with ease. "Glad to see ye're finding yer balance."

"*Bollocks!*"

"Would ye like to hear what yer lovely wife was up to all day—in between asking me if I'd heard from ye—every few hours?"

The censure in his cousin's voice was not lost on him, but he didn't have time to get into an argument. The worry creeping into the back of his mind throughout the long day had him by the throat. He needed to see Mignonette. Now! "Where is me wife?"

"In yer room, last I checked."

"Why isn't she in the sitting room? Did something happen?"

"Are ye worried then, Sean?"

Anger raged within him as the worry that held him by the throat threatened to spill over. The sound of carriage wheels behind him, brought him back to the present and the fact he was standing outside the duke's town house about to punch his cousin.

Emmett's eyes gave away the fact that he'd welcome the chance to go a few rounds with him—but not here...not now. O'Malley swallowed the overwhelming need to pound the living daylights out of his cousin to say, "Thank ye for watching out for the lass. Is there anything I need to know?"

"Nothing happened," his cousin remarked. "She had two visitors today."

"Did she?"

"Madame Beaudoine and Yvette Augustin."

"I hope she met with them in the sitting room."

"That's just it," his cousin said with a frown. "She asked them to meet with her in yer room."

"Why?"

"That was the question I put to her."

O'Malley raked a hand through his hair, making it stand on end. "What did she say?"

"She's afraid one of the servants will think she's getting above herself, playing at being a lady."

O'Malley's frustration simmered. "She *is* a lady."

"Ye bloody well know what she means." Emmett shook his head and turned to lead O'Malley's horse to the stable. "Go talk to yer wife first. Once ye've assured her all is well, and that ye didn't forget ye were married...I want to know how yer meeting went."

"There's a wager..."

Emmett paused to look over his shoulder. "Is there now?" He waited a beat before asking, "Involving?"

"Me, me wife, and Lady Aurelia."

"Bloody hell!"

Satisfaction filled him. His cousin understood and would have his back as they fought to uncover the perpetrator of these lies, rumors, and innuendos...and the wager the elite of the *ton* would by now have laid coin on.

"I have to tell her but I'm not sure how."

"The wager?"

"Aye."

"Just tell her what ye told me," his cousin advised. "It involves the two of ye and Lady Aurelia."

"Coventry gave me the same advice."

"Ye'd best listen to us then," his cousin grumbled as he led the horse into the alley leading to the back of the house.

"Emmett?"

"What now!"

"Thank ye."

"Ye're bloody welcome. Now go talk to yer wife!"

Ignoring the exhaustion plaguing his steps, O'Malley headed to the side door. "Franklin," he greeted one of King's men. "Anything to report?"

"All's quiet," the Bow Street Runner informed him. "Mrs. O'Malley retired to your room an hour ago."

"Thank ye."

The Runner gave a brief nod and resumed his post.

O'Malley passed by the kitchen but didn't stop to speak to anyone. He sprinted up the servants' staircase and strode to the room he shared with his wife. He lifted his hand to knock when the door abruptly opened, and he was nearly bowled over by his petite wife.

"Have a care, Lass."

"Sean!" she rasped, flinging herself into his arms, surprised when he asked her to help him settle his injured arm around her waist.

"Where were you all day? I was so worried. How is your arm? Are you hungry?"

He chuckled as the warmth of his wife's concern washed over him. "Do ye want me to answer the first question or the last?"

She eased back to meet his gaze. "Mrs. O'Toole promised to feed you the moment you got home."

He did not want to go back downstairs. What he wanted was currently wrapped around him, firing questions at him. "I'm tired to the bone, Lass. Can we sit?"

"*Oui*. I am sorry for not thinking how tired you must be." She slipped out of his arms, opened the door, and pulled him inside.

He was about to sit when she bid him to wait. "Let me help you out of your frockcoat."

Hands to his buttons, she frowned. "Did you take this coat off?"

"Aye."

Boldly meeting his gaze, she asked, "Did you take the sling off?"

He shook his head. "Every few hours, the temptation nearly drove me mad, but I remembered me promise to me lovely wife and did not."

"Sit while I remove it."

"Bless ye, Lass. I'm thinking the knot rubbed me neck raw."

Before she could step around behind him, he had her by the hand and pulled her to stand between his legs. "'Tisn't the back of me neck that's sore," he rasped, placing his hands on the curve of her hips. "'Tis the side." He fought with the need to pull her into his lap and plunder her sweet lips before sweeping her into his arms and onto their bed.

The knock on the door had him thundering, "Go away!"

The low rumbling chuckle from the other side of the door had him cursing.

"Can't. I promised Mrs. O'Toole I'd deliver yer blasted supper. Open the door, ye ungrateful heathen!"

Mignonette pressed her lips to his forehead, untied the knot and took a step back. "Come in, Emmett."

The door opened and Emmett shook his head. "Am I interrupting anything?"

O'Malley glared at his cousin.

Before he could comment, his wife answered, "I was just going to take a look at Sean's neck. The knot from the sling I fashioned for him must have slipped beneath his cravat and rubbed his neck raw. I need to take care of it. Would another infection cause his arm to become inflamed again?"

"As long as ye take care of it as ye did for his arm, ye needn't worry," Emmett assured her.

O'Malley sighed. "Me neck will be fine," he assured her. Turning to his cousin, he said, "Well, ye're in. What else do ye want?"

His cousin shook his head. "Do ye see how he treats me? Is it any wonder I prefer working with his brother, Michael?"

"Thank you for bringing his supper, Emmett."

He shrugged. "Me cousin can be a bear if he's hungry, worse if ye best him in a bare knuckle bout."

"Bare knuckle?"

"Aye," O'Malley rumbled. "'Tis the fact ye're married to Wexford's reigning champion."

"Ye *were* the champion when last ye lived there."

"Aren't ye on duty?" O'Malley countered.

"Aye, but King sent another one of his men just now." His gaze met his cousin's. "Thought ye'd like to know."

"Any message?"

"He asked to speak with ye."

"Mignonette, would ye mind—"

"After I see to your neck and check your arm—"

"I'm not bleeding! 'Tis important, or else King would not have sent a third man to speak to me."

Hurt flashed in her eyes, then disappeared. Concern took its place. O'Malley regretted causing her distress, but he did not have the time to soothe her now. He would deal with his wife's tender feelings after he met with King's man. He rose and placed a hand to the middle of her back. "I'm sorry, Lass. Emmett's right. I am a bear when I'm hungry. I'll ask Mrs. O'Toole to send up a pot of tea and some scones while ye wait."

"*Merci.* I shall *continue* waiting for you."

He ignored her pique and pressed a kiss to her forehead. "I'll be back, Lass."

⤐⟫⟪⟞

AT THE TOP of the servants' staircase, Emmett remarked, "I'm thinking yer wife isn't too happy with ye right now."

"She'll have to get used to me comings and goings," O'Malley grumbled. "We gave our vow to protect the duke and his family. No matter the hour, no matter how long a day we've already put in. Neither one of us would break that vow."

"Ye might be telling yer wife that, Boy-o," his cousin suggested. "Unless ye prefer sleeping in the stables with yer horse."

O'Malley shoved his cousin. "Ye're a horse's *arse.*"

Emmett snorted with laughter. "Faith, doesn't it take a horse's *arse* to recognize his own kin?"

"Mrs. O'Toole," O'Malley called out as he entered the kitchen. "Would ye mind sending a pot of tea and some of yer delectable scones up to me wife?"

"Not at all, Sean. Would you like me to sit with her until you return?"

"Would ye? I'd be obliged."

She nodded. "I'd be happy to keep her company."

Knowing he'd be leaving his wife in good hands did not negate the fact that he'd left her to her own devices since just after dawn. In the duke's town house, where she did not feel comfortable. After they'd exposed the lying lord who posted that wager—and who'd paid him to, he would be taking his wife to their new home in Sussex. *Home.* And wasn't that a wonder, receiving the gift of his own home?

"Franklin," O'Malley greeted King's man. "What do ye have for me?"

"Lord Brownwell was seen leaving Lady Kittrick's town house just after dawn."

O'Malley nodded. "And?"

"His carriage was spotted dropping him off on her doorstep half an hour ago."

"Me contacts have confirmed he hasn't paid his staff's wages in three months. Two of his footmen mentioned the disappearance of small valuables and were immediately dismissed."

Franklin nodded. "Someone tried to pawn the *Brownwell Sapphires* at Grimsby's shop as he was closing for the night."

O'Malley slowly smiled, recognizing the name. "Grimsby's an honest man. Came to Her Grace's rescue—before she married His Grace."

Franklin agreed. "He's well-known, honest, and respected. He's alerted King more than once whenever he's been asked to pawn jewelry."

"Have you spoken to Grimsby?"

"Aye. The man trying to pawn the jewels looked like he was more accustomed to working the docks at night. Grimsby let him know he never accepted jewels at his shop."

"Any trouble?"

"Not for our friend Grimsby."

"Any instructions from King?"

"We wait."

"Aye." He'd wait…until five minutes *after* Franklin left to confront the bloody bastard and beard the lioness in her den of iniquity!

Lady Kittrick crossed the line when she escalated her campaign to ruin the earl and his wife by adding O'Malley's wife. Brownwell crossed over the line when he added the wager to White's betting book to help perpetuate the lies.

It was time for them to pay.

CHAPTER THIRTY

EDWARD, EARL LIPPINCOTT, arrived as O'Malley was about to mount his horse.

"Going somewhere, O'Malley?"

He hadn't noticed the carriage, or the fact that the earl was standing on the sidewalk. Shocked that he'd let his guard down while planning the downfall of two members of the quality, he laid a hand on his horse's neck and replied, "Aye, yer lordship."

The earl's eyes narrowed as he walked over to where O'Malley stood. "Mind if I join you?"

He paused before replying, "Nay, I wouldn't. But I'm thinking His Grace would."

"My brother isn't here, is he?"

O'Malley noticed the intensity in the earl's gaze and hesitated. "He isn't, but I gave me pledge to protect His Grace and his family. Ye're his family." Bloody hell...one of the guard should have ridden with the earl. "Did ye forget something, yer lordship?"

"No. Why do you ask?"

"I don't see me brother or any of me cousins traveling with ye."

"Given the circumstances, I felt it was more important to leave my wife under the protection of your brother and your cousins."

Jenkins opened the front door to greet the earl. "Your lordship. It's wonderful to see you. Is her ladyship with you?"

"She's visiting Lady Calliope and the viscount."

O'Malley thought to make his escape while the earl was distracted but stopped in his tracks when he heard the earl say, "O'Malley and I were just leaving. I have an urgent appointment."

"Will you be riding with his lordship?"

"Nay."

"Yes," the earl replied at the same time. "Please have someone see to his horse and send word to Mrs. O'Malley that I asked her husband to accompany me."

"Of course, your lordship."

"Thank you, Jenkins." Turning back to O'Malley, the earl frowned. "Where were you going?"

O'Malley did not want to confide in the earl or have the earl accompany him. The duke would sack him on the spot if he got wind that O'Malley had dragged the earl with him to confront the two individuals responsible for this latest round of attacks on the duke's family.

"May I remind you that my brother is not here."

O'Malley knew when he was beaten. "No need, yer lordship."

The earl got into his carriage. "Then may I remind you, in his absence, you report to me?"

"Nay, yer lordship."

The earl growled, "Get in the bloody coach, O'Malley!"

Without another word, O'Malley entered the carriage.

"I repeat, where were you going?"

"Lady Kittrick's town house."

"Bloody hell."

"Aye."

"I only have one question for you."

"Yer lordship?"

"If the person responsible for placing that wager at White's is with her, are you prepared to act as my second?"

"I'd rather our roles be reversed."

"One cannot always have what one wishes." The earl waited a beat before adding, "I highly doubt Brownwell would ever entertain a challenge from someone he did not feel his equal in society."

O'Malley ground his teeth together. "I will gladly act as yer second—unless for some reason, he accepts me challenge first."

The carriage was a block away from the lady's town house when the earl knocked on the roof, signaling the driver to stop. The earl met O'Malley's questioning gaze, musing aloud, "You do not wish to neglect your vow to protect our family."

"I do not."

"What if I let you go in alone, challenge Brownwell—and he accepts."

"Ye'd agree to be me second?"

"I'd gladly act as your second, O'Malley."

"And if he refuses to acknowledge me challenge?"

"You gracefully accept his decision. When I see you leaving the town house, I will enter and challenge Brownwell."

"What if he refuses?"

"What if he doesn't," the earl countered.

"Does Coventry know what ye intend?"

"I would assume so."

"And King?"

"If Coventry knows, King knows."

O'Malley drew in a breath, let it go and opened the door to the coach.

"O'MALLEY TO SEE you, your ladyship,"

Lady Kittrick jolted at the name before glaring at Lord Brownwell. "I told you not to attempt to pawn off *entailed* jewels," she hissed. "Why did you not listen to my advice?"

"I'm not about to listen to the advice of a third-rate actress."

Lady Kittrick flushed. "How dare you!"

Brownwell's gaze slid from her coiffure to her toes, his knowing look unsettling her. "Would you prefer Cyprian?"

Lady Kittrick drew in a breath, prepared to lambast him, but her butler interrupted, reminding her that he had heard the insult.

"I beg your pardon, your ladyship. Shall I send O'Malley on his way?"

"No!" she shouted. "Send him in."

O'Malley entered the drawing room, prepared to goad Brownwell to accept his challenge. "Lady Kittrick. Yer lordship."

"Who the devil are you?" Brownwell queried.

"Mr. O'Malley is one of the Duke of Wyndmere's personal guard," Lady Kittrick drawled.

The image in his mind was not how Brownwell appeared in person. O'Malley stared at the tall, dark-haired man with the sneer on his lace-framed face and wondered if there was a mistake. The man was the antithesis of Earl Lippincott.

"Are you here on behalf of your employer, the duke?" Lady Kittrick inquired.

O'Malley didn't answer quickly enough.

"The lady asked you a question," Brownwell spat out.

O'Malley stared at the lord, ignoring the question. "Ye will publicly announce that ye lied about me wife, Lady Aurelia, the earl, and me."

"Or what?"

"I'll meet ye at Chalk Farm at dawn over a brace of pistols."

Lady Kittrick's theatrical gasp of shock and near swoon was not as believable as the woman intended. O'Malley made no move to catch her.

Brownwell sputtered. "You dare to dictate to me? Do you realize who I am?"

O'Malley sneered. "Aye. Ye're the one helping to spread Lady Kittrick's lies. When ye marked it down in White's betting book, ye crossed the line."

"I don't give a bloody damn what you think, O'Malley." The man turned to Lady Kittrick, asking, "Aren't you going to have this person removed?"

"I'll leave on me own, just as soon as I hear yer answer to me challenge. Not a moment before."

"I do not converse with those of your station in life." He turned his back on O'Malley.

"Well then, ye're in luck, because I often speak to those who are of a higher station in life than me. As a matter of fact," O'Malley remarked, "ye're not the first bloody lord I've met who thought he was far above me."

"What did you call me?"

O'Malley slowly smiled. "I called ye a bloody lord, though in truth, I should have used a different word altogether."

"You shall be sorry for insulting me."

"Aye, I am sorry," O'Malley relented. "What I should have said, is ye're not the first bloody bugger who thought himself far above me."

Brownwell vibrated with anger.

O'Malley knew he had goaded the man to the point where there was now the possibility of a fist being thrown! "Aye. 'Tis always a man with a puny cock that tends to expound on how great he is in front of others."

O'Malley's eyes gleamed as Brownwell closed the distance between them. Anticipation sang through his veins. His hands itched to plow into the man's face, pummeling him until the man cried out for him to stop.

Remembering every slur, every threat against the earl and his wife—and his own beautiful wife, he knew he wouldn't be stopping until the man begged him to stop.

"Is that fear I smell on yer fine frockcoat, Brownwell?" O'Malley taunted. He refused to believe he could not goad the man to accept his challenge. He tried one last tactic. "I know exactly who ye are and don't give a bloody feckin' hell that I'm a commoner and ye're a feckin' titled lord. I may be crossing the line I should never have crossed…but ye crossed the line when ye maligned me wife!"

Brownwell's face flamed, then paled a moment before he tilted his head back and laughed in O'Malley's face. "I do believe you are a few rungs below a commoner."

He curled his hands into fists, wishing the earl was not waiting outside for him. He imagined what it would feel like to club the blackguard in the mouth and then watch the blood gush from his nose when he flattened it against the man's face. *Immensely satisfying.* "That's yer final answer?"

"Have your butler remove him at once!"

"I do not take orders from you, Lord Brownwell."

O'Malley was halfway to the door when he heard the pompous lord spout, "Someone should take you in hand, Melisande and teach you to listen to your betters."

In two strides, he was at Lady Kittrick's side. "Do ye need me to remove this person for ye, yer ladyship?"

Emerald eyes wide with shock, her gaze darted between O'Malley and Brownwell before she finally managed to rasp, "If you would, please."

O'Malley grabbed the back of the lord's frockcoat and dragged him to the door. "Get your hands off me! Melisande, *do* something!"

She followed O'Malley and Brownwell into the entryway. "Who would listen to a third-rate actress, a Cyprian like me?"

Lady Kittrick's butler rushed to open the front door.

"Ah," Earl Lippincott intoned from the other side of the doorway. "I was hoping someone would eventually answer the door."

Lady Kittrick's face paled. "My lord, what are you doing here?"

"I've come with a proposal for Brownwell." Lippincott glanced at O'Malley. "I was beginning to wonder how long it would take."

"How long what would take?" Lady Kittrick asked.

Brownwell struggled but could not get free. "Lippincott, call off your lackey!"

"'Fraid not, Brownwell—O'Malley answers to my brother."

"Summon the Watch!"

The earl ignored the man to ask, "O'Malley, what did he say?"

"He laughed."

"Coward."

"What was that?" Brownwell asked.

"I called you a coward," Earl Lippincott repeated. "Only a true coward would refuse a challenge to meet on the field of honor."

"Bloody prig!"

"You will publicly apologize for attempting to shred my wife's reputation and Mrs. O'Malley's reputation."

"Or what?" Brownwell demanded.

"I shall meet you at dawn over a brace of pistols."

Brownwell mistakenly did not realize the peril he was in, or he may have kept the condescending tone from coloring his words. "Did the two of you rehearse your lines on the drive over together?"

O'Malley kept his expression blank, keeping thoughts of pummeling the man until he wilted to the floor to himself for now. "With yer permission, yer ladyship?"

"Er…yes, quite. Please assist Lord Brownwell through the door."

The Irishman slowly smiled. "Shall I boot him to the curb while I'm at it?"

A flash of regret flickered in her eyes, and O'Malley knew the woman remembered the day her cook had booted her scullery maid out the door and to the curb. He'd been certain more than one of the lady's staff had witnessed the event—and the young maid's rescue, before Garahan spirited her away.

Lady Kittrick quickly recovered, stating, "I think not."

With no sign that anything out of the ordinary was occurring, her butler stood straight and tall, continuing to hold the door open.

O'Malley nodded to the butler before forcing Brownwell to goose step out the door. He saw the humor in watching the earl's stiff-kneed step, though he doubted the man would ever have the courage to buy his colors or march proudly with his military brothers. It took his considerable control to fight the urge to plant his boot in the lord's backside.

Earl Lippincott prodded Brownwell the moment his foot touched the sidewalk. "I demand you answer my challenge!"

Brownwell spun around. "I'll see you in hell first!"

O'Malley chuckled. "Faith, isn't he the bold one? Everyone who knows ye, yer lordship, knows ye've earned yer wings twice over since His Grace assumed the title."

The earl stared at Brownwell. "Name your weapon and your second."

O'Malley wondered if the man would rise to the challenge. He had high hopes, as he'd never had the honor of acting as anyone's second. His decision made, he taunted, "He doesn't have the spine to meet ye on the field of honor, yer lordship." Seeing the hatred burning brightly in Brownwell's gaze, he added, "He's not fit to wipe yer boots, yer lordship. Don't waste yer breath."

Brownwell growled, "Smithers." The man slowly smiled. "Rapier."

O'Malley noted the brief flare of surprise, but the earl inclined his head, accepting Brownwell's weapon of choice. "Chalk Farm. Tomorrow. At dawn!"

The challenged did not refuse. Therefore, the terms of the *code duello* had been met.

Lady Kittrick threw herself at the earl. While the earl was busy extricating himself from her clinging grasp, O'Malley wondered what the woman's game was. He'd felt sorry for her predicament when the man had insulted her—in her own home, in front of Earl Lippincott.

His lordship was not one to gossip—ever, having been the recipient of more than his share before…and after marrying Lady Aurelia. Lady Kittrick should not worry that the earl would repeat what had transpired. But Brownwell bloody well would!

Thinking to intervene and discuss the situation with the earl—asking how in the bloody hell he planned to defeat Brownwell with a rapier, he looked to the earl. "Begging yer pardon, yer lordship, but ye asked me to remind you about yer meeting with Gavin King."

The earl placed his hands on Lady Kittrick's arms to gently ease out of her hold without harming her. "Thank you." He bowed before the woman. "I shall let King know that you have had a change of heart and will retract the false allegations you have made about my wife, myself, Mrs. O'Malley, and Sean O'Malley."

"What does Mr. King have to do with it?"

The earl smiled at her question. "He has been instrumental in helping my family uncover who is behind these heinous rumors rioting through the *ton*." His jaw clenched and his eyes narrowed. "The latest vicious rumor, posted as a wager in White's betting book, is slander… defamation of character—mine and my wife's…O'Malley's and his wife's. That will not be tolerated!"

O'Malley fought not to laugh at the look of astonishment on her pale face. "I'm certain her ladyship would not want it known that she is associated with the rumors or Lord Brownwell, yer lordship." With a glance at the white-faced woman, he added, "I would not trust the man *not* to cast aspersions on ye, yer ladyship, saying that yer ladyship was behind the plot from the start."

Knowing full well that she *had* been the one who had started the ugly rumors, O'Malley knew it was not the issue here. Getting her to cooperate, have a change of heart, and publicly apologize was.

"I have no idea what you are talking about," Lady Kittrick professed. "I demand that you leave at once, else *I* shall summon the Watch!"

O'Malley's gut clenched. He'd actually felt sorry for the woman. Her reaction when Brownwell insulted her, his innate need to protect those weaker than himself, pushed him to take charge of removing the man from her town house.

With a glance at the earl, he bit back the retort on the tip of his tongue.

"King awaits, O'Malley," Earl Lippincott stated. With a brief nod in the lady's direction, he entered the carriage.

O'Malley followed. Sitting across from the earl, he apologized. "I never should have stood up for the woman after all she's said and done to ye and her ladyship."

The earl sighed. "I understand why you did, O'Malley—not that I approved."

"Whenever I see someone at the mercy of someone else or unable to feed their family—forced to resort to unlawful means to do so…I find meself in the thick of things."

"You've more than earned the moniker, *The Duke's Protector*. Although, I must admit, Jared and I would prefer if you would not get involved with those who are bound and possessed to shred our family's reputation."

He accepted the censure in the earl's voice as his due. "Aye, yer lordship. I shall do me best to refrain." *God help him, he'd die trying.*

"Excellent. Do I have an appointment with King?"

O'Malley grinned. "Ye do now, with her ladyship all but confessing to ye that she'd been the one to start the ugly business."

"She did not admit to anything," the earl reminded him.

"Ah," O'Malley's eyes were alight with humor, "but she did not *deny* our claims, did she?"

"No," the earl replied.

"Well then, we'd best let King know what's happened. He's certain to have a plan in mind to deal with it."

Earl Lippincott slowly smiled. "I appreciate the twisted way your mind works, O'Malley. I'm glad you were here."

"Me pleasure, yer lordship." He held the earl's gaze for long moments before asking, "Would ye care to cross swords with me to practice for the morning?"

The earl snorted out a laugh. "I may prefer to face an opponent over pistols at dawn, but that does not mean I am unskilled with a rapier."

O'Malley nodded, pleased that the earl was confident in his skill with a blade. "Me sources tell me Brownwell is a fair hand with a rapier."

This time, the earl laughed out loud. "I'm better."

Relief filled O'Malley. Relaxing for the first time since leaving Grosvenor Square, he asked, "What will Lady Aurelia have to say when she learns about the duel?"

The earl's eyes blazed. "She's in Sussex and will not find out about it. Will she?"

O'Malley was quick to respond. "Not from me or any of the men." Knowing Lady Aurelia, he had no doubt she would eventually hear. News traveled fast—salacious gossip traveled faster! His immediate concern was whether Lady Aurelia would have time to make the journey to London before dawn, and if Lady Calliope would be traveling with her.

CHAPTER THIRTY-ONE

"WHY DID HIS lordship ask ye to be his second?" Emmett argued. "I'm on duty here in London—ye haven't been in months!"

"I've worked closely with his lordship from the beginning."

"The lot of us have worked closely with the earl and His Grace," Emmett countered.

"I was there," O'Malley bit out. "Ye weren't."

His cousin sighed. "Word travels, Sean."

O'Malley's gut iced over. He knew what Emmett meant. "When did she find out?"

"Before ye got home."

"How is it possible news of the duel reached the lass?"

"Mrs. O'Toole was doing the marketing and happened to hear the rumor from the sister of the cousin whose brother is Lady Kittrick's butler."

O'Malley raked a hand through his hair. The urge to rip it out had him by the *bollocks*.

"I cannot believe Mrs. O'Toole would tell me wife about the duel."

"She didn't," his cousin remarked. "Yer wife overheard one of the footmen speak of it."

"How in the bloody hell do ye know?"

"She told me what she'd heard and demanded I tell her the

truth."

"Bloody *bollocks*! Ye couldn't have lied?"

Emmett's direct gaze had O'Malley shaking his head. "Faith, I'm an *eedjit*. Of course, ye couldn't lie to me wife. She trusts ye as she trusts me."

"Aye, she does."

"Does the lass know it's tomorrow?"

His cousin shrugged. "She didn't ask, and I didn't offer what me own cousin hadn't told me himself."

"Bloody hell! I didn't want ye acting as me second, I wanted ye to protect me wife!"

"What would have happened when yer aim faltered, and yer blasted shot missed the bugger?"

O'Malley wouldn't admit he'd had the same worry. "Why would me aim would be off?"

"I was there when yer arm was sewn back together, and watched the fever begin to build. Yer wife and I took turns fighting to break the hold it had on ye. 'Twas the O'Malley cure that I'd mixed together in a poultice and herbal draught for ye to drink that helped ye heal so they wouldn't chop yer blasted arm off!"

His gut roiled at his cousin's words, and O'Malley's shoulders slumped. "Ye saved me life—and me arm. I'll be grateful to ye for the rest of me days."

"Start acting like ye are and start thinking about how yer actions affect that sweet wife of yers! The lass doesn't deserve to become yer widow a sennight after she married ye."

"Ye're right."

Emmett paused and cupped a hand to his ear, "What was that ye said?"

O'Malley snorted. "I'll not be repeating meself."

"Ah, such a heartfelt apology from me stiff-necked cousin."

"Bugger it."

"Thank ye, but no." Emmett clapped a hand against O'Malley's back. "I'd rather not."

O'Malley snickered, nudging his cousin with his shoulder to move him out of the way. "I'd best speak to me wife."

"Don't tell her when or where," Emmett warned.

"I'm not an *eedjit*, O'Malley countered.

His cousin snorted with laughter. "Are ye certain of that?"

O'Malley shook his head as he ascended the servants' staircase. It was time to apologize to his wife for having to leave so unexpectedly this evening. As far as he was concerned, there was no need to apologize for being gone all day—it was part and parcel of his job. She'd best get used to it.

For the second time that evening, he found himself standing outside the door to the room he'd been sharing with his wife. Odd, but he never imagined he'd be sleeping in bed as soft as a cloud on the privileged side of the duke's town house. To tell the truth, he and his kin were more comfortable sleeping in one of the outbuildings, barns, or stables on a pallet than in a house like this.

What would it be like to have a home of his own—one he shared with the lovely lass on the other side of this door?

He raised his hand and pulled back at the last minute, or he would have knocked on his wife's forehead.

"Lass, where are ye going?"

Her eyes widened. "I did not know you were back."

"Ye didn't answer me question," he reminded her. "Where are ye going?"

"I have business to attend to."

He raised his brow in silent question. When she didn't answer, he frowned at her. "If we're going to get along, Lass, ye'll have to answer when I ask ye questions."

"Does the same hold true when I ask *you* questions?"

He paused to think before answering. "'Twould depend on the question."

"*Merde!*"

O'Malley struggled to keep from laughing. He didn't want his wife to think he was laughing at her. "I may not know many

French words, but I know that one. Should ye be cursing in front of yer husband?"

She tilted her chin up and saucily replied, "*Oui.* He curses in front of me all the time."

"Now, Lass," he began, but she lifted her hand to caress the side of his jaw and his thoughts evaporated.

"*Oui, mon coeur?*"

"Lass, I wanted to say—" Blast it all if she didn't place her hand over his heart and bat her incredibly long, dark lashes at him. A female ploy he'd learned of years ago. It had never affected him before...but right now, he'd be bloody well damned if he could recall what he wanted to say.

"You look tired. Come, let me tend to your neck. You rushed off before I could smooth healing salve on it. Then I will need to change the bandage on your arm." With a hand to his elbow, she steered him into the bedchamber.

He willingly let himself be led.

"Mrs. O'Toole promised she'd have something warm for you to eat when you got home. Did you see her already?"

"Nay, Lass. I spoke to Emmett...no one else."

She guided him to a chair. He sat quietly while she gathered what she needed. With a glance, he recognized the small jar of his cousin's healing salve along with clean bandages and knew she was ready. He'd already kept her waiting the whole of the day, he wouldn't add to her time worrying and caring for him. He tried to remove his shirt without assistance and ended up struggling.

With the touch of a hand on his shoulder, she told him without words to wait. "Let me help you."

"Aye, Lass. Thank ye."

His wife concentrated on removing his injured arm from the tight sleeve. He'd successfully ignored the fit until she'd helped him slip it free and he realized just how tight it had been. "Much better."

Soft brown eyes met moss green. "I let out the seams of one of your cambric shirts and your other frockcoat." She looked away, but not before he saw the concern in the depths of her eyes. Did she think he'd be upset that she hadn't waited to ask his permission?

Humbled, he rasped, "Thank ye, for thinking of it—and me, Lass."

"Don't thank me until we see if the thickness of the bandage fits inside the new width of the sleeve and frockcoat."

Slipping his hand beneath her ear, he was rewarded when she rested her head against the cup of his hand. "Thank ye for seeing to me comfort. I never would have thought of seams and such."

She smiled and his world turned upside down. His wife was a beauty, but it was the love, care, and concern shining in her eyes that touched his heart.

"It is what I do. Why would I not use my ability with needle and thread…when I know how much you disliked wearing the sling?"

"Ye care about others, Lass. 'Tis an admirable trait."

Heart in her eyes, she dipped her head so he could not see what she was thinking. He vowed he wouldn't push her anymore tonight. The light touch of her fingertips on the back of his neck cooled while the salve soothed the angry skin there.

"Have ye ever worked with a healer?"

She paused for a moment before continuing to blot his arm dry, careful not to rub against it. She tended to his wound with a light, loving touch. "I always helped *Maman*. She took good care of us. Emmett will be happy when I tell him your injury shows no further signs of infection."

When she moved away from him, he felt the immediate change in the air about him—as if a cloud covered the warmth of the sun. O'Malley shook his head at the fanciful notion as he watched her graceful movements, marveling that such a small thing would give him pleasure.

"Here." She held out one of his shirts to him. "Try this on."

O'Malley stood and slid his bandaged arm into the sleeve easily. Grinning at his wife, he bent his arm, then extended it.

"Much better."

"Wait!" She hurried over to the wardrobe and reached for his spare frockcoat. "Now, see how this sleeve fits. I may need to let out the seam a pinch more. We won't know until you try it on."

Allowing her to help him with his coat was not something he wanted to get used to. He'd be relieved when it was no longer necessary. Another day or two, he reasoned. The difference may not have shown, looking at his coat from the outside, but the difference was remarkable to him. "Me arm won't feel constricted as it did most of today."

With a slow smile, he added, "I'll be able to lift me arm and hold any of me weapons."

"Weapons," she muttered beneath her breath.

He'd heard what she'd said but asked just to hear her say it aloud. "What was that, Lass?"

"Weapons. Why would you need to hold weapons?"

"'Tis an important part of me job protecting the duke, the earl, and their families." Sensing that part of his job added to her worries, he teased, "Did ye think I only used me impressive size and powerful fists?"

Her light, musical laughter filled the air around them. "Your broad shoulders and the width of your chest would deter many from ignoring any orders you give. While your height would intimidate others."

"But not ye?"

She shook her head. "Not me. Your size and strength saved me."

Her words wrapped around his heart and stayed there. He hadn't mattered to a woman in a long time. The others had come and gone from his life without touching his heart. Mignonette grabbed hold of his heart from the first...and then she'd touched his soul. Before another moment passed, he needed to find out what she'd heard about the dawn appointment.

"Have you spoken to Emmett recently, Lass?" Should he ask her outright what she knew or tell her what he *wanted* her to know?

"*Oui.* He has been checking in with me all day—although I know what he is really about."

"Do ye now?"

"*Oui,* he is doing as you asked, protecting me." She placed a hand to his shoulder. "I would have rather called upon Madame today, but because you wished it, I stayed here."

"What did ye do today besides moving the seams in me shirt and coat?"

She lifted one shoulder and let it drop. The change in her attitude toward him surprised him. "Does it matter?"

He frowned at her. "Aye, it matters."

"Why? You are off doing whatever your duties require of you. Is there another reason you ask?"

He grabbed hold of her hand and yanked her against him. "As yer husband, 'tis me right to know where ye go and what ye do."

A bleak look of sorrow flashed in the depths of her eyes before she blinked and it was gone. "Ah, but I am not permitted to ask what you did, or where you went today. Am I?"

"Ye know I cannot speak of me duties to His Grace and his lordship."

"Because you do not think I can be trusted *not* to speak of what you confide in me? Is it because I refused to admit that I do know Ruan?" Heart in her eyes, she confessed, "*Mon papa* did not want to hide smuggled goods in his shop, but Ruan had a blade to my throat, promising to slit it before he gutted me if Papa told a soul."

"I'll kill the bloody bastard!"

"No! He is evil. You cannot battle evil and win. I lost both of my parents because of that man. I will not lose my husband to him!"

"What of yer life? Am I not allowed to protect and defend ye from the bleeding bastard?"

"Nay, *mon amor,* promise me!"

"*Mo ghra,* I cannot lie to ye. If he comes anywhere near ye, he'll be dancing with the devil."

"I pray he remains in France."

O'Malley placed the palm of his hand against the middle of her back and drew her close, until their lips were a breath apart. "Kiss me, Lass."

Desire flared brightly in the warmth of her brown eyes. She started to turn away from him, but he placed the tip of his finger on the line of her jaw, drawing her gaze back to meet his.

The urge to sample the sweetness of her lips nearly did him in. The need to kiss his wife would have to wait. He needed her to understand. "I'm grateful ye finally told me the truth. I'll be passing it on to King. He has ears to the ground and will know when Ruan is in England. He'll add to yer protection."

"Merci, Sean, but I—"

"Let me finish the rest, Lass. I swore an oath. Never to speak of me duties or what they entail unless given leave to do so by His Grace or his lordship."

"I see." She closed her eyes.

"Look at me, Lass." His wife did not immediately respond to his request. "I can wait all night."

She huffed out a breath and opened her eyes. "I am looking at you," she snipped.

The irritation she did not bother to hide from him proved what he thought—his wife was not afraid to speak her mind. It would make their life together that much more interesting. "I have never, and will never, ever, break a vow."

She was listening, intently. "So you have mentioned more than once."

"And yet, ye don't believe I would never break a vow."

She looked away, then back. "There are times in life when one has no choice but to break one vow in order to honor another."

"I've yet to find meself in such a position. Have ye?"

"*Oui.*"

"Will ye tell me about it?"

"Mayhap when you tell me about your dawn appointment."

"Ye know of it?"

Her eyes welled with tears and one slipped free. He caught it on the tip of his finger, brushing it away, waiting patiently for her to answer. He'd never made an effort to be patient in his life before marrying Mignonette. For her, he would do so.

Finally, she inclined her head.

"What did ye hear?"

"You are to meet the lord who wrote in White's book at dawn."

"When ye hear a tale from another, ye'd best make certain 'tis the truth and not a tale."

"Mrs. O'Toole told me. She would never tell tales."

He nearly smiled at her quick defense of the duke's cook. "Ye have the right of it. Although, ye must understand, Lass, there are times in life when one hears a rumor and is worried for the person or persons involved."

"What of it?" his wife asked.

"They would speak of it in order to learn whether or not the rumor or rumors were true so that they could do all in their power to protect the people they love."

"You are not fighting a duel tomorrow?"

"I'm to act as second to his lordship."

"Is that not as dangerous as the one who is facing his opponent?"

"Not necessarily."

"Is not the one who acts as second there to ensure the rules are obeyed?"

"Aye."

"He chose a blade, didn't he?"

O'Malley nodded.

"Are you worried that his lordship is not as proficient with a blade as with a dueling pistol?"

"Nay, Lass. His lordship and the duke are expert marksmen and highly skilled wielding a blade."

"What has you worried, *mon amor?*"

"I cannot be in two places at one time. As his second, 'tis me job to ensure a physician is in attendance, check the weapons and the surroundings to ensure no one is concealed, lying in wait to take aim at his lordship's back."

"Do you believe this is possible?"

"Aye," he was quick to respond. "'Tis happened before."

Her eyes widened. "You have been involved in more than one duel?"

His gaze locked with hers. "It sounds as if ye have yerself. Have ye?"

They stared at one another, neither answering. O'Malley sensed she was going to be difficult about what he needed her to do. So there would be no question, he told her, "Ye'd best not try to follow us tomorrow. Ye're to stay where I put ye!"

She planted her hands against his chest and shoved away from him. Rounding on him, hands to her hips, she declared, "When you cease to order me about, I shall consider obeying your many dictates."

His wife opened the door and sailed through it before he could stop her. O'Malley let her get a head start and was smiling by the time he'd reached the door to the servants' staircase.

"Faith, but I love a feisty woman!"

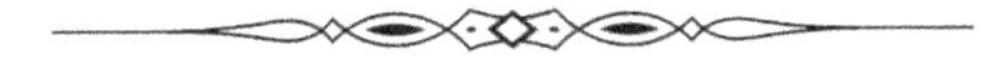

CHAPTER THIRTY-TWO

O'MALLEY FOUND MIGNONETTE in the conservatory. From the way her shoulders were slumped, he knew he'd somehow managed to upset her. He was not accustomed to watching what he said, or how he said it.

Mayhap he should have asked Coventry's advice on how to reason with one's wife. Especially when one's wife was *not* listening to commands. Wasn't that her job, to do as she was told?

A whisper of a memory flashed through his mind of his ma giving Da fits over the way Da had ordered her to do something his ma did not want to do. He smiled as the reality of his situation shifted and he put himself in his da's place, with Mignonette in Ma's place. "Ye've stepped in it this time, Boy-o."

Memories of day long arguments with neither his ma nor his da giving an inch filled him. Newly married, he did not want to draw a line in the sand, tempting his wife to cross it, just to prove her point.

Resolved to right the situation before it declined any further, he softly called her name.

She whipped around and his gut clenched. "Ye're crying."

The lass wiped at her eyes and sniffed back her tears, immediately contradicting him. "I am not crying."

He closed the distance between them and held out his arms. Without a word, she flung herself into his arms. The slight weight of her soothed him, while her heartbreaking sobs tore at his soul. "Are ye crying because I ordered ye to stay put?"

She didn't lift her head when she answered him.

He eased his hold on her. "I cannot hear ye. What did ye say?"

She shook her head against his chest in reply. From the way she'd burrowed closer, he sensed she needed him to hold her. Not batter the lass with questions. Content to let her cry herself out in his arms, he stroked his hand up and down her spine and waited for the storm to pass.

Finally, she quieted in his arms, turned her cheek to rest against his chest and whispered, "I am afraid."

"What do ye fear, Lass?"

"Tomorrow."

"Ye have nothing to fear. There's never been an O'Malley who died before siring a son to continue our line."

She pushed away from him. "Do not speak of such in the same breath!" she warned.

"'Tis the truth. I didn't say we O'Malleys never die. We're not that arrogant."

"For my sake, Sean, do not speak of dying when you will be in harm's way just hours from now."

"Dying is a part of life, Lass, and should not be feared."

Her bone-deep sorrow bothered him. "Let's go back upstairs."

She shook her head at him.

"I'm wanting a private conversation with ye, *mo chroi*."

"We are surrounded by plants—"

"With footmen stationed within hearing distance," he reminded her.

"Forgive me. I did not think others would hear our conversation."

"'Tis the way the privileged live their lives—not the rest of us. Ye'll become accustomed to it the longer ye work and live among them."

Leaning close, she pitched her voice low. "Do we have to live among them?"

"Nearby them, aye. Among them, in a manner of speaking. I cannot promise ye'll be having a lady's maid, Lass, if that's what ye're asking."

"I would not know what to do with one, unless she knew how to sew. Then I could put her to work."

O'Malley smiled. "There's the feisty lass I married. Are ye tired?"

She tilted her head to one side. "Why do you ask?"

"If ye're not tired, we can walk together to our bedchamber."

"And if I am tired?"

He swept her off her feet and into his arms. "Then I'll carry ye."

She sighed, leaning against him. "How does your arm feel?"

"Fit enough to brace me weight on it."

"Why would you…" her lovely lips formed an "o" as understanding filled her.

"I've a powerful need to make love to ye, Lass."

"What if—"

His lips cut off her words, but she did not complain as she boldly kissed him back.

She tightened her arms around his neck. "Hurry, Sean."

With his wife in his arms, O'Malley strode from the conservatory, through the darkened hallway to the servants' side of the town house.

Taking the stairs two at a time, he carried his precious burden back to the privacy of their bedchamber where he would spend the rest of the night proving the depth of his love to her.

MIGNONETTE WOKE ABRUPTLY to find herself alone. Her face flamed remembering how he'd spent most of the night worshiping every inch of her. She'd done the same, reveling in the strength of him, the sheer size of him...so much more to touch, to caress, to love.

With a shaking hand, she touched the sheets where her love had slept beside her—*still warm.*

Slipping from the bed, she picked up the chemise he'd tossed to the floor, and the gown that quickly followed. Reveling in the prelude to their lovemaking, she felt the warm glow of it returning. She dressed quickly, then walked to the adjoining dressing room and back before noticing the clothing she'd helped him discard so eagerly a few hours ago were no longer strewn about the room.

Shaking with fear, knowing where he'd gone, she slipped into her shoes and yanked the door open. She'd flown down the servants' staircase and ran past the kitchen not caring who saw her. No one—no one would stop her from going after Sean!

Using the same doorway she had the day before, she slipped out of the duke's town house, into the alley, heading around the back to the stables.

With trembling hands, she opened the door and saw a horse—saddled and waiting for a rider. She sent up a silent prayer and walked straight into a wall. Before she landed on her backside, a strong hand wrapped around her arm, catching her.

"Where do ye think ye're going?"

"After my husband. Do not try to stop me!"

Emmett crossed his arms in front of his chest. He was nearly equal in size to Sean, but that was not going to stop her. The foreboding sense that something terrible was going to happen filled her the moment she discovered him gone.

"Ye are to stay put," Emmett reminded her.

"*Merde!* I will not." She feinted to one side when he reached for her.

The big man tried to box her in, but she was shorter—lower to the ground, and faster. She slipped past him.

"If ye know what's good for ye, ye'll obey yer husband."

She whirled around to face the only thing standing between her and freedom. "I have to go to him. I cannot explain why, but I have this soul-deep feeling something awful is about to happen."

Emmett stared down at her without speaking.

"Come with me, please? You can protect me until we get to wherever Sean is. He needs me," she pleaded.

"Ye promise to listen and do whatever I tell ye to once we get there?"

"*Oui.* Hurry!"

One minute she was standing beside the horse, and the next she was being swept off her feet onto the horse in front of Emmett. "Find Franklin!" Emmett ordered the stable lad. "Tell him Mrs. O'Malley and I just left. He'll know where to find us."

With Emmett's strong arm banded around her waist, they rode off into the lightening sky.

"Will we get there in time?"

"Aye."

Worry had tears threatening, but she refused to give in to them. She could cry later when Sean was safe. Heat poured off the man riding behind her, and she was grateful for the warmth in the pre-dawn chill.

He slowed the horse to a fast trot as they neared an open field. "We're here?"

"I'm going to trust ye to keep yer word, Lass."

"*Oui*, Emmett. Tell me what to do."

He dismounted and helped her off the horse. "I need ye to stay out of sight while I see if yer fears are founded."

"Founded?"

"See that stand of trees over there?"

"*Oui.*"

"Perfect spot for someone intent on shooting his lordship or me cousin in the back."

Hands to her mouth to stifle her gasp, Mignonette could only stare. "Are there any other places one could hide?"

He narrowed his eyes, scanning the lay of the land. "A few, if ye count the tops of the carriages."

"Carriages?"

"Look over there." Emmett pointed toward three carriages. Two together and one off by itself. "Sean will have sent word to his lordship's physician."

"Dr. McIntyre?"

"Aye."

"Is that his lordship's carriage behind it?"

Emmett nodded. "Now the other one—"

"Belongs to the man who will try to kill both Earl Lippincott and Sean."

He locked gazes with her but didn't ask how she knew. She couldn't explain other than it was a feeling that had her by the throat. Sean and the earl were in danger.

Just then, the sound of hoofbeats pounded toward where they stood. Emmett waved to the riders approaching. "'Tis King's men."

"Mr. Franklin?"

"Aye and Jackson."

Mignonette moved to stand closer to Emmett. "Who are those men?"

She felt him stiffen, then relax. "Coventry's men."

"Captain Coventry?"

"Aye. He and his men are former soldiers and sailors, serving the king before they were injured and relieved of their duties."

"You know them?" she rasped. "Can they be trusted?"

"Every one of them would give their lives—and nearly had for King and Country."

She reached for his hand, holding it tight. Trying desperately not to panic, she asked, "Does Sean know them? Does he trust them?"

Emmett drew her against his side, leaned down and told her, "Trust me as ye trust me cousin."

"I don't—"

"Those men would give their lives for Captain Coventry."

"What of the earl and Sean?"

"Any friend of the captain's is under their protection as well."

"Including you?"

"Are ye worried about me?"

Tears filled her eyes and she struggled to blink them away. "You saved the love of my life. How could I not worry about you, too?"

He brushed a kiss to the top of her head. "Now, then, Lass. Ye stay here with me horse. Do not leave this spot."

She nodded.

"Ye promise?"

"*Je promets.*"

He frowned. "What?"

"I promise. Unless I have no choice."

"Ye'd best be keeping yer promise and forgetting about having a choice."

"You do what you have to do, Emmett. I shall do what I have to do."

"Ye have to do what I tell ye to do," he growled.

She shrugged and turned her back on him. It wouldn't do to anger the man when he needed to protect her husband…and the earl.

"I cannot protect ye if ye don't mind me."

"I shall try."

"Don't try—just do it."

She nodded but did not give her promise again when she sensed she would be breaking it before the duel was over.

Mumbling curses she'd heard her husband use more than once, Emmett glared at her and slipped away. She saw him pop up behind a tree a few feet away, but then lost sight of him again. The man moved like a wraith. Did all of the O'Malleys have that ability? For as massive a man as Sean was, he, too, moved silently.

From her spot a distance away from those gathered to observe the duel, she noted Captain Coventry's men were no longer standing beside him. Where had they gone? How could they have slipped away without her noticing?

"Gentlemen!" She turned at the sound of her husband's voice carrying through the stillness of the last minutes before dawn. "Ye have agreed to disengage at first blood."

The earl inclined his head in answer.

Brownwell glared.

"I'll have yer agreement now, Brownwell."

"*Lord* Brownwell," the man barked.

"Well?" O'Malley demanded, not deigning to show an ounce of respect to the man.

"You either agree to disengage when either of us draws first blood," Earl Lippincott drawled, "or you may accept defeat."

Brownwell inclined his head.

O'Malley gave the signal. The two men circled one another and they advanced and retreated. Thrusted and parried.

The feeling of impending doom swept up from her toes. Out of the corners of her eyes, she saw a branch appear in the "v" of the tree to her left. She blinked and the bottom dropped out of her stomach. It wasn't a branch—it was the thin barrel of a rifle!

A twig snapping had her glance shifting toward the sound. Another rifle was aimed at the field of honor!

She dared not interfere with her husband's duties as second. Earl Lippincott's skill with a rapier would soon have him drawing first blood! There was no time to find Emmett…she knew what she must do.

Mignonette screamed Sean's name as she ran toward the rifle closest to her. Searing pain brought her to her knees as her vision narrowed and men's shouts became muffled whispers in her ears. The last thing she heard was her husband roaring her name before darkness claimed her.

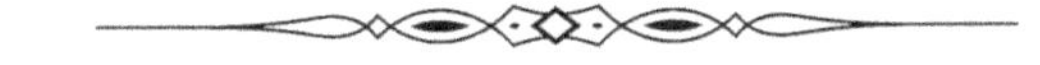

CHAPTER THIRTY-THREE

THE EARL LUNGED and felt a grim satisfaction as his blade sliced through the fine lawn of Brownwell's shirt sleeve to the flesh beneath. It wasn't a deep slash, but he'd drawn first blood!

"Damn your eyes!" Brownwell raised his sword hand in the air.

Two things happened simultaneously—a woman screamed Sean's name, and a rifle shot echoed through the early morning air.

"MIGNONETTE!"

At the guttural sound of Sean O'Malley screaming his wife's name, the earl turned his back on his opponent and was immediately tackled to the ground as the unmistakable sound of a lead ball whizzed past his head.

"Don't move, your lordship!"

"Franklin?"

"Aye."

"What is O'Malley's wife doing here?"

"Emmett brought her."

Before he could ask what in the bloody hell the man had been thinking, a deep voice called out, "Drop yer blade, or I'll gut ye where ye stand!"

"Who in the bloody hell do you think you are to threaten

me?" Brownwell exclaimed.

"I'm your second worst nightmare," Emmett O'Malley replied.

"Second worst?" Brownwell queried.

"Aye, me cousin, Sean, is your worst. 'Tis his wife one of yer lackies shot!"

⇛⇚

"SHE'S BLEEDING!" SEAN fell to his knees beside his wife applying pressure to the wound in her shoulder. "Where's Dr. McIntyre?"

"Here." The physician knelt beside Sean. "I'll need you to keep her calm and still when she comes to."

"What if she doesn't?" O'Malley's gaze was riveted to the physician's.

"She's a strong, young woman, O'Malley," McIntyre replied, nodding to Emmett who had dropped to his knees beside them. The physician removed the sleeve O'Malley had ripped from his own frockcoat to stanch the flow of his wife's blood.

"Use this," he directed, handing O'Malley a folded length of clean linen. "I need to apply a field dressing. I will thoroughly cleanse the wound once we reach the duke's town house."

A high-pitched scream rent the air.

Emmett looked over his shoulder toward the sound and told them, "'Tis Lady Kittrick. Proof that she is involved. We have witnesses enough to convict Brownwell."

"Will ye have to remove the lead ball?" O'Malley rasped, brushing a strand of midnight hair from his wife's lashes.

The physician ignored his question. "I will know in a moment. As soon as I secure this bandage around her, I'll lift her to look for an exit wound."

Sean's heart hammered in his chest. His wife—his life, had risked hers to save the earl...to save him. Her life's blood stained his hands, but he had to ignore the emotions rioting through him to do as the physician bid him.

"There!" Dr. McIntyre indicated a spot high on her back. "O'Malley, hand me that bandage!"

Cradling his wife to his heart, he did as he was asked, watching the physician fold another length of linen and press it to her back, He willed the bile rushing up his throat to recede as the physician secured the bandage around her.

"When I give you the signal," the physician instructed, "pick her up and carry her to my carriage." Dr. McIntyre locked gazes with O'Malley and nodded.

O'Malley shifted to one knee, lifted his wife in his arms, and slowly stood. Jaw clenched, heart pumping like mad, he strode to the physician's carriage. He heard his name being called but ignored it. The only thing that mattered was his wife. The earl and the duke could go to blazes for all he cared! The woman who held his heart needed him.

He didn't remember climbing into the carriage but felt the jerk as the horses began to move. Within minutes, the horses picked up speed until they were galloping through the streets of London.

"She'll be fine, O'Malley," McIntyre assured him.

"How much longer?"

"Nearly there," the physician replied.

O'Malley didn't acknowledge the response. He was too busy willing every ounce of his strength into the woman cradled in his arms.

The carriage jolted to a halt and the door swung open. O'Malley blinked in surprise. "Coventry?"

"Hand her to me," the captain commanded. "I'll hold her while you get out." Sean passed his wife into the captain's waiting arms, leapt from the carriage, accepting his precious burden the moment his feet touched the sidewalk.

Jenkins stood white-faced as shouts for Mrs. O'Toole and hot water sounded behind him.

O'Malley blocked it all out, listening for the thready sound of his wife's labored breathing. He looked up once when he felt a steadying hand on his shoulder. Coventry was beside him, guiding him into the kitchen. Grateful for the support, he met the other man's gaze, then looked back at his wife.

"In here." Mrs. O'Toole was waiting for them in the small room Mignonette had insisted was more comfortable when he'd first brought her to the duke's town house.

"You need to let go of her," Coventry urged.

"I can't."

"Dr. McIntyre needs—" the captain began, only to be interrupted.

"Me help," Emmett announced striding into the room. "After we wash up, Sean and I will be yer extra hands, Dr. McIntyre."

"Excellent."

In short order, the men were on either side of Mignonette as the doctor began the arduous task of cleansing the entry wound, then with their help lifting and holding her, the exit wound.

"Mrs. O'Toole, do you have the boiled threads ready?" the doctor asked.

"Right here, Dr. McIntyre."

Working quickly, efficiently, the physician closed the first wound. He was halfway through stitching the second closed when Sean heard a low moan.

His heart stopped when he heard the sharp intake of breath that followed. "Lass? Can ye hear me?"

"Why couldn't she have stayed unconscious until ye'd finished sewing her back together?" Emmett wanted to know.

Mignonette's eyes shot open, and she immediately tried to move away from the pain. She fought them, until she realized what was happening. His wife bit her lip until it bled but did not move again until the physician tied off the final knot.

Emmett rose from where he was sitting and quietly spoke with Dr. McIntyre. Mrs. O'Toole bustled about them, straightening the room, collecting the blood-soaked linens, and handing them off to one of the maids.

Sean ignored them all. The only thing that mattered now was taking care of his wife. He'd already put his job in jeopardy by ignoring the earl when he rushed from Chalk Farm. His position with The Duke's Guard didn't matter. His vow to the duke and the earl didn't matter—not a bloody thing mattered, except his wife.

God help him, he never thought it would be possible, but his wife was right. There had come a time in his life when he would break one vow to honor another. "'Tis finished, Lass," he murmured, stroking the tips of his fingers across her forehead. Back and forth, back and forth. Hoping the motion would soothe her.

Her eyes met his. "What happened?"

He felt the anger begin to boil. "Before or after ye threw yerself into the line of fire and screamed me name?"

She did not answer, but she did not look away.

"I've never in me life known such fear, Lass, as in that moment."

"I heard a sound," she rasped. "When I looked in the direction it seemed to come from, all I could see was a branch…moving—until I recognized it as the barrel of a rifle." Tears filled her eyes and spilled over as she continued, "I was terrified when I heard another twig snap—on the other side of me. *Two rifles!* Both aimed at the field of honor. What would have had me do?"

Though her voice sounded weak, the woman lying on the cot was anything but. The lass was brave, loyal, hardheaded, and the love of his life. "Ye could have screamed for help."

"And waited for it to come? What if a lead ball struck you?"

"I'm a larger target than a slip of a lass like ye," he reminded her. "The chances were on me side that it wouldn't hit anything vital."

"What if it struck the earl?"

"We'd be attending a hanging."

She brushed aside his words to tell him, "I could not take a chance that either of you would be shot."

Sean ground his teeth together. "So ye took a lead ball to save me and the earl?"

She closed her eyes. But was it against the pain or to avoid answering his question? He opened his mouth to speak when a hand squeezed his shoulder to the point of pain.

"Shut yer *gob*, Sean. Let the brave lass rest. She's been through hell, don't be adding to it."

Sean shrugged off his cousin's hand. He needed to hear his wife tell him why she'd put herself in danger. "Did ye think to save the earl's life?"

When she did not answer, he asked the question burning in his soul. "Did ye think to save mine?"

MIGNONETTE COULD FEIGN sleep, thereby avoiding her husband's question, or she could tell him why she made the split-second decision to throw herself in front of the rifle. One look at the agony ripping through him, and she rasped, "You. *Mon coeur.* I thought only of you."

He fell to his knees beside her. "Ye could have been killed! Would yer sacrifice have been worth it?"

She lifted a hand to trace the line of his jaw and felt the tension there. Her brave and beautiful husband was holding on to his emotions with the strength of ten men. *Mon Dieu*, how she loved him!

"*Oui.* I would willingly give my life for you. You are so brave, so strong. You fight for what you feel is right—no matter what the law of the land dictates. Families matter to you. Being forced to commit a crime for the sake of family matters to you. Your duty to put yourself in between the duke, the earl, their families and anyone who means them harm matters to you. Today could have been the last time you performed your duty…"

Her eyes welled with tears as she opened her heart fully to him. "I do not wish to live in a world without you, *mon amor.*"

His lips claimed hers in a kiss that burned through her worries, and her fears, leaving no doubt of the fullness of his love and devotion.

Her lips acquiesced, accepting his kiss, before pouring herself into the kiss so that *her* lips laid claim to his. Promising the fullness of her love, devotion, and the new life neither knew lay just beneath her heart.

EPILOGUE

Three months later…

S EAN O'MALLEY AND his wife descended from the duke's carriage. One look at his wife and he knew she was more than ready to be on steady ground. "I'm sorry the movement of the carriage nauseates ye."

"It is not your fault…" Mignonette paused and glared at her husband. "It *is* your fault."

O'Malley chuckled. "If memory serves, I wasn't alone in our bed."

She sighed. "Forgive me, *mon coeur*, I am tired of being tired."

Earl Lippincott was waiting to greet them. "We've been expecting you for the last few hours. Was there any trouble with the changes of horses along the route?"

"Nay," O'Malley replied. "The motion of the carriage made me poor wife ill."

"Ah." The earl nodded. "I recall making numerous stops, and journeys taking twice as long when Aurelia was newly pregnant. Thankfully, the symptoms did not last more than the first few months."

Mignonette sighed, louder this time, and O'Malley drew her closer. "Would you like to lie down?"

"No! Er…forgive me. The thought of closing my eyes and

lying down when I can still feel the motion of the carriage is worse than riding in the carriage."

"I'm thinking that does not make sense, but if ye say it is so, I won't be arguing with ye."

"*Merci*."

"Would ye care to go for a walk to stretch yer legs and clear yer head?"

"That would be wonderful."

"If you don't mind a bit of a stroll," the earl remarked, "I'd suggest a walk to the stables and the fields just beyond."

"Do ye now?" O'Malley knew what the earl did not say but remembered the earl's instructions and did not spoil the surprise. "What do ye say, Lass. Are ye up to it?"

"*Oui*. The air is refreshing after the close confines of the coach."

"Are ye joining us, yer lordship?"

"I need to see what Aurelia is up to. I don't like to leave her for long periods of time. Our babe is due in a few days."

"We won't be long."

"Take your time. We'll have some of Mrs. Wyatt's triple berry tarts and teacakes when you return."

"Thank ye, yer lordship."

As they strolled along the path leading to the stables, Mignonette inhaled deeply. "The air is so fresh after being in London."

"Ye get spoiled breathing in country air after being stuck drawing in London's sooty air."

They paused to watch a few of the earl's horses grazing in the grassy field under the midday sun. "I've missed this," Sean remarked.

"It seems like a lifetime ago since I was in the country." Her gaze swept the land beyond the stables and the field where the horses grazed. "Oh, look!"

O'Malley slowly smiled, then hid his expression when she turned back to remark, "Over there!"

"Where?"

"There's a thatched cottage just over the rise. By that stand of trees." She took hold of his hand and held on. "Isn't it lovely? I wonder who lives there."

"We could walk over and find out. Mayhap they'll invite us in for tea."

Her face clouded. "It sounds lovely, but the earl and countess are waiting for us to have tea with them. I wouldn't want to slight them on our first visit to Lippincott Manor."

"Why don't we borrow the carriage and take a ride over to see the cottage after tea?"

"I would love that."

"Consider it done, Lass."

O'Malley let his wife speculate as to who lived in the quaint cottage she'd spied as they returned to the manor house.

The earl's butler greeted them with his customary flourish. "O'Malley! We've missed you. Mrs. O'Malley, welcome to Lippincott Manor. Their lordships are expecting you in the sitting room."

"Thank ye, Finch."

The butler announced them from the open doorway.

"Ah, come in!" the earl expounded, making introductions all around. Once seated, Lady Aurelia poured their tea while the earl urged the tarts and teacakes on their guests.

"Excuse the informality," Lady Aurelia explained. "We do not stand on ceremony when we are with friends." Turning to Mignonette, she confided, "I know we shall become good friends, living so close to one another." With a hand on her burgeoning belly, she asked, "When is your babe due? Ours is due in a sennight."

"Not for at least five or six months. I'd be honored to call you friend, your ladyship."

"Have you heard?" the earl asked when his wife paused to sip from her teacup.

O'Malley's gaze locked with the earl's. "Heard?"

The earl set his teacup on the table and announced, "I had a missive from King early this morning."

O'Malley nodded. "And?"

"According to King," the earl replied, "the woman refused to admit any culpability, nor did she admit to maliciously setting out to destroy my name and that of my wife!"

"What about the destruction of Madame's shop?" Mignonette asked.

The earl raked a hand through his hair. "She denied having any knowledge—nor would she admit to hiring anyone to injure you, Mignonette."

"What of me wife's reputation?" O'Malley rumbled. "Did she deny that she had Brownwell add that bloody wager to White's betting book?"

The earl's angry gaze met his. "She denied everything. We cannot prove anything unless someone comes forward to speak out against Lady Kittrick. She has more friends than we counted on. Those who owe their existence to her."

"That is how it is with bullies who bribe those to do their dirty work, holding them hostage," O'Malley rasped. "What's to be done? This cannot go unpunished!"

The earl's expression changed. "It won't. The wheels are already in motion."

"Wheels?"

"Indeed. My sister-in-law in the Lake District, and my sister in the borderlands, have begun their campaign to bring the truth to light. Between the two of them, their friends, contacts, and staff are many. Word has already reached the village here of Lady Kittrick's cruelty to former servants she has dismissed without cause, references, or pay they are entitled to."

"Unconscionable behavior!" his wife declared.

The earl nodded. Turning to O'Malley and his wife, he added, "Madame Beaudoine has added her experiences dealing with Lady Kittrick, letting it be known she severed ties with the woman. Immediately after doing so, her shop was destroyed, leaving you and Mignonette injured."

"How will any of this help?" Mignonette inquired.

Lady Aurelia rose to stand beside her husband, leaning against him as she told of their experiences before they were wed and the cruel rumors that were spread about them. "The truth always wins when one is brave enough to bring it to light."

"And has connections in the working class as well as the elite of society," O'Malley added. "Do ye think ye will succeed this time, too?" he asked the earl.

"Without question." Meeting O'Malley's direct gaze, he told him, "Word has it the lady's accounts with the shops on Bond Street have been closed. Once the hard-working shopkeepers heard of her treatment to her current and former staff—and that of Madame Beaudoine's seamstresses, they refused to extend her credit."

"I wonder how long it will be before she leaves London with her tail between her legs," Lady Aurelia murmured aloud.

"Not soon enough," the earl remarked. He walked over to the bell pull and gave it a tug. "We have time to see to that errand, O'Malley, while your wife and mine enjoy another pot of tea."

"Aye, yer lordship." O'Malley rose, walked over to his wife, and pressed a kiss to the top of her head. "I shall return shortly."

The earl murmured softly to his wife before kissing her cheek. "Send for me if you feel any more twinges."

"Of course," Lady Aurelia replied. When the door closed behind the men, she turned to Mignonette. "I thought they'd never leave!"

Mignonette's laughter mingled with Lady Aurelia's. "Edward hovers. He's more nervous about me birthing our babe than I am!"

"Sean watches me like a hawk. If I wake in the night, I'll find him staring at me, watching me sleep."

The countess nodded before she changed the subject. "I hope you'll enjoy living here at Lippincott Manor. I am so looking forward to having you close by."

Mignonette slowly smiled. "There was a beautiful cottage on the rise…just past the stables and the field. Who does it belong to?"

"Why do you ask?"

"The moment I saw it, I could imagine Sean and I living there, raising our family beneath the thatched roof."

"Do you like surprises?" Lady Aurelia inquired.

"Not especially."

Looking over her shoulder, she leaned close and whispered, "If I tell you a secret, will you promise not to tell?"

"*Oui. Je promets!*"

"You."

"I do not understand," Mignonette remarked.

"The cottage. It belongs to you and Sean."

Mignonette's eyes filled with tears. "Our gift from you and the earl?"

"For saving his life, Mignonette. I would stand up so that I could bow before you, if I did not fear I would tip over under the weight of the babe in my belly." The countess gave an exaggerated sigh and motioned grandly with her hands. "Then my husband would come running, demanding to know what I was thinking."

At the image the countess painted with her words, Mignonette's tears stopped. "It is Sean and I who are beyond grateful to you and his lordship for all you have done for us. By all rights, the earl could have let Sean go for abandoning him on the field of honor."

"Don't be ridiculous! Edward would have done the same thing had it been me who'd been shot in front of his eyes."

"But—" Mignonette began only to be cut off by the countess again.

"Not another word. Now do not forget to show surprise and delight when your handsome husband takes you for a carriage ride when they return."

"Is there more news from Mr. King?" she queried.

"Not that I know of. Although I would not put it past my darling to keep news from me, I am quite certain Edward is showing Sean the cottage. The two have been corresponding about it for months now. With Edward seeing to all of the details Sean has asked for on your behalf."

"Me? But I do not remember him asking me anything about the cottage."

"Your husband and mine can be quite canny when keeping something from us." The sound of heavy footfalls and deep voices reached them. "Now remember," Lady Aurelia instructed, "surprise and delight!"

Mignonette reached for Lady Aurelia's hand and gently squeezed it. "*Oui!*"

"Are ye ready for that carriage ride, Lass?"

"If I must," she sighed, letting him lead her from the room.

"Is everything in place?" Aurelia whispered as her husband joined her on the settee.

"Aye, my love."

"Flowers? Basket of food?"

"Yes, my love. Do stop worrying. You'll wear yourself out."

Aurelia sighed and leaned against her husband. "If I must."

"Aye, you must."

"It's not far, Lass. Just up the lane."

Mignonette moaned as the motion had her belly turning upside down. "Could we please get out and walk the rest of the way?"

"'Tis a quarter of a mile!"

"I'm not weak," she reminded him. "But I will lose every tart and teacake if you do not stop this carriage immediately!"

O'Malley shouted for the coachman to stop. The carriage rocked, but he'd swept his wife off the seat, into his arms, and out the door before it came to a full stop. "Now then, Lass. Shall I carry ye the rest of the way, or would you prefer to walk?"

She linked her arms around her husband's neck and kissed his jaw. "Your arm does not ache?"

"Nay. I keep telling ye it's healed, Lass."

"You are not tired?"

"From spending the day riding on me *arse*?"

As he'd hoped, Mignonette giggled at his coarse expression, tightening her hold on him. "Hang on, Lass."

O'Malley carried his wife down the lane, stopping in front of the freshly painted white fence. "Open the gate, Lass."

She did as he bid, and again when he asked her to open the door.

He carried her over the threshold and set her on her feet next to a round oak table with four sturdy chairs. "Oh, Sean! Look at the flowers!" She bent to sniff the bouquet, drawing in the sweet scent of blush-colored faery roses. "My favorite."

He grinned. "Have a look in the basket. Ye may be hungry now that we're not riding in the carriage."

She shook her head at him. "I'm not hungry...for food."

"Before I let ye lure me to bed, Lass, tell me. Do ye like it? Can ye see us living here, raising our family here?"

Mignonette threw her arms around her husband and poured herself into the kiss. When at last she could bear to pull away from him, he locked gazes with her. His love shone in the soft green depths. His words confirmed it. "Faith, I love a fiery woman."

"Just any woman will do?" she teased.

"Nay, Lass. I'll not have ye thinking any woman will do when ye're the one holding me heart." He strode to the door, locked it, and turned back to her.

Mignonette could not wait, she rushed to him, throwing herself into his arms. "I love you, Sean."

Immeasurably grateful to have strength in both of his arms, he tightened his hold around her and lowered his lips. When they were a breath apart, he rasped, "Faith, I love ye more."

About the Author

Historical & Contemporary Romance "Warm...Charming...Fun..."

C.H. was born in Aiken, South Carolina, but her parents moved back to northern New Jersey where she grew up.

She believes in fate, destiny, and love at first sight. C.H. fell in love at first sight when she was seventeen. She was married for 41 wonderful years until her husband lost his battle with cancer. Soul mates, their hearts will be joined forever.

They have three grown children—one son-in-law, two grand-sons, two rescue dogs, and two rescue grand-cats.

Her characters rarely follow the synopsis she outlines for them...but C.H. has learned to listen to her characters! Her heroes always have a few of her husband's best qualities: his honesty, his integrity, his compassion for those in need, and his killer broad shoulders. C.H. writes about the things she loves most: Family, her Irish and English Ancestry, Baking and Gardening.

C.H.'s Social Media Links:
Website: www.chadmirand.com
Amazon: amazon.com/stores/C.-H.-Admirand/author/B001JPBUMC
BookBub: bookbub.com/authors/c-h-admirand
Facebook Author Page: facebook.com/CHAdmirandAuthor
Facebook Private Reader's Page ~ C.H. Reader's Nook:
facebook.com/groups/714796299746980
GoodReads: goodreads.com/author/show/212657.C_H_Admirand
Instagram: c.h.admirand
Twitter: @AdmirandH
Youtube: youtube.com/channel/UCRSXBeqEY52VV3mHdtg5fXw

www.ingramcontent.com/pod-product-compliance
Lightning Source LLC
Chambersburg PA
CBHW071220210726
48293CB00002B/513